C000119059

SHARPS AND SPRINGFIELD
PEACEMAKER

MORGAN BRICE

Peacemaker

Sharps & Springfield
Book 1

Morgan Brice

eBook ISBN: 978-1-64795-043-9
Print ISBN: 978-1-64795-044-6

Peacemaker, Copyright © 2023 by Gail Z. Martin.
Cover by Deranged Doctor Designs.

The right of the author to be identified as the author of this work has been asserted in accordance with the Copyright, Designs and Patents Act 1988.
All rights reserved. No part of this book may be reproduced in any form or by any electronic or mechanical means, including information storage and retrieval systems, without written permission from the author, except for the use of brief quotations in a book review.
This is a work of fiction. Any resemblance to actual persons (living or dead), locales, and incidents are either coincidental or used fictitiously. Any trademarks used belong to their owners. No infringement is intended.

Darkwind Press is an imprint of DreamSpinner Communications, LLC

For everyone who believed.

Chapter 1
Owen

September 1897

O wen Sharps chuckled as he read his book on the train to St. Louis. He had been waiting to get a copy of *Dracula*, the sensational new book from England, and had found one in a New Pittsburgh bookstore before heading to the station.

It's got flair, and I like how splashy Van Helsing is, but it's obvious Stoker never fought a real vampire.

Owen had heard about the book and its growing reputation for being frightening and violent. *So far nothing he's written compares to being covered in blood in an ice-cold cemetery at midnight, hammering a stake through a vampire's heart, and trying not to get bitten. Then again, maybe I have a skewed perspective.*

"Pardon me, is this seat taken?" A drop-dead gorgeous man waited for an answer. He had raven black hair, bright blue eyes, and plush lips that filled Owen with impure thoughts. The stranger carried a suitcase and an overcoat, with a newspaper folded under his arm. Owen took one look and would have booted his granny to the cargo car to free up the seat for the man.

"It's all yours." Owen gave a dismissive wave, tearing his gaze away so he'd quit staring. It wouldn't do to drool.

"I think this might be the last open seat on the train." The man stowed his suitcase and coat, settling in across from Owen with his newspaper.

Owen couldn't help giving him the once-over. He figured the man to be slightly shorter than his own six-foot-two inches, and from the cut of his suit jacket, he had a trim, muscular build. Owen made a mental note to be sure to get a glimpse of what was likely a prime ass when they left the train.

"Where are you headed?" Owen thought that a little conversation couldn't hurt. He wanted to remember the man's voice to go with his image on nights when he sought relief alone with his hand. This fellow would never know he'd been promoted to the lead in Owen's secret fantasies. Owen particularly liked the contrast between the man's dark hair and athletic body to his own rangy build, blond hair, fair skin, and green eyes.

"St. Louis." The man returned Owen's scrutiny with an assessing gaze.

Owen sat up a bit straighter, oddly wanting to make a good impression on this person he was unlikely to see again. He felt the weight of the man's inspection, which made him wonder. *Is he a cop? Private investigator? Or maybe…like me?*

They were both dressed equally well in suits that were department store quality but not bespoke. The stranger's hair was fairly short but more fashionable than military, and he was clean-shaven. Owen wondered what a hint of dark stubble might do to heighten those high cheekbones and accentuate the impossibly blue eyes, and he felt himself chub in his pants.

None of that, he admonished silently. *It wouldn't do to raise suspicion. He probably just wants to make sure I'm not the sort to steal his suitcase when he's not looking.*

"I'm headed there myself," Owen said. "Business or pleasure?"

The man looked amused at the question but not annoyed, which boded well. "Business. You?"

Owen nodded, surprised that he wanted to continue the conversation instead of returning to his book. "The same. I've heard the food there is good, but I doubt I'll have time to do any exploring." He found himself at ease with the stranger. "Will you be staying in the city, or going on from there?"

"I'll meet with my boss, but I spend most of my time traveling," the fellow replied. "I don't get to stay long in any one place."

So we have that in common too. Makes it unlikely that we might meet up again the next time I come back to St. Louis. "Me, too. I'm a bit of a rolling stone."

"You hail from the South?" the man asked after silence stretched for a beat. "Just a guess from your voice."

Owen tried not to preen at the attention. "Baltimore. Are you from New Pittsburgh?"

The stranger shook his head. "Boston, originally. Although I've been here and there."

Much as Owen wondered about his new companion's work and what kept him traveling, he shied away from that line of conversation. *It's not like I can fess up to being with the Supernatural Secret Service. And I'd rather not lie. He seems like a decent sort. Unfortunately, there's a driver who'll be waiting for me at the station, so even if he did lean my way we'd have no time to find a cheap room or a dark alley to do anything about it.*

"That your book?" The man pulled Owen out of his thoughts.

"Yes—quite fantastical, but a lively read." His acquaintance carried a newspaper, and Owen braced for a dismissive comment about "penny dreadfuls."

"I've heard good things. Do you like it?" Nothing in the man's blue eyes suggested mockery.

"I'm only halfway through, but it's been interesting so far," Owen replied. "Lots of stuff from legends and superstition—but then again, it *is* about a vampire."

"Does it scare you? They say it's bloody and terrifying." Those blue eyes were alight with curiosity and held a hint of teasing. *Is he flirting? Surely not. Don't imagine things. I don't need that sort of trouble.*

If he didn't have a driver waiting for his arrival, if he had at least an overnight before he met his contact, Owen might have been tempted to try to arrange dinner, perhaps test the waters to see if his acquaintance was just a platonically friendly businessman or if he might share Owen's proclivities, good for an anonymous roll in the sheets. *Probably for the best. With those wet dream good looks he could be one of those Pinkertons who try to trap men like me. Better to leave him alone—except for in my imagination.*

"I don't scare easily." Owen was unable to resist a little banter. He'd become a master of knowing how to walk the conversational line between good-natured humor and real intent.

"Oh, you don't? Don't tell me you're one of those Pinkertons," the man joked.

Owen tried to hide his startle as the comment mirrored his thoughts. He took a hard look at his companion but met guileless blue eyes. "Hardly. Just very practical. I'm afraid my mind keeps interrupting the story to point out the things that strain credulity."

"Like what?"

The question sounded casual, but Owen thought he saw a flash of something more serious in the man's face before the pleasant smile erased all traces.

Damn. I can't tell the truth—regular people don't believe vampires exist let alone know anything about fighting them. "Undead creatures. People turning into bats. That sort of thing. Although it makes for an exciting read."

He could have sworn he saw something spark and then shutter in the stranger's eyes at his answer. And he had the strangest feeling that while he had given the plausible reply, he had somehow disappointed the man.

"Anything interesting in the news?" Owen nodded to the folded paper.

"Can I admit that I wasn't reading the articles?" The dark-haired stranger dropped his voice as if confiding a secret. "I always start with the funnies. *Hogan's Alley* is my favorite. Never fails to make me laugh."

Damn. Handsome, built, and has a good sense of humor. Probably for the best I'll never see him again. Not like I could hope for more than a quick fuck.

Owen had resigned himself to a solitary future not long after he accepted the truth about his preference for men. He didn't worry about the opinions of other people, and he felt no shame about his desires. But Owen knew that not only would his position with the Supernatural Secret Service end if he were ever found out, he could be arrested, jailed, and worse.

He mostly contented himself with jacking off, a private and discreet way to handle the problem. Sometimes he broke down and searched out the establishments for men like him, "nancy" bars that were as secretive as their clientele.

Owen had tried keeping company with Eli, a fellow he'd liked well enough when his work let him stay in Denver, a while back, but then his lover had come down with pneumonia and died, leaving Owen alone once again.

Much as he longed for a real relationship, the kind other couples had, Owen knew it wasn't in the cards. While he accepted that fate, he hadn't entirely extinguished the pesky spark of hope that flared whenever he met someone he could imagine keeping around—someone like his seatmate.

"Nothing wrong with a good laugh." Owen feared he'd been lost in his thoughts for too long. "Just like reading an adventure tale—takes your mind off your troubles."

The trip to St. Louis would take most of a day, and while part of that would be overnight, Owen and his new "friend" had a long ride together. Owen resolved to make the best of it, indulging in good conversation and a bit of harmless, deniable flirting.

They chatted about the weather and the World Series, and the price of good shoes. At the other man's behest, Owen read a few pages of his book aloud, and in turn his seatmate shared the funny pages with him. By unspoken agreement, they never exchanged names or personal details.

Owen couldn't help noticing the stranger's hands. While the man dressed well and spoke as if he'd been educated, he had the swollen knuckles of a brawler. Owen had seen hands like that on men who boxed for money or sport and those who couldn't seem to avoid bar fights. It seemed at odds with the rest of his polished presentation, and Owen wondered about the story it revealed.

"Bourbon, please—neat," Owen told the server who came to take their dinner order. It would make a good end to a beef stew entrée and might help him sleep.

"Whiskey," the stranger ordered, also choosing beef over the chicken.

"Do they have good bourbon in Boston?" Owen was invested in keeping their conversation going.

"Passable," the other man replied. "Not as good as what I've had in Knoxville or New Orleans, but the company here is friendlier."

"Glad to hear it." Owen didn't question that the other man's Boston accent had earned him animosity in the South, where the scars of the war were slow to heal. He didn't bother adding that his own welcome would be equally frosty given his family's allegiance to the Union, which had cost them everything.

After dinner, Owen and his companion went back to reading, and he noted that the other man did indeed start over from the front page when he'd dispensed with the comics. *Intelligent and a sense of humor. Not exactly the sort I'm going to meet for a quick hand job in the back room of a bar.*

He'd put the hope for a true life partner behind him—or so Owen had thought. *Apparently not,* he thought with a sigh. His brain unhelpfully offered one reason after another why the stranger would be perfect "husband" material.

All of which might be true, but it doesn't change my life, and it doesn't change the world. But it'll make a nice daydream.

A good dinner, two fingers of bourbon, and the rocking of the train made it easier to sleep sitting up than Owen had expected. He and his seatmate negotiated the space between them to unfold their legs as much as possible. If Owen appreciated every second of the accidental brushes and the times their knees knocked together, he made sure to keep it to himself.

When the lights dimmed to signal quiet time, the stranger rose to use the men's room. Sliding out of his seat made his suitcoat catch on the velvet upholstery, and Owen caught a glimpse of a revolver in a holster underneath.

The stranger froze for just an instant, then continued as if nothing had happened. Owen stared after him as he made his way down the corridor, matching the train's motion to keep his footing with the grace of an athlete.

His ass is as nice as I imagined it would be.

A more ominous thought followed. *I know why I'm carrying a gun on a train. Why is he?*

Several possibilities spun through Owen's mind. *US Marshal. Pinkerton. Private investigator. Hired security—the railroad sometimes puts plainclothes officers on trains if they expect trouble.*

Train robber?

Owen had difficulty imagining his seatmate as a latter-day Billy the Kid. But he had to admit that no matter how charming the man seemed, he was a stranger. Before Owen joined the Supernatural Secret Service, he'd been a soldier in the County Seat Wars and the Cattle Wars out West. He'd seen suave killers and grouchy heroes, enough to know that appearances could be deceiving.

Shit. That ruins a perfectly good fantasy. Not to mention that now I'll need to sleep with one eye open, just in case.

When the man returned, Owen availed himself of the facilities as well, but he was careful to keep his jacket from revealing his weapon. He wasn't worried about being robbed. What little he had of value was in his locked valise in the overhead rack, and with the train at full speed his companion wouldn't be leaving before morning.

When Owen returned to his seat, he had already moved his gun to a pocket so he could keep it on his lap overnight, just in case. The stranger was sprawled in his seat with his overcoat as a pillow but considerately left plenty of room for Owen's long legs beneath the table that separated their forward and backward-facing seats.

Owen got comfortable and slipped his gun from his jacket to rest on his thighs.

The other man sighed but didn't open his eyes. "I hope you aren't planning to shoot me during the night. It'll cause a ruckus and stain the seats."

Owen's gaze snapped to the stranger, whose mouth quirked in a crooked grin. Whatever his thoughts about Owen's gun being pointed at him beneath the table, he didn't seem frightened.

"Are you going to give me a reason to shoot you?" Owen countered, fascinated despite his better judgment.

"Many people might say it's a talent of mine, but no. And I should be asking you the same question since you drew first."

He's a cocky sot; I'll give him that. Cool as a cucumber. Looks like he's no stranger to a fight. Wouldn't doubt he can handle himself. But who is he, and why is he going to St. Louis? Is his gun to protect himself? From whom? Or part of his job, like mine?

"I've had a long day, and tomorrow's going to be busy, so if it's all the same to you, I suggest a truce to shooting each other," Owen said, his voice a deep rumble from the bourbon and the late hour.

"I can honor that." He didn't bother to open his eyes. Either he had read Owen as being trustworthy, or he had uncommon faith in the speed of his own quick draw.

"Good. That's settled." Owen made himself as comfortable as possible given the tight quarters, and if his traitorous cock twitched when his leg bumped against the stranger's knee, the table hid the evidence.

OWEN WOKE SOON AFTER DAWN, pleased to see he had neither been robbed nor shot. His seatmate didn't stir, but thankfully also hadn't snored—much—through the night. Owen regarded the man while he could, appreciating the handsome features, long lashes, and full lips. For a man carrying a hidden gun, the stranger looked oddly vulnerable.

What's his story? Why is a Boston man heading to St. Louis with a gun under his jacket? Is he in trouble with the law? Running from debts? I'll have to give him a history if he's going to be my imaginary lover.

"If you're going to stare, at least sketch my profile." His acquaintance opened his eyes and yawned, giving Owen more indecent ideas of what might fit between those lips. His sleep-mussed dark hair drooped into startlingly blue eyes.

"Funny," Owen replied in a droll voice. "Note that neither of us fired a shot."

The man sat up and stretched, giving Owen a chance to appreciate the broad shoulders and trim waist. "Good for us. The conductor would not approve. I'd rather not be put off in the middle of nowhere."

"Of course you assume you'd draw first," Owen countered.

The stranger shrugged. "I'm good with a gun."

The breakfast cart brought hot tea and coffee plus a selection of pastries and breads. They didn't speak much as they ate, then took turns heading for the lavatory.

"It's too bad I have to head out as soon as we arrive," Owen chanced since there was nothing to lose. "We might have had dinner before we went on our way."

The other man flashed a brilliant smile that made Owen's heart pound. "That would have been nice but…duty calls." He actually sounded regretful, making Owen wonder once again if his interest was truly unrequited.

They pulled into the St. Louis station just after lunch. Owen gathered his coat and valise, as his seatmate did the same. "I have a driver coming for me—can I drop you somewhere?" Owen offered, wishing to extend their company a bit longer.

The other man shook his head with what might have been regret. "Thank you, no. I have someone waiting for me as well. Best of luck with your business dealings. I hope St. Louis is good for you."

"Same for you." Owen was surprised at the disappointment he felt. He hadn't known the man for a full twenty-four hours, but the unknown possibilities felt like a tangible loss.

They stood in line to leave the train, then launched into the hubbub of the station. Owen willed himself not to look for the stranger in the crowd and sighed, resigned to the loss.

He searched for the carriage that would take him to the regional headquarters for his new assignment. A dozen cabs waited near the platform, and he wondered how to find the right one.

"They all look alike." His seatmate had come up beside him. "I imagine I'll have to knock on each one to find my driver."

"Mr. Sharps! Mr. Springfield!"

Owen and the stranger both turned toward the voice. A man in a cabbie's uniform waved to them. "Over here!"

Owen's stomach dropped like a rock. *Oh dear God. Please tell me that man isn't my new partner. Just let the ground open up and swallow me now.*

No, don't think of swallowing. Or those lips. That throat. That prime ass...

I am so screwed.

For a second, Owen thought he saw the same poleaxed look on the other man's face that he was sure was on his own. Cocky self-assurance wiped the expression away. "Looks like we'll be riding more trains together. Good thing we've got novels and comic strips to discuss," the other man said.

The cabbie took their bags and the two men got into the carriage. His companion confirmed the address with their driver—the same as on Owen's letter from the agency—and they headed off through the city's crowded streets.

"Calvin Springfield." His new partner held out his hand to shake.

"Owen Sharps." Owen took the proffered hand and returned the shake with a firm grip. He did his best to push everything from the past twenty-four hours out of his mind.

"You know, I wondered when you didn't introduce yourself on the train," Calvin commented without making eye contact. "But since I wasn't keen to share my name either, I figured it was just as well."

"I guess it's not all that strange that we'd end up on the same train to St. Louis. New Pittsburgh is a hub," Owen said.

Aside from the initial surprise, Calvin didn't seem to have any difficulty about adjusting to their new working relationship. That signaled another unwelcome likelihood to Owen. *He's not like me. I must have imagined any interest. He wasn't flirting, just being polite.*

I am stuck with a crush on my very not-interested, excruciatingly handsome new partner.

Oh just shoot me now.

"Have you been with the service long?" Calvin found his tongue more easily than Owen seemed to manage.

Don't think about his tongue. Or his lips—

"Two years. Before that, I was in the Army, County Seat Wars, Cattle Wars," Owen replied. "You?"

"Three years. They had me at the War Department for a bit, but even in the Army I didn't always color inside the lines," Calvin admitted. "Then someone decided it was a better fit to send me on the road. Probably to get me out from underfoot."

The Supernatural Secret Service recruited people who had at least a touch of paranormal ability. Owen could see ghosts and, if the circumstances were right, could talk to them as well. He wondered what Calvin's talent was and how they might work together. *Platonically. Completely platonically.*

Shit. I hope he's not a mind reader. Owen wondered how much he could concentrate on safe things like shredded wheat or oatmeal to keep him from fantasizing about his sexy partner.

The ride across town was quieter than their time on the train. Owen figured they were both adjusting to the shift from casual strangers to working together in close quarters and dangerous situations.

The service's headquarters was a large, non-descript building downtown without signage. Not too surprising since the service's supernatural protections weren't public knowledge.

The cabbie and doorman carried in their luggage and put it behind the reception desk. Owen and Calvin followed signs to the office number in the assignment letter they both received. That turned out to be a conference room, where two agents in their early thirties rose from their seats to meet them.

"Agents Sharps and Springfield," the taller of the two men greeted them. He was dark blond with a long face and an Eastern European accent. His partner had dark hair with a prominent five o'clock shadow and the rakish look of a penny dreadful hero.

"I'm Mitch Storm," the brunet said, "and this is my partner, Jacob Drangosavich. We've been on loan from the New Pittsburgh office of the Department of Supernatural Investigation until new Supernatural Secret Service agents could be assigned to St. Louis. Welcome."

Owen wracked his brain to recall the difference between the two agencies, both of which dealt with issues involving paranormal crime. The only thing that came to mind was that while DSI didn't require its agents to have some sort of magical or psychic ability, the SSS specifically recruited people with special talents.

They all shook hands and sat at the table. "What happened to the previous St. Louis agents?" Calvin asked.

Mitch and Jacob exchanged a look. "We don't know yet, but the situation is being investigated," Mitch said.

"Hold up. Our predecessors disappeared and you don't know where they went?" Owen echoed incredulously.

Mitch rubbed his neck. "It sounds really bad when you say it like that. Jacob and I have only been here for a month. We got temporarily reassigned to cover the gap, but we're getting sent back to New Pittsburgh, and we wanted to tell you what we've learned so far."

"So we can investigate our own future murders?" Calvin asked with a deceptive smile.

Owen fell a tad more in love with his new partner right then, despite himself.

Jacob glared at Mitch. "I told you this wasn't going to go well, explaining it like that."

Mitch glared back. "Then by all means...do it your way."

Owen read the friendship and trust beneath the men's bickering, despite their difference of opinion. *Like an old married couple, my mother would have said.*

"Forgive my partner for leading feet-first." Jacob gave a long-suffering sigh. "He does that. You get used to it."

Mitch looked daggers at him. Jacob ignored it.

"St. Louis has been fragile since the war," Jacob said. "There've been bank panics and fears of more instability. The town is still trying to find its footing in the post-war economy, and there are plenty of divided loyalties. Not just lingering North/South tension, but human/paranormal sides too."

"There have been several gruesome murders in the past few months where only pieces of the bodies were recovered," Mitch picked up. "Our attempts to match the body parts to the people reported missing hasn't accounted for everyone, but those we have identified all had one thing in common—they opposed the new railroad expansion."

"Do the police have any leads?" Owen suspected he already knew the answer.

Jacob shook his head. "We're pretty sure the chief of police is either paid off or in cahoots. The deputy seems honest, but he hasn't come forward with anything. The chief has stonewalled us through official channels. But we do have a list of suspects, some of whom were being investigated by Harris and Davis—your predecessors— before they went missing."

He slid a couple of papers toward Owen and Calvin.

"Pastor Ronald Thomas gets his name in the newspaper by being continually outraged about one thing or the other," Mitch continued, heavy on the sarcasm. "Benson Tucker is a local lawyer whose reputation for winning cases is second only to the rumors about him taking bribes. Ross Swanson is a prominent St. Louis businessman with investments in restaurants and hotels, corrupt enough to feed the rumor mill but not substantiated enough to get indicted."

"Last but not least, Lillian Webb," Jacob took up the tale. "A rich man's daughter and a wealthy man's widow who now specializes in being seen with all the right people at all the right places. She's been linked to all three of the other suspects, some romantically and others socially, and she had spoken to at least two of the missing people— plus Harris and Davis."

Owen frowned. "So how is this a job for the Supernatural Secret Service? Don't the regular feds handle corporate corruption?"

Mitch leaned forward, pushing one more item across the table, a newspaper with a grainy photo of a man with his hat pulled down to hide his face. "We think this man is behind the railroad trouble—Leland Aiken. He's a vampire."

Calvin gave a low whistle. "A vampire who wants to run a railroad? Strange—but not actually illegal."

"We can confirm Aiken is a vampire. We know he's told the press that he wants to be the next Rockefeller, making his fortune in railway lines to underserved cities. We just don't know if there's more to the undead angle," Mitch replied.

"Did the mutilated bodies look like there was a ritual component? Are we talking about blood magic?" Owen asked. He'd gone up against a dark witch or two, and was really hoping never to do so again. Not that vampires were an improvement.

"Harris and Davis were looking into that—and maybe they got too close for comfort," Jacob admitted. "We retraced their steps from the notes they left behind, but their contacts have all either gone to ground, turned up dead, or clammed up. Both men had a reputation for not always working entirely by the book, so they might have been investigating side angles they didn't put in the official report."

"I'm sorry that we're dropping this in your lap." Mitch looked regretful enough that Owen believed him. "We didn't ask to get sent in as pinch hitters, and we didn't have a say in getting pulled back to New Pittsburgh. But we aren't deserting you. We've got some friends with significant abilities who know a lot of people in the supernatural community. We've already got them putting out feelers on this, so if we hear from them, we'll let you know."

"I have a contact who was in St. Louis the last time we talked," Owen mused. "Haven't been in touch for a while—worth a try."

"I knew a Pinkerton in town, worked a case together a year or so ago," Calvin spoke up. "Good person to have in our pocket—and no stranger to supernatural trouble."

Mitch looked around, then leaned forward and dropped his voice. "The St. Louis office isn't the most efficiently run. Sinclair Chambers is the Agent in Charge. He had some big wins back in the day and knows how to gladhand politicians to avoid publicity and bury inconvenient stories. The higher-ups like him because he's polished and keeps a low profile, and he's also good at charming the local movers and shakers.

"Chambers has done field work. He knows what's out there. But he's very political, and he likes the perks of his position. Don't expect him to have your back if the shit hits the fan," Mitch warned.

"And at least for now, don't count on meeting him soon," Jacob added. "He's gone on vacation somewhere in Canada for two weeks."

"With any luck, you'll wrap up the case and be on your way before you have to encounter him." Mitch's smirk conveyed how little he liked Chambers. Jacob elbowed him, but Mitch didn't look contrite.

"We've already sent the boxes of files to your train car," Jacob said. "Both what Harris and Davis compiled and what we added to them."

"Train car?" Owen remembered mention of needing to travel frequently with his new position, but had just assumed that meant finding a boarding house at each destination.

Mitch grinned. "Oh, you're going to love this. Jacob and I just moved out so everything could be freshened up for you. This assignment comes with a private Pullman car and a dedicated assistant."

Calvin's eyebrows rose. "It does? The pay is higher than my last position, but I just figured that meant more people would be shooting at me."

"That too," Jacob remarked. "But the Pullman car is an attempt to keep you safer than taking a random room-for-let and giving you more control over secret or sensitive documents."

Owen frowned. "That didn't keep our predecessors from going missing."

Jacob shrugged. "We know they didn't disappear from the train car. Since their valet was one of the people who turned up dead, we believe Harris and Davis were ambushed on reconnaissance. They didn't leave notes about their last theories or movements, so we don't know for sure."

Note to self: leave a paper trail so the next guys can pick up the job after we disappear.

Calvin leaned back with an assessing look. "Do you have any of Davis's or Harris's personal effects? Something they might have carried with them or used frequently?"

Owen gave his new partner a measured look, wondering about the request.

Mitch nodded with a knowing smile. "You're the psychometric. Handy talent to have."

Weariness flashed across Calvin's face. "Useful, but I'd be glad to part with it. Tells me more than I want to know most of the time."

Jacob glanced at Owen. "That means you're the medium."

Now Owen felt Calvin's gaze re-evaluating him. "Yes. But I'll say this upfront—that doesn't mean I can just interrogate ghosts and get all the answers. It doesn't work like that—unfortunately."

Owen had the feeling Calvin wanted to ask questions, but restrained his curiosity—for now. He wondered about Calvin's unfamiliar talent as well. *I imagine we'll have time to figure it out since we're going to be living and working together.*

Shit. We're going to be sharing a sleeper car—permanently? Guess I'll be taking plenty of cold showers.

"I'll see what I can find that belonged to Harris and Davis," Mitch said. "Go ahead and ask Jacob whatever questions you've got." He ducked out of the room, seemingly oblivious to the side eye Jacob gave him at the handoff.

"How much of a case do you have against Leland Aiken?" Calvin asked.

Jacob grimaced. "Not as much as we'd like. Tangential connections, but no smoking gun. Nothing that would stand up in court. He's too smart to do the dirty work himself, and so far, his people haven't slipped up, or we haven't caught them in a mistake we could leverage."

"So we look into him—carefully?" Owen asked.

"Very carefully. He's wealthy and he's got a lot of powerful friends. His vampire nature isn't public knowledge. Aiken has been devilishly clever about stage managing his appearances to avoid problems. Don't try to come at him directly. Director Chambers hates having to clean up bad publicity."

Owen took the warning to heart. The smirk on Calvin's face made him suspect that tact might not be his new partner's strong suit.

"HERE'S what I could find, without getting lost in the bowels of the storage area." Mitch hurried into the room with a tray that held a few small items.

He set the collection down in front of Calvin, who sat up and leaned forward, visually inspecting the pieces while keeping his hands well clear.

"The wallet belonged to Davis. It was found in the stable behind a bar where he often met his contacts. From the scuff marks and footprints nearby, it's clear there was a scuffle, but there wasn't enough blood to suggest a mortal wound, and no body," Mitch said.

"The single cufflink and the watch chain belonged to Harris," Jacob chimed in. "They turned up in the bushes outside of the Lindell Hotel. The bellman remembered seeing a man matching Harris's description who appeared to be in distress being helped into a carriage by another man who asked directions to the hospital. None of the hospitals have a record of him arriving, and he hasn't been seen since."

Owen stretched his legs beneath the table and bumped knees with Calvin, who did not jerk away from the accidental touch.

"Let's start with the wallet." Calvin squared his shoulders and set his jaw. He looked to Owen.

"You need to know how it works when I 'read' an object. Most of the time it's not too bad. But if it's intense, I can pass out or fall over. Having a glass of water and a couple of cookies helps me recover faster."

Jacob left the room and returned a few moments later with a pitcher and glass as well as a container of mints. "Sorry—it's what I could find."

"That'll be fine, thank you." Calvin stretched out his arm and let his right hand hover above the wallet, hand open and palm down. "It's nice to have an idea of how much of a punch something is going to pack before I touch it."

He closed his eyes, and Owen watched, fascinated. The corner of Calvin's lips quirked and a tic twitched his left eye. "I'm going to make contact." He pressed his palm against the worn leather.

Calvin's sharp gasp made Owen and the others move toward him protectively. His throat worked, but no sound came. Tremors ran up and down his rigid form, and Calvin's breath came in sharp pants. Owen shifted to grab Calvin's hand away from the wallet, but Mitch shook his head.

"Let him be. He's not in danger," Jacob said.

Owen sat back, not fully convinced.

Calvin groaned, then began to slide sideways from his chair. Jacob grabbed at the tray as Owen slid to his knees, catching Calvin before he hit the ground.

"You're safe," Owen assured him, worried when Calvin didn't immediately open his eyes. A sheen of sweat covered his forehead even though his skin felt clammy.

Day one and I'm cradling him in my lap. God help me, this is going to test my patience.

Calvin took a deep breath and blinked several times before he seemed to come back to his senses. He hesitated just a few seconds before he pulled away from Owen and sat.

"Well, that was interesting," he said with an attempt at humor that fell flat. "Thanks for not letting me break my head open," he said to Owen.

Owen shrugged. "That wouldn't be a good way to start a partnership." He tried to ignore how solid Calvin felt, with a build that fit perfectly in his lap, making his cock chub in his pants.

Calvin got to his feet, waving off further help, and reclaimed his chair. "Davis was jumped. Caught by surprise, overpowered. Pain—a stab wound, possibly. He fought. That must have been how the wallet got dropped. I didn't pick anything up after that. He...feared... whoever grabbed him."

"Feared?" Mitch echoed.

Calvin nodded. "Usually when I scan something dropped in a fight I pick up on a lot of anger, tension, and the rush of danger. Davis was an experienced agent?"

"Yes," Jacob replied. "Nearly ten years in the field."

"So he knew how to handle himself in a normal scuffle. Confidence and experience should have tempered his reaction. But Davis was terrified. Which makes me wonder if his attackers weren't human," Calvin suggested.

Mitch and Jacob shared a look. "Vampires?" Mitch asked.

Jacob shrugged. "Dunno. We don't have enough information."

Calvin drank the water and ate a couple of mints. Owen refilled his glass and Calvin shot him a grateful smile that warmed something deep in Owen's belly despite his effort to stay professional.

"Let me take a look at the other stuff," Calvin said.

"Are you sure?" Mitch's eyes narrowed. "I'd rather not have to carry you out feet-first before you've even gotten the keys to your Pullman car."

"I'll be fine," Calvin assured them. "I've seen a lot worse." The emotion that glinted in his eyes, quickly there and gone, told Owen that the other man had glimpsed horrors he'd rather not remember.

Jacob pushed the tray closer, and Calvin once more let his hand hover over the cuff link and broken chain. Calvin's eyes closed and he slipped into a trance. As his palm neared the jewelry, Calvin frowned, looking worried and then puzzled. When he finally touched the items, his eyes flew open in alarm and he bolted from his chair toward the waste can in the corner, where he promptly emptied the contents of his stomach.

Calvin leaned against the wall with one hand, shoulders hunched, and wiped his mouth with his fist. Owen sprang up to follow and handed him a handkerchief and the water glass, receiving a nod in acknowledgment.

For a moment, Calvin stayed still, breathing hard, tense as if trying to avoid a repeat performance. Finally he turned and leaned against the wall, looking pale.

"Pretty sure Harris was poisoned. He was suddenly, violently ill. And suspicious, in spite of everything. He dropped the cufflink and broke the chain on purpose. Probably hoping that Davis would find the clue and know to look for him."

"They were last heard from within hours of each other," Jacob said. "So if they were snatched, it seems likely to have been planned because that's too much of a coincidence."

Calvin made his way back to the table. Owen stayed close, not touching but near enough to grab him if he stumbled. After more water and mints, Calvin seemed to sort through his impressions.

"Whatever hit Harris hit quickly," Calvin said. "I'm thinking something injected instead of tainted food or drink. He just collapsed. I picked up confusion, surprise, realization that he was in trouble, and fear."

"Want to bet that the Good Samaritans who said they'd take him to the hospital were the ones who dosed him?" Owen theorized. "Especially since he never showed up at a hospital."

Mitch swore under his breath. "Very likely. But both men were still alive at the moment captured with the impressions?"

"Yeah. That doesn't mean they still are. Which raises the question —why capture two agents, especially if they're hot on the trail? Too much chance for rescue or escape," Owen said. "There's been no ransom note?"

"No. Interrogation maybe?" Jacob asked in a flat voice, eyes cold and hard. "Someone wanted to know how much we know. Once they got their information, Davis and Harris would no longer be useful."

"So where are the bodies, if they weren't among the…pieces…that turned up?" Calvin asked, still looking nauseated.

Mitch shook his head. "I suspect they'll turn up—or we'll find someone who will squeal. Probably too late to help them, but maybe we can give their families closure."

"Do the families know they're missing?" Owen wasn't close to his own kin. They either faulted him for working for the government or for not having already married. Both situations required far too many lies to paper over the truth, so he kept his distance. If the two kidnapped agents had people who expected to hear from them, his heart went out to them.

"Not yet. We generally don't notify next of kin until we have a body," Jacob replied. "So if in the course of your investigation you find out what happened to them, the service will take it from there."

"That's all we have," Mitch said.

"Are there other Supernatural Secret Service agents based in St. Louis aside from Special Agent Chambers?" Owen asked.

"No. The head office dispatches agents to where there are cases to investigate. This was an oddity happening in and around St. Louis," Jacob replied. "Which is why we were brought in to cover until they could get your paperwork finished. Once you handle the situation, you'll be shipped out too. Hence the Pullman car."

"Speaking of which," Mitch said, standing, "I'll have the doorman put your luggage in the carriage and we'll drive you to the station. The car is on a siding until you need to leave. Winston is no doubt waiting for you."

"Winston?" Owen didn't remember hearing that name before.

"He comes with the car," Jacob told him. "The new valet. Semi-retired former field agent who now specializes in research, errands, and protection—as well as cooking and taking care of the living quarters. Winston's a bit eccentric, but he's good at what he does. Don't underestimate him. He's a valuable ally—and one hell of a good cook."

Calvin's shoulder brushed against Owen's as they jostled to get into the carriage. Although the vehicle held four, squeezing grown men inside made for a tight fit. Owen didn't object to being pressed hip to knee against Calvin for the ride. *Might as well enjoy my hopeless fantasy while I can.*

Chapter 2
Calvin

When Calvin looked back over the past day and a half, he didn't think things could get any weirder.

First, he couldn't believe his luck when he found a seat across from a handsome man who was traveling by himself. Even if the man was—quite probably—not interested in other men, Calvin had a nice view for the long trip, a bit of conversation, and a new face for his late-night jack-off sessions.

Then the stranger turned out to be fascinating, which upped Calvin's interest even more, especially when he got a glimpse of the tall, muscular body beneath the tailored suit. Calvin had long-ago mastered deniable flirting, and was delighted when the other man seemed inclined to play along.

Calvin usually refrained from seeking partners outside of the private men's clubs that catered to his tastes. Membership organizations were far less likely to have undercover police looking to bust men like him, and Calvin had no desire to be caught in a roundup. *But for my very interesting seatmate, I'd consider making an exception, if I thought he played for my team.*

That night on the train, as he lay awake listening to the clack of the wheels and the rails, Calvin remembered his last conversation with Serena, his best friend, before leaving Boston.

"Change is good for you, Cal," she'd said, toying with a glass of gin while her girlfriend watched the band play. For all that Boston was known for its propriety, there were secret corners for bars and clubs that offered gathering places with relative safety for those who didn't fit the mold.

"Maybe you'll meet someone," Serena continued, ignoring Calvin's derisive snort. "Hey, it could happen!"

"You're an optimist and I love you for it, but guys like me are lucky to get a quick tumble without getting arrested. Happily ever afters aren't part of the package."

"You didn't believe that when you were with Jeremiah," Serena said gently.

Calvin tried to hide his wince. "And look where it led." Jeremiah was a bookish artist, quite a contrast to Calvin's dangerous work and his rough-and-tumble past. They'd shared a connection Calvin had almost dared to call love, something beyond physical attraction. Jeremiah didn't question Calvin's frequent absences, welcoming him back with a willing body and a warm bed.

Then Calvin returned from an assignment to find Jeremiah's loft deserted, his whereabouts unknown. Calvin suspected foul play and used his law enforcement connections to make enquiries—using a non-existent case to dispel curiosity. Jeremiah had been murdered, and his unclaimed body buried in a pauper's field. No one had investigated because he'd been rumored to be one of "that sort."

Serena was one of the few who knew that before the Army and the Supernatural Secret Service, Calvin ran with Irish street gangs. His father had given him a choice to enlist or be turned over to the police. But he'd never forgotten what he'd learned in those switchblade years.

He spent a couple of nights undercover and sussed out the killers. He'd gotten them blackout drunk, stripped them naked and posed them in compromising positions, planted a dozen stolen wallets and watches among their things, and tipped off both their gangs and the cops. Jeremiah wouldn't have wanted Calvin to do murder, but his dark sense of humor would have felt satisfied at the men's humiliation and the likely repercussions.

"You deserve better than fucking frat boys and spoiled heirs for one-night stands." Serena tossed her dark curls over her shoulder as she watched her girlfriend sway to the music.

"Like you didn't lick your way through Miss Pomeroy's School for Young Ladies." Calvin gave her a pointed look and knocked back his whiskey.

"Of course I did. It was a finishing school and I didn't stop until I was finished," Serena replied with a wicked grin. *"That was then. But we're both in our thirties now, Cal. Time to settle down. I like the life Deanna and I have. It's solid. Nice to come home to the same person every night."*

"And that, my dear, is why it will never work for me." Calvin beckoned the bartender for another shot. *"I travel constantly. People shoot at me. I make very powerful enemies. I'm not home long enough to have a proper relationship or keep a partner safe."*

"What happened to Jeremiah wasn't your fault. Don't use him as an excuse to hide your heart."

Calvin kissed the top of her head. *"I hear what you're saying. I'm just planning to ignore you. You'll always be my best girl."*

Serena snickered. *"The word you're looking for is 'beard'. Don't worry— I've got a friend lined up for you in St. Louis who won't blow your cover. Pinkerton agent, posing as a showgirl. You'll be perfect for each other. She doesn't fancy men, and you don't cotton to women. It's a match made in heaven."*

Calvin had snuck a glance at his sleeping companion. *Was he really flirting with me? I wish I had extra time in St. Louis to find out. Do dinner. Have a romp. Serena was right—I do want more, but when do we ever get what we really want?*

Discovering that his train acquaintance was his new SSS partner had nearly put Calvin in a panic, going back over his words and gestures to make sure he hadn't accidentally let too much slip. When Owen didn't react strangely, Calvin relaxed. The immediate attraction he felt was going to be difficult to hide, as well as the way his dick hardened when Owen brushed against him.

He's probably not interested. Even if he is, it's dangerous mixing work and play. But…it could be the perfect arrangement. A reason to be with each other at all hours. Traveling together. No need to lie about my job. Perfect…and unlikely. Guess I'll be taking more cold showers than usual.

The damnable part was, the more time Calvin spent with Owen, the more he liked him. They played off each other well at the headquarters briefing, and Owen had been quick to lend a hand when Calvin passed out from touching the dead man's wallet.

I really didn't mind waking up in his arms. I just had to get away before my cock woke up too.

"Penny for your thoughts." Owen bumped his shoulder as they rode in the carriage, jostling Calvin out of his silence.

Calvin cleared his throat. "Just thinking about what I saw when I read the wallet's energy. I can get stuck in my head a little after one of those sessions."

"Understandable," Owen replied. "I've got to say—that was pretty impressive."

"The vision part or the fainting part?" Calvin turned away to hide his blush at Owen's praise. He'd learned early to use humor to deflect, and he definitely needed to gently keep Owen at a safe distance or he'd be plagued with blue balls for the entire assignment.

"Both." Owen chuckled. "Should make for interesting times."

"How about you? What's it like seeing ghosts?" Calvin's natural curiosity melded with his desire to learn more about his new partner.

Owen hesitated, and then let out a deep breath. "I've been able to sense spirits all my life, although I didn't realize what was actually going on until I was older. I just thought I had a good imagination."

"Can you see them, or do you just get a feeling that they're around?" Calvin could imagine the benefits to having that sort of talent, but he guessed there were also drawbacks, like with his own abilities.

"It depends." Owen seemed a little uncomfortable talking about the subject, and Calvin wondered if he'd run into a lot of skeptics through the years.

"Sometimes the ghosts almost look alive—solid, no wounds. In other cases, they're more like fog or shadows. Certain ghosts can move objects. Usually the temperature drops, and there might be a cold draft—most people can feel that, even without being a medium."

"And they can talk to you?" Jacob leaned forward, elbows on knees, giving Owen his rapt attention. Calvin felt an irrational stab of jealousy, and did his best to squelch it, knowing that the other agent's interest was purely professional.

"Often, but not always," Owen answered. "Sometimes they can write in the dust or on a foggy mirror. Occasionally a ghost can direct me to write for them."

"Automatic writing," Mitch said. "I've heard about that with Spiritualists."

Owen shook his head. "It's just part of being a medium, not tied to philosophical views. If a ghost can't speak or write, sometimes we can work out a code—two taps for 'no,' for example. And there's always the Ouija board."

"Those actually work?" Calvin's eyebrows rose with surprise.

"They do for me," Owen replied with a shrug. "Can't say for sure about other people."

"Do you have to go looking for the spirits or do they find you?" Calvin asked. "Are we going to have a bunch of ghosts in our parlor every morning?" Picturing a haunted train car was safer than imagining Owen sleeping and showering just a few feet away, so close but out of reach.

"We'll take the usual precautions—salting the doors and windows, iron filings, holy water. You don't have to worry about having ghosts invade your sleeping room, if that's what you're worried about." Owen laughed.

"Given that the Pullman belongs to the Supernatural Secret Service, many of those protections were built in," Mitch said.

The carriage finally drew up at its destination in the train yard. They stopped alongside a streamlined beauty of a sleeper car, gleaming black with chrome accents, sleek and aerodynamic.

"This is where we'll live?" Owen asked, looking as stunned as Calvin felt at the unexpected windfall. Calvin had endured plenty of bland apartments in his time with law enforcement. The Boston office didn't outfit its agents with sleeper cars, but then again, it didn't send them as far afield.

Jacob grinned. "Yep. Nice, huh? Mitch and I clearly picked the wrong branch of the government. We get rooming houses with stern landladies."

"It was fun squatting here while they finished your paperwork," Mitch said. "Come on—we'll give you the tour and see if Winston is here."

Calvin couldn't stifle an awed gasp. At the back, the Pullman had a generous observation platform, which opened into a well-appointed parlor with dark wood walls, a hammered tin ceiling, and furnishings in emerald green velvet. Couches, arm chairs, and side tables gave the room the look of a fine hotel.

"Cars like this tend to have six sleeping rooms, but Nighthawk—that's the car's name—has been customized to what agents need in the field," Jacob added, playing tour guide. "You've got three sleeping quarters—complete with private baths. One for each of you, plus Winston."

He led them down a narrow hallway with dark wooden walls and a deep green carpet. "The dark colors help hide bloodstains," Mitch noted before opening a door into one of the bedrooms.

"Full-sized bed, chair, and desk, ample room to store your things, a large window, and a sink, shower, and toilet," Jacob tag-teamed the description.

"The other bedrooms are identical, but this is where the changes were made," Mitch jumped in. He opened a door to reveal a room with white tiled walls and stainless steel tables. Glass-fronted cabinets held a wealth of scientific instruments and medical supplies. At the other end of the room, a wooden worktable and apothecary cabinets clearly had a more occult vibe.

"Everything you need to handle medical emergencies, do just about everything you could in a full laboratory, and work a rather astonishingly wide variety of magics," Mitch continued.

"While in here, we have the library and a telegraph station," Jacob said, leading Owen and Calvin into a room filled floor to ceiling with bookshelves.

Dark wooden shelves, a small reading table, and a couple of comfortable chairs rivaled anything Calvin had seen in London's tony private gentleman's clubs. The lamps reminded him of the copper-shaded reading lights in the New York Public Library.

"There's also a little surprise." Jacob went to one of the bookshelves, pressed his fingers into a niche in the cabinetry, and the shelf swung forward on a hinge, revealing racks of guns, knives, and other assorted weapons.

"Is that a flame-thrower?" Calvin asked, awed.

"Yes. As well as machine guns, hand grenades, land mines, a couple of hand mortars, plus some experimental technology courtesy of inventor friends at Tesla-Westinghouse," Jacob said. "Winston can fill you in on those."

Jacob slid the bookshelf back into place and they returned to the corridor where he led them to a dining room. A mahogany table dominated the space, with dark green velvet draperies and matching upholstery on the chairs. One wall held glass-fronted cabinets with bottles of liquor and wine.

"You can wine and dine contacts or suspects here in privacy, with protections," Mitch said. "Up front there's a full kitchen and pantry. Just let Winston know what you need and he'll make arrangements and get supplies."

"You've mentioned 'protections' a couple of times," Calvin ventured. "What does that include?"

Mitch grinned, and Jacob groaned.

"He thought you'd never ask," Jacob said in a jokingly put-upon tone.

"The steel walls and ceiling are reinforced to stop most gunfire, and the glass is an experimental prototype that will fracture but not shatter from bullets," Mitch replied. "You've got a special air filtration system—top secret—in case of a gas attack. The undercarriage can withstand driving over a significant TNT explosion."

"Every room except the laboratory has pipes of salted holy water with iron filings built into the frames for the doors and windows and other openings," Jacob continued. "The lab and spell room were omitted for obvious reasons, so if you need to do a séance, that's your best bet. Warding sigils against demons, dark magic, and a fairly exhaustive list of supernatural nasties have been worked into the steel behind the walls."

"There are some other hidden weapons and supernatural goodies —Winston can explain," Mitch added.

Calvin struggled to keep his jaw from dropping. Owen seemed to be equally surprised while Mitch and Jacob shared a grin at their reaction.

"It's really something, isn't it?" Mitch said. "We think the Supernatural Secret Service gets fancier digs than DSI because you technically represent the President."

"Do we have a cover story?" Owen asked. "Because riding around in a car like this isn't my idea of 'secret.'"

"Actually, yes." They turned to look at Jacob. "They've created background stories for both of you. You're agents for a group of private investors looking for good business opportunities. The dossiers on your fake personas are waiting for you in the library."

"We also forgot to mention that you've been issued three fine riding horses, battle-trained so they won't spook from gunfire," Mitch said. "They have their own stock car for when you travel. Winston will arrange to have them stabled nearby for extended stays."

"When do we get to meet this elusive Winston?" Calvin asked.

Mitch checked his pocket watch. "He went to check on the horses, so I assume he'll be here any minute."

"Winston is a rather remarkable jack-of-all-trades," Jacob added. "He's a trained field medic, a chemist, and a tinkerer. He's also a witch and a damned good cook."

"He's a fellow with a fascinating story, but we'll let him share that," Mitch said. "You'll be spending plenty of time together. Don't underestimate him—he's a valuable asset, and I think he'll make a good traveling companion."

"My ears are burning—are you telling these gents about me?" A man with thinning brown and gray hair and a full beard bustled toward them from the front end of the car. He stood a few inches shorter than either Calvin or Owen, with a stocky build, round face, and a glint of mischief in intelligent, bespectacled brown eyes.

"Winston Smith, these are Agents Sharps and Springfield. Agents, this is Winston," Jacob said.

"Pleased to meet you." Winston greeted them with a firm hand-shake. "And I'm sorry that you'll be moving on," he added with a look to Mitch and Jacob.

"You took great care of us," Jacob acknowledged. "And I dare say these guys will keep you on your toes."

"Which means—the handoff is complete," Mitch said. "This is where we bow out and let you get down to sleuthing. Jacob and I will be on a train to New Pittsburgh this evening. Good luck—and Winston knows how to reach us by telegram if you have questions."

After another round of well-wishes and handshakes, Mitch and Jacob returned to their carriage.

"Well lads, how about a cup of tea? I'll unpack your bags and then let's meet in the library where I can go over your documents and get you properly settled in. Tomorrow, we can go to the stable so you can meet the horses," Winston told them.

Calvin guessed that their new assistant might be in his late forties, but despite the gray in his hair and beard, his voice and manner exuded energy.

"The stove keeps water warm most of the day, handy if you need tea or coffee," Winston told them as he headed back to the galley and returned with two porcelain cups with saucers, which he set on the dining room table. "Take a moment, catch your breath, and when you're ready, I'll see you in the library."

At that, he turned toward the sleeping compartments, leaving Calvin and Owen alone in their new home on wheels.

"Fancy." Owen held his cup as he made a slow turn to take in the details.

"Pretty damn impressive," Calvin admitted. He was completely poleaxed at the sleeper car's amenities. His previous work with the service had not included anything like this, but then again the new job included a promotion and clearly required more travel.

Now that they were alone again, Calvin felt acutely aware of Owen. In the carriage, he had picked up on the scent of Owen's pomander and cologne, a woody, musky fragrance that had his cock at half-mast and made him want to bury his nose in his partner's hair.

Between the close quarters of the drive to the train station and the narrow corridor in the Pullman car, the two men had brushed shoulders, arms, and hips. Each time it sent a frisson of awareness through Calvin like a live spark.

Owen's attention seemed to be fully on their new accommodations. Calvin took the opportunity of the distraction with Mitch and Jacob playing tour guide to take another look at the man who tormented his libido.

I wonder what he'd taste like—lips and cock. How would he do it? Top, bottom, or maybe change it up? Is he quiet or a screamer? I'd like to find out.

Most of Calvin's escapades had lasted a few hours, a night at most. Only with Jeremiah had there been anything resembling an actual relationship with time spent together, and given his travel, that had gone by far too quickly.

Being in each other's pockets will make it harder to slip away to scratch an itch. Could Owen possibly share the same interests? And if so, how colossally stupid would it be to mix business and pleasure?

Best to keep up appearances, until I know for certain. Too high a price to be paid for guessing wrong.

Calvin had heard of other agents who were blackmailed for their sexual interests. In the Army, he'd seen some unlucky fellows receive court-martials for getting caught with their pants down and their dicks up. He'd known others who took beatings or worse just on the basis of rumors or suspicions.

Still, when he and Owen headed to the library, Calvin couldn't help taking in a deep breath to catch the other man's scent and imagine for just a second what it might feel like to press together, skin to skin.

"Welcome to the library and armory," Winston said with a broad smile. Laid out on the desk were two dossiers, half a dozen fake badges for each of them, and some items Calvin had never seen before.

"I'll let you take your time reading up on your new selves." Winston handed them the thick envelopes. "We'll have contacts with the service wherever we travel, but otherwise, we stick to the cover story. You're investors, and I'm your harmless valet." His smile flashed a glimpse of teeth, putting the lie to the descriptor.

"That doesn't mean you have to use your real names. You have your official badges, but we have others with various names and titles for different agencies. If we need something different, I can make that happen." Winston dusted his hands together.

"I trust you've brought your personal sidearms?" he asked, and both nodded. "Good. I manage the armory's assets. Anything you need, I'll make sure you have. The library is stocked with all sorts of helpful books, and some classic literature and penny dreadfuls as well," he added with a conspiratorial wink. "Plenty of lore, grimoires, and volumes on legends and monsters. It should serve for the kinds of things we'll be chasing."

"Are you really a witch?" Calvin couldn't help asking. Owen gave him a side eye, but Calvin bet his partner wondered too.

Winston folded his arms over his chest. "I am. Is that a problem?" His jovial smile flattened, and Calvin saw steel in his eyes.

"Not at all," Calvin hurried to assure. "Just been a while since I've worked with someone who could do more than a few simple spells."

Winston seemed to relax at the admission. "I've been working the craft all my life, trained with some powerful folks. I prefer being out of the line of fire, supporting folks like the two of you. But if the chips are down, I'll be right there with you, and my magic can hold its own."

Calvin and Owen stayed in the library to review their files while Winston headed for the galley to make dinner. As Owen settled in at the desk, Calvin detoured for a look at the telegraph setup.

"It's done right, I'll give them that," he said appreciatively, checking out the equipment. "There's also a telephone for when we're in the station. Won't work when we're moving, but it's a nice option."

"Assuming that whoever you need to talk to has a telephone," Owen observed.

"There is that," Calvin agreed. He sat in the lounge chair closest to Owen.

"Here's your folio," Owen said, passing the folder to him. On the front was a symbol identical to those of the mundane Secret Service except that the star in the center was clearly a pentagram, and the line of Latin beneath came from the Rituale Romano exorcism.

"What are the other badges?" Calvin nodded toward several more slim wallets.

"For undercover work, I assume. When our fake personas need to be even more fake." Owen sounded vaguely amused and handed over the stack.

Calvin examined them with a mixture of amusement and incredulity.

"Department of Justice. US Marshals. Texas Rangers. Is it still illegal to impersonate a government agent if you actually *are* a government agent?" Calvin mused aloud. He frowned, taking a closer look at the names. "Wait a minute. Is this Winston's idea of a joke?"

"What?"

"These names. George Gaskin and Steve Porter, Dan Quinn and Frank Stanley," Calvin read aloud. At Owen's perplexed expression, he sighed. "Don't you get out much? They're famous singers. I saw Gaskin perform in New York once, and I was at a vaudeville show in Chicago where Porter sang."

"Huh. Well—I guess we just hope anyone we use those on doesn't live the high life," Owen replied, drolly teasing.

"Take a look at your folio. I can't wait to hear what you think of...yourself."

Calvin opened the folder, but he couldn't resist glancing at his partner, who seemed to be completely engrossed in reading. Owen was personable and had asked plenty of questions, but the easy-going —possibly flirtatious—side he'd shown on the train to St. Louis seemed to have been buttoned up as neatly as his suit coat.

Maybe I misread him. Perhaps he was just being off-duty friendly and didn't mean to flirt. Or he's changed his mind and doesn't want to risk the partnership. Probably smart. But still...

Calvin couldn't help smarting a bit at the tinge of rejection. Owen was the first man since Jeremiah who had caught his attention for more than carnal reasons, and letting go of the fantasy—however short-lived—stung.

Take a deep breath and give it up. We'll be working together indefinitely. It's less complicated this way. Owen certainly seems like he'd be a good work partner and a loyal friend. Those are in short supply. But if anything else did develop over time...that would be amazing.

"So how is 'fake you'?" Calvin asked after they read for a while. Whatever Winston was cooking for dinner smelled fantastic and made his stomach rumble.

"Both fake and real, I'm apparently just as hungry as you are." Owen chuckled when his gut made an answering growl. Calvin found himself lulled by Owen's soft drawl, something he'd never found arousing before.

"It looks as if they kept most of the story as close to the truth as possible. They fudged details about my family, of course, made me an only child and a widower. Instead of my time with the Army and the service, I apparently traveled through the South buying up hotels and cotton mills. That's actually sort of funny."

Something sharp-edged in Owen's tone caught Calvin's attention. "Why?"

Owen looked away. "My real grandfather was a wealthy businessman in Georgia who refused to support the Confederacy. He and my grandmother and their small children had to flee for their lives since that wasn't a popular opinion. He lost everything and was disowned. I was probably safer in the Army than I would be going anywhere south of Baltimore."

"Huh. Interesting. My real grandfather was an abolitionist merchant," Calvin said. "Had no tolerance for slavery or indenture. Managed to make his way even though Irish Catholics weren't always welcome." Calvin wasn't sure he'd ever want to admit his time with the gangs. Even if he and Owen were only work partners—and maybe friends—he didn't want Owen to think badly of him. That mattered to a degree that surprised him—and was better left unexamined.

He flipped through the folder. "I'm apparently a confirmed bachelor according to this," Calvin added. "Oldest son of a rich banker in

Boston. No tragic history. Although they suggest I have a weakness for betting on card games—and a talent for winning. I'm rumored to have won a couple of duels in New Orleans against angry husbands and jilted boyfriends. I'm something of a rake, girl in every town."

Owen flashed him a grin that didn't reach his eyes. "I could believe that. It suits you. Much better than my story—they made me an accountant. How much more boring can it get?" He sounded seriously aggrieved, which made Calvin smile.

"You're clearly the moneyman, which is not too awful. And much less likely to be shot by a cuckolded husband than 'fake me' is." He leaned forward conspiratorially. "Less likely to have the clap too."

Owen rolled his eyes. "Ew."

Calvin leaned back, laughing at his partner's annoyance. "Well, it's true. They've set you up to be the good, analytic, reasonable one. I'm the wild card, unpredictable and maybe a little dangerous. We can work with that." He shrugged. "The details might be fake, but they seem to have gotten the basics true to life."

Owen raised an eyebrow. "Oh, you think so?"

"Am I wrong?" Calvin's teasing challenge hung between them, stretched a bit too long, fraught with tension.

"Dinner is served." Winston's announcement over the speaker tube broke the moment, and both stilled with sudden awkwardness.

"Damn, I hope there's some good whiskey for afterward," Calvin said as they filed out of the library. He couldn't help a glance at the way Owen's trousers showed off a fine ass. *I don't know what was going on a few minutes ago, but I've got to be more careful. Owen's got an effect on me that's more spunk than spell. I need to rein this in before it gets dangerous.*

WINSTON'S MEAL OF BRISKET, baked beans, and mashed potatoes hit the spot. Both Calvin and Owen had seconds, and Winston beamed at their praise.

"We're in St. Louis. I do my best to adapt to the local foods," he told them.

"We're going to have to do a lot of running to keep from gaining weight if you feed us like this every night," Owen joked.

"The job keeps you active. I need to keep your energy up."

Dessert was a chocolate torte with good whiskey. Calvin felt some of the tension ease from his shoulders. Owen seemed a bit less distant, though not as approachable as when they first met. Winston remained properly reserved, but with a hint of mischief that made Calvin suspect their new assistant had secrets of his own.

"What did you think of your folders?" Winston nursed a cup of coffee as they sipped their drinks.

"Amusing," Calvin replied.

Owen looked resigned. "Why do I always have to be the boring partner? Just once, I'd like to be a high-rolling riverboat gambler or maybe the wastrel son of some exiled nobleman."

"But that would leave me being the responsible one," Calvin protested. "And who would believe that?"

Full bellies and good whiskey gave them back the repartee they'd shared as strangers on a train. Calvin didn't realize how much he missed that connection until it vanished in propriety and professional distance.

"What are your plans for tomorrow?" Winston asked. If he noticed the back-and-forth between Calvin and Owen, he didn't react.

"I have a contact in town, a reporter who helped me on a previous case," Owen said. "I thought I'd start there. See what she knows."

"Is she pretty?" Calvin fell into the kind of teasing that he'd perfected as a cover.

Owen shrugged. "Pretty enough, I guess. She's smart, connected, and knows how to dig up dirt. I like that in a woman."

Calvin didn't know what to make of that, so he smiled in defense. "Better make sure you're wearing your best collar and cuffs. Women notice that sort of thing. Good impressions and all." He nudged Owen with his elbow as if he had imparted dating wisdom.

"What about you?" Owen's mellow mood seemed to have faded.

"I've got a friend in town. Showgirl at Kearson's Palace." Calvin did his best to sound off-handed. "She's popular with the customers and hears plenty of gossip. Always saves the best for me." He gave a conspiratorial wink. Calvin left out that Louisa was a Pinkerton and berated himself for hoping Owen looked jealous.

He didn't. Calvin felt his heart sink.

"Girl in every town. Maybe your folder really did have you pegged." Owen knocked back the rest of his whiskey and stood. "Winston— thank you for a great meal. Calvin—I'll see you when I see you."

"I'll have coffee and breakfast ready by seven," Winston told them. "We'll find a rhythm. I'll be working on a few spells that might come in handy, and it's my day to sharpen the blades."

Owen hesitated. "Which room is mine?"

"Mr. Springfield is the first room on the right. You're in the second, and I'm in the third," Winston replied. "Everything is stowed away, and your beds are turned down. Sleep well."

Owen thanked him with a nod and lumbered off. Calvin lingered at the table, bothered by the thoughts that swirled in his mind like the whiskey in his glass.

"Will you be requiring anything else, sir?" Winston's question roused Calvin from his musings.

"No. No, thank you. Everything's been great. I'm not an early riser, so please save me a couple of cups of coffee," Calvin replied.

Winston chuckled. "You can count on me." He headed into the kitchen, leaving Calvin alone.

Calvin finished his drink and set the heavy leaded glass down with a thump. He hadn't drunk enough to silence his worries, but he'd had enough to make it difficult to push troublesome thoughts aside.

He took a hot shower, glad to sluice away the sweat of the day and a night spent on a train with completely different amenities. Calvin tried not to think that Owen was on the other side of the stateroom wall, stripping out of his clothes, maybe showering and letting the water run over his lean body.

Calvin's soapy hand fell to his neglected cock, already erect and leaking from being half-hard all day. He jerked himself off quick and rough, punishingly fast, angry at himself for not being able to rinse Owen out of his mind, desperate for release.

He pictured himself on his knees, sucking Owen's cock. It would be long and generously sized, Calvin fantasized, circumcised and flushed pink with arousal. Owen would buck and jerk under Calvin's practiced attention, begging for release, offering increasingly filthy suggestions of what to do next, and promising to return the favor.

Calvin bit his lip to stifle a gasp as he came hard, spurting against the wall of the shower and nearly buckling his knees. He steadied himself as the jizz washed from the tile and swirled down the drain.

I've got to stop thinking like this. It's going to ruin a good assignment. There's no reason to think Owen shares my interests. We could be friends and excellent partners. That's enough. I just need to get laid. That shouldn't be too difficult to arrange. Take the edge off. It's been a while. Then I can put everything in perspective and get back to normal.

Calvin toweled off and put on pajamas, making sure his gun was under his pillow. The full-sized bed afforded the chance to stretch out, far more comfortable than the cramped seating of the train to St. Louis the night before.

He'd always found the clickety-clack of the rails and the train's sway to be like a nightcap and a lullaby combined. Their car wasn't traveling tonight, and he struggled to fall asleep despite a good meal, a stiff drink, and a tiring day.

I'll talk to Louisa, and while I'm out on the town, I'll stop by the club Serena suggested. Maybe I'll find a rancher's son or a cattle baron's heir to fuck into the mattress. That'll do it.

Despite his promise to himself, Calvin dreamed of Owen's body pinning him down, pushing his legs apart, sliding down to encase his cock in the wet heat of his mouth. It was Owen's long fingers that opened Calvin's ass with practiced, careful skill and prepared him to ride his long, elegant prick. It was Owen's voice that groaned in ecstasy when he slid into Calvin's tight channel, his lips and hands exploring all of Calvin's skin.

Calvin woke in the middle of the night, sweaty and panting with a tell-tale wet spot on his sleep pants. He could still hear the faint echo of Owen's imagined endearments and sexy talk.

I am in so much trouble.

Chapter 3
Owen

Owen woke to the smell of bacon. He took a deep breath, steeled himself to face daylight, and opened his eyes.

He'd slept well, happy that the bed was big enough for his lanky frame, which contributed to a good, but short, night's sleep. A hot shower before bed had done wonders to ease the tension in his neck, and the whiskey on top of a hearty meal should have made him drowsy.

At first, Owen had laid awake, mind still racing, long into the night.

Calvin seems like he'll be a good work partner. We might get to be close friends. If that's all it ever is between us, that's better than many assignments. Assuming we're successful, we could be working together for years. The pay is right, the sleeper car is amazing, and Winston is a bonus.

So why do I want the one thing I can't have?

His memory had unhelpfully cataloged Calvin's movements and comments throughout the day, analyzing them to see if there might be any hidden intentions. He had been painfully aware of his handsome partner's body all day—how he sat, walked, and inhabited space. Owen had studied Calvin's expressions and gestures, as well as his tone and word choice.

It all boiled down to being inconclusive. Maybe Calvin's words and actions hid a dangerous subtext of mutual desire. Quite probably, Owen admitted, anything beyond platonic interest and friendship was all in his imagination.

Accepting defeat hadn't stopped Owen's overactive brain from serving up a wet dream of Calvin's naked body twined with his own, exploring everywhere, trying everything. He woke sticky and chagrined, and the only thing that kept him from taking a shower in the wee hours of the morning was the fear that Calvin and Winston might hear the water running and deduce the reason.

Just because I'm attracted to Calvin doesn't mean anything has to happen. We're adults. Professionals. We'll be trusting each other with our lives. Living together. Maybe we'll be like brothers. Having someone in my life like that would be wonderful, even if it never crosses that line.

But if there were ever a situation where two men could hide in plain sight and have a real relationship, this would be it.

He took a quick—cold—morning shower and hurried to dress, lured by the aromas of breakfast. Winston looked like he had been up for hours already.

"Good morning, Mr. Sharps."

"Please—call me Owen."

Winston smiled and nodded, but didn't promise a change. "Breakfast is ready. Coffee, pastries, bacon, scrambled eggs, and potatoes. Have a seat. I'll bring you a plate and the morning paper."

"Have you seen Calvin?"

Winston shook his head. "I don't believe he's awake yet."

Owen figured that was probably a good thing since he wasn't clear-headed enough to encounter Calvin before he'd had his coffee. He glanced at the headlines, looking for anything that might be associated with their case, and saw nothing that was the slightest bit irregular.

Then again, people in power can keep information like that out of the public eye.

"Here you go." Winston placed a full plate in front of him. "Enjoy! And there's more if you'd like seconds." He brought a pot of coffee and a pitcher of cream, for which Owen was grateful. He knew he'd need several cups to make up for the past two sleep-challenged nights.

"Do you know your plans for the day?" Winston seemed to be avoiding the use of any salutation as a compromise. "I recommend always giving me an idea of your whereabouts so that someone knows where you've gone, just in case."

"I appreciate having someone looking out for us," Owen told him, pausing to let his first bites settle. "The last time I was in St. Louis, I met a reporter who had a keen eye for details and a good grasp of who was pulling the strings. I'm sure she's been looking into the murders, and I'm interested to see what she's made of it. Seems like a good place to start."

"You'll be able to hire a carriage to take you into the city at the station platform, and the trolley isn't far," Winston replied. "There's always something to eat here if you happen to come back mid-day. I plan supper for eight unless I'm told otherwise."

"If every meal is like the one last night, I will not be late," Owen said with sincere appreciation. He drank another cup of coffee, waved off seconds, and pushed his chair back from the table.

"I have some research and spell work to tend to and a trip to the market early in the day. Our horses are boarded at a stable where they'll be well cared for, but at some point before you need to ride, I'd suggest we take a trip over so you know where to find them and can make their acquaintance," Winston added.

Owen had always had a soft spot for horses. "I'm looking forward to it. With luck, today will be a useful scouting expedition, and Calvin and I can compare notes when we both return."

He left the newspaper for his partner, grabbed his coat with his badge already in a pocket, and tucked his gun into its holster. "Thanks for holding the fort, Winston. See you later." Owen snagged his hat from a hook near the door and headed outside.

The fresh air helped to clear his mind, and he walked briskly toward the main platform. Owen had Ida's calling card from his previous visit and hoped that she was still working for the *Post-Dispatch*.

Morgan Brice

Owen remembered Ida Hardin as diligent and clever. She was tough, making her way in the newspaper business where there were few other women who weren't secretaries. Ida asked hard questions, refused to be intimidated by powerful people, and possessed the unswerving integrity most journalists Owen had met only pretended to maintain.

If he liked women, he'd have fallen for Ida head over heels.

Owen suspected that Ida had guessed his secret. Maybe she'd felt relieved to know he had no hidden agenda. At least for now, she'd eschewed any romantic entanglements for her craft. That single-minded determination shone through in her work, especially the exposés that others hesitated to pursue.

In other words, the gruesome deaths sounded like a story Ida was born to investigate.

Owen fidgeted as he rode in the cab into downtown St. Louis, offering one-word answers to his talkative driver and paying little attention to the passing cityscape. When they arrived outside the *Post-Dispatch* building, he paid the driver and looked up at the sturdy stone building that hunkered like a bulwark.

The receptionist met his gaze as Owen approached. "I'm here to see Ida Hardin."

"She's a busy lady. Gotta give me a name and a reason," the woman said.

Owen shared one of the calling cards Winston had made for them. Ida knew he was Secret Service, and she'd understand the subterfuge about the supernatural part.

The receptionist placed the card in a pneumatic tube and pulled a chain that sent the capsule zipping away on an elaborate metal track, shooting it upstairs to the newsroom.

Five minutes later, Owen heard the click of heels on the marble staircase, and Ida came into view, grinning broadly.

"I wondered when something would bring you back to St. Louis." She held out her hand, offering a solid, firm shake.

"Still defending truth and justice?" he joked.

"Every day. How about you?"

"Giving it my best shot," Owen replied.

Ida was a tall, spare woman. Her dark hair was coiled around her head in a spiral braid. She wore a gray fitted jacket that nipped in at the waist and flared at the shoulders over a full "skirt" that was actually wide-legged flowing pants over sensible high-button shoes. A casual observer might not notice the split skirt.

"Come this way. We need to talk." Ida led him to an empty meeting room and partially closed the door, still respectable within the watchful gaze of the receptionist through a partial window wall.

"I'm sure this isn't a social call." Ida sat on the opposite side of the table from Owen. "What's going on?"

"Gruesome murders, missing people, body parts. Sound familiar?" Owen enjoyed working with Ida. Their conversations felt like verbal sparring, a good-natured competition to solve a riddle, and a matching of wits.

"Unofficially, yes. Not something the editor wants to see on the front page. Or the mayor, the chief of police, and probably not the governor either."

"So you're investigating?"

A grin brightened Ida's features. "Of course. Depending on what I find out—and whether I lose my job for disobeying a few direct orders —it might set some folks on their ears."

"And the reason you have to investigate unofficially?" Owen suspected he already knew.

Ida shrugged. "All the usual nonsense—avoiding a public panic, murder is bad for business, warning people about a monster might harm the city's reputation. Nothing new."

Owen nodded, unsurprised. "And yet, you persist."

"Stubbornness is my best trait. Right next to intransigence." Ida smiled.

"Unofficially, my new partner and I are in town to have a look at the situation and see if it's our kind of case."

Ida knew about the supernatural and paranormal side of Owen's job. They had worked together on a werewolf case the last time he'd been in town, so maybe it was only right that they could be tracking a rogue vampire now.

"Which means you think it's more likely to be a creature than a homicidal human," Ida theorized. "And you're concerned that it's connected to something bigger, or you'd chance leaving it to regular law enforcement."

"Two for two," Owen said. "Any leads?"

Ida made a tutting noise. "Share and share alike. Tell me something I don't know."

Owen had already weighed how much he could divulge. "There's a railroad line doing some aggressive expansion. People who make big plans don't like it when others get in their way. We'd like to rule out the railroad's involvement." He didn't mention vampires, knowing that Ida would know that something, somewhere, was supernatural.

Ida's investigative instincts were good enough that Owen wondered whether she had more than a touch of clairvoyance.

"That thought has crossed my mind," Ida admitted. "Because money and murder usually go together. There's no obvious link between the people who have gone missing or whose parts have shown up."

"How about what's not obvious?" Owen pressed, enjoying their game.

Ida touched a finger to her nose. "Exactly. They all had some link to properties or businesses that would be close to the new rail line. Some of them owned land, others managed farms or factories. A few had special knowledge—a doctor, a lawyer, and a bookkeeper who dealt with people who were either part of the railroad company or in its way."

"Who directly benefits from the deaths? And why kill people so spectacularly and risk drawing attention when bodies can disappear pretty easily?" Owen voiced the questions he'd been mulling since the briefing with Mitch and Jacob.

"Well, that's the rub," Ida admitted. "It's not that direct. If my theory is right, whoever's behind this likes puzzles. But I feel in my bones that there's a bigger agenda."

"That's mostly what I'm working on too. Gut instinct," Owen admitted. "Which is why I was hoping you could take me out to the places the bodies were found, and I'd see if the ghosts have hung around."

"Happy to play tour guide," Ida replied.

IDA LED him first to an alley behind a furniture store. Any police barricades or chalk markings were long gone. The place smelled of piss and stray cats.

"The first victim—at least the first that anyone noticed—was found here. Harold Walner." Ida recited the details by heart. Owen knew he could have read the police notes or the newspaper's scant coverage, but he trusted Ida not to hold back details.

"Harold had no connection to the furniture store. He was a drover and carried influence among the wagon men who handle freight at the train station," she added. "Apparently, Harold had voiced some worries that expanding the rail line without hiring more drovers would dramatically slow down deliveries. He was someone other people listened to. Then he went missing and turned up in pieces."

"I imagine no one is complaining about the possible problems since then?"

"Quiet as a tomb," Ida confirmed. "But here's another detail you won't find in the official record. Harold's body was missing a hand."

"Was he killed here or dumped? Maybe the hand got lost on the way," Owen asked.

"Definitely wasn't killed or cut up here—not enough blood." The sanguine details didn't seem to bother Ida. "Not sure where he died, but he was stabbed in the heart. As for the hand...my bet is that the killer kept it. Why, I don't know—yet."

Owen closed his eyes and listened for Harold's ghost. Alleys like this one had more than their share of restless spirits who had either gotten lost or didn't want to go onward. Most of those passed Owen by with a disdainful glare or a curious glance. The specter of a belligerent drunk careened toward him, shouting and waving his hands, but Owen's mental shields pushed him away.

He frowned when he saw a ghost dressed in a workman's jacket and pants sitting on a crate near the end of the alley. Owen didn't know whether Harold's ghost would be able or willing to communicate. That ability varied by an individual's desire to make themselves known.

"Harold?" Owen said quietly. He opened his eyes and could still see the ghost. Ida's confused look told him that she didn't. The ghost looked surprised.

"Can you speak?" Owen asked. Harold shook his head.

"Just nod then for yes. Did you die here?"

Another shake of the head.

"Do you know where you were killed? Did you know the people who killed you?"

Once again, negative.

"Had you seen them before?"

Harold raised his arm and pointed in a direction that could encompass most of downtown. Owen took a chance. "Had they been at the railroad?"

Harold nodded.

Owen had plenty of other questions, but they didn't have simple yes or no answers. "You don't have to stay here," he said, taking in the ghost's despondent manner. "There's nothing holding you to this world. Go in peace."

Owen watched the ghost dissipate and hoped wherever Harold went was truly better. His branch of the Sharps family had broken with the Southern church over its support for slavery, and Owen doubted his talents would be any more welcome than his convictions. He didn't know what lay beyond, but he'd seen enough injustice in life that he sincerely hoped that the next world—if there was one—improved on that.

"Impressive." Ida sounded curious but not frightened. Owen realized that while she knew about his mediumship from before, she hadn't seen him do much in person.

"He wasn't killed here, doesn't know where he died, didn't know his killers but recognized them from something to do with the railroad," Owen summarized. "Unfortunately, he couldn't speak, and he wasn't a strong enough ghost to let me channel him. But we got some validation."

"Let's see how the next one goes," Ida said gamely.

She led him to a disreputable area down by the river. Owen marveled at her confidence. Even with his gun and badge, this wasn't the kind of place he'd want to be alone at night.

"Victim number two: a John Doe," Ida told him. "This time, missing a foot. Stabbed through the heart, like the others. I paid the coroner for information. He confirmed that the bodies were cut apart, not ripped."

"So not a werewolf—unless it's a were-surgeon," Owen remarked. The area was dodgy enough that he was surprised even a dismembered corpse drew anyone's notice. "I'm hesitant to let down my guard to reach out to the spirits."

Ida withdrew a revolver from her voluminous skirt pants. "Don't worry. I've got you covered."

Owen concentrated, trying to locate the ghost. The sudden press of angry spirits made him slam down his mental shields and use his ability to repel instead of attract.

"We need to get out of here." Owen hurried Ida toward the main thoroughfare and the safety of the crowd.

"Did you get anything?" she asked once they were again surrounded by pedestrians.

"Too much. Your John Doe wasn't the first body to be dumped there, and a lot of them haven't moved on. Unsurprisingly, they're miffed about that, and had a bone to pick with anyone who could hear them. If our man was among them, he was drowned out by the competition."

"There have been seven bodies found, each missing a part, all stabbed to death, over the past two months. Over the same period, a total of twelve men went missing," Ida recounted.

Owen knew those details from the briefing documents. "Does that include Harris and Davis—the agents who were here before us?"

She nodded. "But that's not the whole story," she added with a raised eyebrow. "There were four more missing men—ones the police aren't counting."

"Why not?"

Ida gave him a look. "The cops don't care about men of that sort. Sad, but true. Our chief has definite opinions about some things."

Oh. Shit. "Men of that sort." Men like me.

Ida bumped his elbow in camaraderie. "Come on. Let's check the other sites, and then get coffee somewhere we can talk."

The rest of the places body parts were found were equally dismal, their ghosts either gone or unwilling to be much help. Some refused to talk to Owen at all. None of those who were able to communicate knew why they were taken or who abducted them.

"I feel like I've seen the underbelly of St. Louis," Owen remarked. "We've hit the loading docks, wharf, back alleys, and a seedy stable. You're quite a tour guide."

"Stick with me. I can take you to all the best places," Ida rejoined. They'd struck up a comfortable camaraderie devoid of sexual tension, which Owen enjoyed. He didn't know whether Ida guessed his inclination or was like-minded, but the lack of flirtatiousness freed their company of bothersome subtext.

Ida abruptly grabbed Owen by the arm and yanked him into an alley, hiding them behind stacks of discarded crates by the garbage cans.

"Shh," she warned before he could ask. "Stay down."

Owen couldn't see anything from where Ida wedged him behind the pallets, but he heard men's voices pass by the alley's entrance.

Several minutes later, Ida stepped out from their hiding place and made sure the way was clear before beckoning for Owen to join her.

"What was that all about?" He dusted himself off.

"Chief Wyman was heading our way. I didn't want to answer uncomfortable questions," she replied. "He considers me a general nuisance, working my way up to menace. If he thought the newspaper would let him get away with it, he'd probably figure out how to arrest me for disturbing the peace."

Owen's already dim view of the chief grew darker. "He sounds like a real peach."

"A rotten one." Ida ducked into an Italian restaurant. "Good morning, Vincente. Can I borrow the back room for a bit?"

"Of course, Miss Ida. I'll bring coffee. Good to see you," the man behind the counter replied with a wave of his hand.

Ida and Owen padded to the back of the small restaurant to a room Owen guessed was used for private gatherings. "Have a seat." Ida slid a chair out from the bare table in the center. "I helped them deal with a crooked landlord a couple of years ago. Vincente lets me use the room for interviews. Good for not being seen or heard. And the food is amazing."

Vincente brought cups of strong black coffee. Ida ordered lunch for both of them without needing to see a menu. "Put it on the *Post-Dispatch's* tab," she told him.

"You got it, Miss Ida," Vincente replied and hurried off.

"I figured we could compare notes on what we saw today, and go over some of the suspects. No one's going to bother us or overhear, and since we've got to eat somewhere this is some of the best Italian food in the city," she told him.

Since Owen's stomach already growled just from the aromas coming from the kitchen, he wasn't going to complain. "Tell me about the police chief. He sounds corrupt. Do you think he's in on the murders?"

Ida leaned back in her chair and sipped her coffee for a moment. "Corrupt? Definitely. St. Louis isn't Chicago, but it's not for lack of trying. As for the murders—I don't think he's the one killing people. But I also don't think he's trying hard to find out who is."

"What about the Deputy Chief?"

Ida tapped her fingers on the table as she thought. "I'm not sure. My interactions with him have been vastly better than with the chief. Deputy Chief Rourke is always polite and professional. I don't have evidence of him taking bribes or kickbacks. He isn't overly violent—

for a cop. And I get the feeling that there's some tension between him and his boss, but no one knows—or will say—why. He's a wild card."

"Did you know Davis or Harris, the agents who were assigned here before me?" Owen asked. A swallow of his drink revealed it to be scaldingly hot and eye-poppingly strong.

"I knew who they were. Didn't work with them. They weren't around for a while. Then two new guys showed up, poking around. Now you. What's the deal?"

"Davis and Harris disappeared. Missing—probably dead. They were investigating the railroad expansion and might have gotten too close for comfort," Owen replied. "Mitch and Jacob were just pitching in until I could be reassigned with my new partner, Calvin."

"Railroad troubles don't usually involve the Supernatural Secret Service," Ida noted. "So where does your angle come in?"

Owen debated how much to say. "We're not entirely sure yet. The murders and dismembered bodies with missing pieces make me think dark magic. A witch, or maybe some kind of bound creature. The killings only look random if you don't notice that all the victims owned land or businesses near the proposed railway expansion—or had some other connection. But what's worth killing people for or why dark magic is involved, I don't know."

Ida was quiet for a moment. "Have you heard about the gates of hell?"

Owen raised an eyebrow. "Can't say that I have."

"St. Louis isn't the only place rumored to have gates—there are stories about a number of locations across the country. According to old tales, there are seven gates of hell in St. Louis. Pass through all seven with the required tribute and if you survive, you gain some sort of unholy reward," Ida said.

She set down her cup and leaned forward. "The stories vary about what that reward entails. Immortality, wealth, revenge, power...the usual. But the version that has always struck me as most likely—assuming there could be any such thing as the gates themselves—is that anyone who opens all seven gates wins demonic allegiance. Hell spawn, at their beck and call."

That sent a shiver down Owen's spine. *A rich, ambitious vampire with demon henchmen. That definitely wouldn't be good.*

"That certainly ups the ante." Owen took a drink of coffee to settle his nerves. "Any details on where to find the gates and how to unlock them?"

Ida shook her head. "There have always been 'bad places' that people avoided because they felt unlucky or cursed. It's possible that the railroad intends to go through such a place, and someone is hedging their bets. Or...the gates could be a sequence of rituals instead of locations."

"Interesting," Owen agreed. "The cut up bodies and missing pieces could certainly fit with some sort of twisted ritual."

"I started looking at the gates of hell out of curiosity some time ago. Turned up when the editor wanted a piece on local legends and ghost stories," Ida said. "It struck me as the kind of thing that's true and not true at the same time, if you know what I mean. True in the sense that there's something behind the story, but that the story itself has been fabricated or changed over time."

"I can see that. Most spooky stories have a kernel of truth."

Ida pulled a folded piece of notepaper from her bag. "Back when I did the article, I spoke with a woman whose family had been some of the first settlers in this area. She was very old when I interviewed her. Some people said she had the Sight, or at least a bit of psychic ability. She's the only person who had details about the gates...and even that wasn't a lot."

She slid the paper over to Owen, who scanned it and frowned as he read it aloud. "The awakening of the sigil. The summoning of the servants. The destruction of the rival. The commanding of the dead. The corruption of the pious. The desecration of the damned. The sacrifice of the faithful."

Ida nodded. "It feels right, doesn't it? I don't know what it means, but I've never forgotten that old lady or the gates. But if someone wanted to wake up a dormant power, bloody deaths and body parts would fit the bill."

"May I keep this?" Owen indicated the paper.

"For what it's worth. I made the copy for you."

Vincente returned with their meal and refreshed their coffee. He brought a big bowl of rigatoni with meat sauce, a plate of meatballs in marinara and a basket of garlic bread, as well as two cannoli and a small plate of lemon cookies. Owen and Ida thanked him profusely, and Vincente beamed with pleasure. Ida signed off on the tab, and then they left conjecture aside as they dug into their meals.

When Owen had finished his half of the feast, he figured that between Winston's cooking and St. Louis's temptations he needed to spend more time chasing bad guys on foot if he didn't want to burst the buttons of his vest.

"Thank you for a fine meal," he said, and Ida inclined her head in acceptance. "Now—what about suspects for dessert?"

"Ronald Thomas, the minister, is a terrible person who dishes up fear and anger instead of comfort, but he's also incompetent," Ida replied. "I've been watching him closely for years. I can't see any way the railroad hurts or benefits him or his flock."

"How did he make the suspect list?" Owen wondered aloud.

"The man oozes rage. The cops haven't publicized all of the disappearances, but they haven't missed that Thomas condemns everyone who doesn't live by his rules. I can't see him doing violence himself, but he might incite some of his followers enough to bash a few heads. Although dismemberment seems a bit much—even for him."

"The socialite—Lillian Webb? Where did her money come from?"

"Slaughterhouses and meatpacking. Not the kind of thing one brings up in polite society, but it made buckets of money for her daddy. The railroad connection would be moving cattle from ranches to St. Louis or on to Chicago. She's not hands-on in the business since both her husband and her father died. I think the Board of Directors pays her handsomely to ignore the company altogether."

"So she isn't scheming to open a portal to perdition to spite a social rival?" Owen couldn't keep the humor out of his voice, although the threat was hardly funny.

"The idea might appeal, but I can't see her getting blood on her new frock," Ida commented in a dry tone. "And while she technically owns an abattoir where people could be cut up as easily as cattle, the men who've gone missing are not the type she'd notice."

Ida sighed. "Lillian Webb might be persuaded to bankroll something shady, but from everything I've seen, she's actually fairly savvy about people and money. She has more cash than she can spend right now. What's the benefit of risking everything to help someone build a longer railroad?"

"Point taken," Owen admitted. "The dodgy lawyer? His type make a habit of consorting with demons—or at least, people who deserve to be downstairs."

Ida snorted. "True. And Benson Tucker embodies every snide remark about the legal profession you've ever heard. Never met a widow or orphan he didn't swindle. I've been digging up dirt on him since I got to town. He's got hands in every pocket, and lots of powerful people owe him favors. So...maybe. But I see him being more behind the scenes and less hands-on. He'd hire a dark witch before he'd learn to work magic himself."

"So you think it's Ross Swanson—the businessman? Makes sense why our cover story is that we're high rolling investors looking for good prospects," Owen mused.

"Swanson's had people go missing around him before," Ida told him and reached for a lemon cookie. "Of course, there's always a 'reason' but none that would really hold up if anyone actually looked hard at them. Business associates, an ex-wife, a nasty neighbor. Of course, those people didn't show up dead later looking like a bad jigsaw puzzle."

"But he's still the one you'd put money on?" Owen felt validated that Ida suspected the same person he did. *I wonder if we can get something that belongs to him for Calvin to read.*

"Given what we know so far, yes," Ida agreed. "Plus, I think he's got some sort of paranormal ability. Not a werewolf—he definitely would have been implicated in the big pack bust from a few years ago."

Ida set her empty cup aside. "He's often seen in daylight, so he's not a vampire. Maybe a witch—that would track with the idea of spells to open the gates of hell. Or a dishonest psychic who reads minds without consent for his own gain. I don't know what woo-woo gift he's got, but I'm positive it's something he can use for his own benefit."

Owen finished his cookie and washed it down with the last of the coffee. "Thank you. For lunch and for your help. I've got to ask—what's in it for you?"

Ida's smile showed a flash of teeth. "I like seeing bad people get what's coming to them. Doesn't happen often enough. And too many times, the so-called 'good' people are the ones helping them get away with it. I do what the paper lets me—and sometimes I have to break the rules for a noble cause."

"Calvin will be running down some leads and contacts of his own," Owen told her, eager to get back to the Pullman and put his head together with his partner.

I'd like to do more than that, but I'll take what I can get.

Putting distance between himself and Calvin today had helped distract Owen. He hoped that once he returned to the Pullman he could keep his mind on the case and off his handsome partner.

It's not the first time I've been attracted to someone I couldn't have. But it's the strongest feeling I've had for someone in a long time, and we're going to be spending a lot of time together in an enclosed place.

Maybe it'll get easier. Or I'll just spontaneously combust.

Vincente sent them off with a wave. Ida looked both ways before they stepped out onto the sidewalk. The restaurant was on a side street, surrounded by offices and wholesale shops, not department stores or boutiques. By now, workers had finished their lunches and returned to their tasks, which left the lighter traffic of delivery people, bicycle messengers, and shoppers.

Owen caught a glimpse of motion out of the corner of his eye headed right for them. He pulled Ida down and into the scant shelter of a recessed doorway before two shots rang out in quick succession, sinking into the building's façade and splintering the stone.

A man on a bicycle careened past, far too fast to chase on foot, and disappeared into the flow of traffic on the main street. Shoppers scattered and screamed.

Owen helped Ida up from her knees, shielding her until she pushed him aside. "Pretty sure that was aimed at us," she said.

"But were they after you or me—or both?" Owen decided that finding out would be his new top priority.

Chapter 4
Calvin

W ell, well. Look what the cat dragged in." Louisa Sunderson sidled over when she spotted Calvin at the bar in Kearson's Palace, a vaudeville theater on the east side of the city.

"Gonna stay for the show? I promise it'll be worth your while," she purred, tracing a finger around Calvin's collar. They both knew it was all pretend, but that didn't keep them from playing their roles. Louisa wore a dress that accentuated her ample curves, with a neckline that revealed a bit more bosom than many might deem respectable. Her dark blonde hair was piled in a Gibson, and well-applied kohl made her blue eyes smolder.

No doubt that made her very popular with the rest of the men here, but it didn't stir Calvin.

"Maybe," he teased. "Give me a good reason to stick around." Louisa was one of Serena's friends. She knew Calvin's interests, and didn't care. As far as Calvin could figure, Louisa preferred men and women equally.

Despite it being ten in the morning, Kearson's had patrons scattered at the tables and seated at the bar. It didn't hurt that the establishment offered Scotch eggs with their beer in the morning and a plowman's lunch with more beer during the afternoon. Sausages, pickles, and boiled potatoes could be had with beer in the evening.

"Palace" was a misnomer. Kearson's was a grand saloon, offering live entertainment that started early and ran late. The traveling acts changed, and the order of the performances, but patrons knew what to expect for the cost of their ticket. Singers, dancers, impersonators, trained animals, magicians, ventriloquists, and acrobats did their bits throughout the day. Evenings sometimes had one-act plays or dramatic readings—or a short film accompanied by a piano player.

"We've got a fancy magic act all the way from Chicago, and the girls and I are doing a new dance routine tonight," Louisa replied. "I don't have to be anywhere for a little while…if you're looking for company."

While the east side of the city was notorious for prostitution, a legitimate venue like Kearson's didn't encourage that sort of business. Jokes might be ribald, and the dancing could be risqué, but patrons knew to look but not touch. Large bouncers stationed by the stage enforced the house rules.

That veneer of respectability drew customers from all walks of life. While the morning and late crowds tended to be men who worked on the docks or the trains, the afternoon and early evening audience ranged from laborers to store owners, office workers, and traveling salesmen. It was a perfect place for a Pinkerton agent like Louisa to hear all sorts of gossip.

"I'd enjoy the company of a fine lady like yourself," Calvin replied. His performative gallantry made Louisa's lip twitch as she tried not to laugh.

"Eugene," Louisa hailed the bartender. "Two beers and a couple of eggs, please—put it on my tab."

She and Calvin retreated to a table in a back corner where they weren't easily seen and the entertainment wouldn't hamper a conversation. A man on stage declaimed a selection from Longfellow's "Evangeline," followed by Hamlet's soliloquy before giving way to a statuesque singer in an evening gown whose makeup didn't quite cover their five o'clock shadow.

"Not bad." Calvin sipped his beer. "Lord knows, I've had worse."

"Jack Kearson runs a good bar," Louisa said. "He pays the performers what he promises them, leaves the dancing girls alone, and won't let patrons spit on the floor. And the house witch keeps the rats and roaches at bay."

"You almost sound like you'd consider a change of profession."

Louisa snorted. "Don't kid yourself. But as gigs go, it's better than some." She nibbled on her egg and washed it down with a swallow of watered beer. "Now, what can I do you for?"

"Know anything about the missing men who show up in pieces?" Calvin kept one eye on the clientele as they talked.

"Is that why you're here?"

Calvin nodded. "The brass thinks there's more to it. Not to mention that the previous two agents have disappeared."

"Huh. Inconvenient." Louisa pulled another piece off the egg and popped it into her mouth. "And you wouldn't be here if there wasn't some woo-woo involved. Coven? Vampire nest?"

"You tell me," Calvin replied. "I just landed in town yesterday. But I figured if anyone would have heard rumors, it'd be you."

"I'm touched to be in your thoughts," Louisa said in a droll tone. "Let me think. I've been paying more attention to the gangsters. The Chicago mob wants a piece of the action, and so do the New Orleans families. There's a war boiling just below the surface—and the railroad expansion Leland Aiken is peddling just ups the stakes. People go missing and turn up dead a lot here."

"Hear much about Aiken?" Calvin tried to sound nonchalant. Louisa's incisive look told him she wasn't fooled.

"Ruthless. Underhanded. Runs a tight operation. Has a bunch of important people on the take. Typical railroad guy," she replied. "Not sure what going all Jack the Ripper on a bunch of no-account drifters would get him that he couldn't already buy."

"Any connection between Aiken and Ross Swanson?" Calvin leaned back and drank his beer.

"Swanson's a swindler and a son of a bitch." Louisa dropped her voice to a whisper. Her smile and the way she touched Calvin's hand were entirely for anyone who might be watching. "He comes in here now and again. Holds court. Likes to have people beg him for favors."

"I already knew he was a rotter. But you didn't answer my question."

She thought for a moment. "I don't know for sure, but if either one thought they could benefit, then I'm sure their morals wouldn't stand in the way." Louisa paused. "I have wondered whether Swanson's got a witch on his payroll. He makes the papers here on a regular basis for one flashy business deal or another. I don't think he's smart enough to make it happen on his own."

"Wouldn't be the first to tap into magic to boost his business," Calvin conjectured. "It always goes badly in the end, but that type never learns."

"I know you prefer to be the bull in a China shop," Louisa said with a hint of a fond smile. "But tread carefully—at least until you know the city and the players. And watch your back around the chief of police. He's a snake—and he has it out for guys like you."

Calvin took her meaning immediately. *Not federal agents. Men who prefer men.* "I'll keep that in mind."

Louisa gave Calvin an assessing look. "Something's troubling you."

Calvin flashed his cockiest smile. "Nothin' more than the case."

"Uh-huh." She stared at him, eyes narrowed, and Calvin wondered if she had a touch of psychic ability. *Or maybe she's just an extraordinarily good detective who can read people.* "What's your new partner like?"

"Owen? Nice enough, I guess. We haven't spent a lot of time working together yet. Although it was funny—we met on the train and didn't introduce ourselves." Calvin kept his smile pinned in place. It usually won over women who paid more attention to his face than his eyes.

Louisa gave him another look. "You like him."

Calvin fought the way his heart raced. "Sure. I mean, he's got a good resume, doesn't smell like a pig sty, and didn't show up drunk, so what's not to like?"

She shook her head. "Not what I meant."

"Doesn't matter," Calvin said, dropping the act. "I don't think we belong to the same club."

"Are you sure?"

"We don't get membership rings." Calvin rolled his eyes. "Finding out would be too risky. If I guessed wrong—"

"Nothing you couldn't brush off as being thanks to too much whiskey," Louisa replied with a shrug. Calvin wondered if she had firsthand knowledge. "But if you're right—"

Yeah. If Owen did bat for my team, and that connection I felt on the train was real, it could make for a real relationship and the perfect cover.

When does anything ever work out like that?

"Neither of us is going anywhere. So there's time to figure things out." He wished his heart believed his mouth. Calvin felt sure the nightmares would return.

"I've got to get back to work." Louisa stroked her finger down his hand for show. "Keep in touch. I'll listen for what you're tracking, and you keep a sharp eye out for my interests. *Capisce?*"

Calvin gave her a thumbs up. He watched her hips sway as she walked away and felt nothing.

Not like I doubted where my interests lie. Lay. Laid.

Speaking of which…Serena gave me an address for a club. I need to work off some tension and put Owen out of my mind.

Calvin filed the club away for later after he ran down a few more details. He took a cab to police headquarters, debating how he wanted to approach meeting the chief. *Our predecessors weren't using a cover story, and they disappeared. So I'll play it the other way and work our story.*

"WE ALWAYS APPRECIATE business owners who want to invest in our fine city," Chief Wyman said. "But I'm not quite clear on what that has to do with me."

Calvin gave him a frosty look. "The spate of unsolved murders —*gruesome* murders—doesn't speak well for St. Louis or your department. How can I attract employees to businesses I invest in when the city is so unsafe? Attracting investors will be difficult."

Chief Wyman cleared his throat. "If I may speak frankly?"

Calvin gave a curt nod, curious to hear the chief out.

"The sorts that are going missing, getting killed…they're a bad element. They hang around the docks all day to pick up odd jobs and then drink themselves blind once they're paid. Not the kind you'd want to attract to your businesses. Regular people, employees of upstanding companies, they wouldn't be in the sort of places the victims have been taken from," the chief said.

Calvin reined in his temper. *That's what I was afraid he'd say. He's exactly the kind of person I feared he might be.*

"Can you give me some assurance that you're doing something to stop the violence—even if you don't consider the victims to be worth protecting?" Calvin couldn't avoid the snippiness in his tone.

"I didn't say that—"

"You didn't have to." Calvin sighed dramatically and started to turn away. "I'm afraid I'll have to advise our investors against expanding here. Of course, the mayor and the city council will get a full report."

"Wait."

Calvin turned back. Chief Wyman's graying hair looked sweat-damp around the edges, and his flushed skin suggested that he was holding himself in check to avoid losing his temper.

"There is an ongoing investigation. We aren't just sitting on our hands here. The circumstances are strange, and the choice of victims seems random. And as for the gruesomeness—we think it's some sort of psychotic killer, another Jack the Ripper. Maybe part of some crazy foreign religious cult. We haven't caught the killer yet, but we're on the case, and I believe we'll stop him."

The saddest thing was Calvin suspected that Wyman believed his theory. Clearly finding the culprit hadn't consumed the chief or his department because the victims weren't people he deemed useful or important. If Calvin had been relocating a real business, those attitudes wouldn't have recommended the city to him.

"If you clean it up before we find a better, safer location, we might reconsider," Calvin informed him with a derisive sniff. "My people will be in touch."

Calvin strode out of the man's office like he owned the world. Once he was outside and several blocks away, he dropped to sit on the stone steps of a building and tried to sort through his swirling thoughts.

The cops aren't going to be any help—but they could be a real hindrance. Wyman isn't taking the killings seriously because he doesn't think they'll ever affect "respectable" people. Fucking bastard. We'll have to work around them and try not to raise any suspicions.

His next stop was the library, where he skimmed newspapers from the past few months, looking for mention of the murders and articles about Ross Swanson. Calvin wasn't surprised that few details about the killings or the discovery of body parts made the paper. True as it was that sensationalism sold newspapers, it also held that terrifying the populace didn't accomplish anything.

The publisher probably thinks like Chief Wyman, that the people reading his paper aren't likely to become victims, and the people who are dying aren't important. Damn. We've already found some of the monsters, and they're human.

Discouraged and frustrated, Calvin decided lunch was probably the best next step. He checked the address of the card Serena had given him for the Southeast Rivers Club, an elite men's social organization that had reciprocity with one of Calvin's other many memberships, and, more importantly, turned a blind eye to the sexual peccadillos of its members and guests.

Calvin arrived at the club after a short cab ride. He'd taken a moment during travel to straighten his tie, dust off his jacket, and smooth his hair to look presentable enough to make it past the front desk, membership card notwithstanding.

He looked up at the four-story brownstone building located just a couple of blocks from the edge of downtown. Everything about it symbolized propriety and wealth. The only indication that the brownstone was not a private home lay in the small bronze plaque by the doorbell.

Calvin couldn't help feeling nervous as he waited for someone to come to the door. This wasn't Boston, where his family name and his father's success opened doors, no questions asked. A man in a formal butler's uniform greeted him with professional detachment. "May I help you?"

Calvin had his membership card in hand. "Boston member, in town on business." He gave it to the butler, along with his personal embossed calling card, placing them both on the man's silver tray.

"This way, sir." The butler turned and led Calvin inside. The club's foyer boasted a grand staircase with an opulently carved mahogany balustrade set off by a massive crystal chandelier sparkling overhead. The intricate marble parquet floor, dark wood wainscoting, and expensive antique furnishings made it clear that the club catered to a selective clientele.

Calvin traveled often enough that he knew the process. The butler would bring the cards to the manager on duty to check against the private directory, a minor hassle to ensure discretion and the security of club members.

"We are always happy to have a member in good standing as a guest," the butler assured Calvin when he returned moments later. "Lunch is being served in the dining room on the first floor, down that hallway." He indicated with a slight tilt of his head to the right.

"If you'd prefer the bar, the lounge is adjacent to the dining room," he continued. "Upstairs is the library, pool table, and several rooms for card games. The third floor is the ballroom, which is closed since we don't have an event at the moment. The fourth floor has guest rooms. Will you be in need of an overnight accommodation?"

Private clubs often provided both a place for members to stay during a short trip and a ready-made community. Use of the rooms for shorter assignations was generally frowned on—there were other nooks where those could be handled discreetly.

"I have a place to stay, thank you," Calvin told him. "But lunch sounds good."

"Please follow me."

The butler led Calvin to the maître d's stand, where another man in a tux asked if he would prefer a table or the bar. Since eating was only part of Calvin's reason for visiting, he chose the bar, passing through the formal dining room to a well-appointed lounge. A massive carved cherry wood barback with mirror anchored the room.

Calvin took a seat at the impressively large bar. The leather chair was comfortable, and the heavy velvet draperies reminded him of the Pullman car.

Don't think about the Pullman, or Owen, dammit. Lunch then laid. That should help me keep my mind on the job.

Many of the men who spent their days in such clubs playing chess or reading were older—either retired or sufficiently senior in their position that they held emeritus status rather than day-to-day management. Those under twenty-one were not welcome in the club, regardless of wealth or family connections. The men in their late twenties to early forties who were regulars mid-day tended to be single men from well-to-do families who were either traveling like Calvin, or stopping in for lunch and socializing amid their busy calendar of engagements.

Calvin's gaze swept over the room, looking for potential companions. He didn't see any promising candidates. He ordered the daily special—roast beef with carrots, onions, and potatoes—and a cup of coffee, and drummed his fingers absently on the bar's brass rail as he waited for his meal to be served.

"Is this seat taken?" a baritone voice asked to Calvin's left. A man who appeared to be a few years younger than his own age, with a sweep of blond hair and hazel eyes, stood next to the adjacent barstool.

"No, help yourself," Calvin replied, understanding the "dance" of a respectable hook-up.

"Thank you. I thought you might be waiting for someone," the stranger said as he slid onto the seat.

"Unfortunately not," Calvin replied. "I'm in town on business and thought I'd stop in for a good meal and some quality company."

"I'm Stephen." The man extended his hand.

"Calvin."

Stephen's handshake was tepid, not nearly as firm as Owen's. He was about the same height but more slightly built. Although from the side, if Calvin didn't look too closely, there was enough of a resemblance.

"I hope you like what you've seen so far." Stephen's smile and the glint in his eyes made it clear he didn't mean St. Louis.

"I do." Calvin returned the smile and kept eye contact just a bit longer than appropriate.

They chatted as they ate—Stephen ordered roast turkey with stuffing—trading comments on sports, the weather, and the latest headlines.

"Read any good books lately?" Calvin asked, remembering Owen's enthusiasm on the train for *Dracula*.

"Can't say I'm much of a reader," Stephen replied. "Too boring. I'd rather take in a show—or spend time with a friend." The bump of their knees beneath the bar was definitely not an accident.

Calvin found himself unexpectedly disappointed at Stephen's admission. While Calvin's tastes ran to the newspaper and penny dreadfuls, he had found Owen's bookishness charming.

"If you're not in a hurry, we could play a hand or two of cards," Stephen suggested, although Calvin felt sure poker was not on the other man's mind. "The game rooms are quiet this time of day."

"I'm not in a hurry." Calvin felt his heart speed up. They paid their tab, and then Calvin followed Stephen to a corridor at the back of the lounge and up the steps. From the back, out of the corner of his eye, Stephen resembled Owen to a point. Except that Stephen had the nurtured hubris of a wealthy scion, while Owen's confidence had been honed under fire.

Don't overthink this. It's just a tug and tumble.

A flick of a switch illuminated the side lamps in a small, comfortable room with a poker table. When the door clicked shut behind them, Stephen stepped into Calvin's space and laid his hand flat against Calvin's chest.

"You got something particular in mind, or can we just get to know each other a little better?" In private, Stephen's flirting left no doubts about his intentions.

"I'm looking for an after-lunch distraction." Calvin turned them so Stephen's back was against the wall and Calvin's thigh was between the other man's legs. He felt Stephen's erection through the thin fabric of their trousers, but to Calvin's dismay his own cock hadn't roused to attention.

Calvin leaned forward, not kissing but taking in the scent of expensive pomander and exclusive cologne, a hint of shirt starch, and French soap.

"Your secret is safe with me," Stephen murmured, trying to turn for a kiss but blocked by Calvin's position. "Our kind have to stick together." His hand cupped Calvin's package, and Stephen's thumb teased against Calvin's clothed shaft.

Calvin returned the favor, stroking Stephen through his pants, willing his arousal to manifest. Stephen's hands roamed over Calvin's shoulders, back, and ass, groping and exploring. Despite his reason for coming to the club, Calvin found himself maneuvering to avoid escalation.

Stephen's breath smelled of sage and onion from lunch. The body beneath his well-tailored clothing was too slight, not the tall, muscled form Calvin had glimpsed filling out Owen's suit. Long, slim fingers worked impatiently at the button to Calvin's waistband, feeling more like a woman's touch than Calvin had imagined of Owen's large, broad hands.

Worst of all, Calvin's cock apparently wasn't accepting substitutions.

"What's wrong?" Stephen sensed Calvin's hesitance and drew back.

"I'm sorry," Calvin said, embarrassed, confused, and angry at himself. "It's not you...I had a bad breakup—"

Stephen stepped away. "Bloody cock tease. Don't start games you can't finish." He walked out of the room, shutting the door hard behind him.

Calvin slumped against the wall, too caught up in a tangle of feelings to think straight. *What the hell just happened?*

He'd never fumbled a roll in the hay before, not even in his teenage years when what he lacked in staying power he made up for in quick recovery. Stephen had been reasonably attractive, undoubtedly interested, and discreet. He was the ultimate no-strings-attached quick fuck, not to mention a Club regular, which would have ensured repeat opportunities for as long as Calvin was in town.

Even worse, Calvin felt vaguely guilty as if he'd cheated on Owen, which was ridiculous.

I can't cheat on a guy who isn't even interested.

My cock picked a lousy time to get monogamous—when I don't even have a lover.

Calvin sighed and rearranged himself, glad Stephen hadn't left any marks. He felt conspicuous as he left the gaming room and knew he wasn't imagining the judgmental looks he got from the bartender and a few other patrons.

Great. He's probably also told them I'm a lousy lay. Maybe I'll just be mortified into chastity.

Calvin held his head high and slapped on his cockiest grin. He swaggered across the lounge and back to the main entrance. "Lovely club, very good food. Thank you."

"Will we be seeing you again, sir?" the butler asked, perfunctory and polite.

Calvin gave a rueful half-smile and shook his head. "Perhaps…but probably not."

Instead of hailing a carriage near the club Calvin decided to walk back toward the library. He needed to clear his head after the disaster with Stephen. His mood veered from murderous to despondent, and he knew he needed to pull himself together before he could possibly go back to the Pullman and face Owen.

Calvin wasn't so lost in his thoughts to lose his edge. He heard the footsteps behind him and turned sharply, deflecting a blow with a weighted sap that would have left him with a cracked skull if it had connected.

He shoved his attacker into the mouth of an alley where they could finish the scuffle in private. Calvin twisted the man's wrist hard, and the sap dropped to the ground. Disarmed, the ruffian came at Calvin with his fists. His skills might have been enough for a brawl, but he couldn't hold his own against Calvin's training.

After what happened at the club, Calvin couldn't deny that it felt good to throw a few punches.

"You picked the wrong guy to pick pockets." He held the man up by his shirt and gave him a good shake.

"Go to hell," the ruffian spat.

"I could drag you to the cops; let them take it from here."

The guy gave Calvin a dead-eye stare. "Go ahead. I'll be out in an hour. And I don't want your wallet."

"Then what?" The man's cool insolence gave Calvin the uncomfortable suspicion that the attack might not have been random.

"I got paid to crack your noggin so you wouldn't cause more trouble," the tough replied. "If you pay me more, I'll leave you alone."

"Who paid you?" Calvin gave him a shake.

The guy managed to sneer despite his split lip. "Didn't catch his name. Gave me your description, said to keep an eye out and give you a good scare."

Would Stephen be pissed enough to set me up?

Wait a second; he said it was "so I didn't cause more trouble." Hardly what a disappointed lunchtime lay would say. So either Louisa's playing both sides against the middle—unlikely—or I put more of the fear of God into the police chief than I realized.

Calvin thought the last option was the most likely.

"How did you know where I was?" Calvin hadn't noticed being tailed but also hadn't expected it since he'd barely been out and about since arriving in St. Louis.

"Some guy said you'd gone inside that fancy building, and so I was supposed to watch for you to come out and teach you a lesson. Figure either he followed you and didn't want to get his hands dirty or paid the cabbies to look for you."

The idea that he and Owen were already being watched sent a chill down Calvin's spine. He knew he'd need to warn both Owen and Winston. *They can't pay off every cabbie in the city. So we'll just need to go farther away from the Pullman to find a ride or switch midway.*

Did whoever grabbed Davis and Harris find out something from them that put a bullseye on Owen and me? And is Leland Aiken behind it?

"The guy who hired you—did he pay you?" Calvin gave the ruffian a shake for emphasis.

"I don't work for free."

"Coin or cash?"

His attacker looked at him as if Calvin had lost his mind. "Why?"

"Just answer."

"Silver dollars."

"Leave what he paid you—don't want anything else, just what you got from him. Then run like the devil's after you before I decide to put a bullet in your back," Calvin warned.

The ruffian hurried to empty his pockets of a few silver coins, leaving them on the street. He got to his feet and regarded Calvin as if he feared a trap, then took off at full speed.

Calvin wasn't really going to shoot the attacker, but the guy didn't know that. And if Calvin's suspicion about who had hired the man were true, turning him over to the cops wouldn't help. He ran his left hand over the bruised knuckles of his right. *I've got plenty of "souvenirs" from when I was with the gang. Fucking up my hand even worse isn't going to help.*

He took a kerchief from his pocket and picked up the coins, deciding he would "read" them in the safety of the Pullman. *I wonder if Owen's had as lively a day as I did. Comparing notes should be interesting.*

Wary of other attackers, Calvin took a street car in one direction, then got off and switched to another trolley line, zig-zagging his way closer to the train station. He walked the rest of the way, noting where other cab stops were so he could tell Owen and Winston.

The aroma of coffee and freshly-baked cookies hit Calvin when he opened the door to the Pullman.

"Welcome back," Winston greeted. "I hope you had a productive day."

Calvin grimaced. "You could call it that. Is Owen back?"

"Not yet," Winston replied, and while he didn't add the "sir," Calvin knew it was implied. "Although I would trust he'll be back before supper."

"That's okay," Calvin said. "But once I get settled, I'd like you to spot me. Got a couple of items I'd like to read—and see if I can find out who hired someone to jump me."

Winston's brows rose, which might be as much alarm as he ever showed. "Are you undamaged?"

Oh, I've got plenty of damage, but it would take too long to tell you. "I got the best of him." Calvin grabbed a couple of cookies from the tray on the table and poured a cup of coffee, adding sugar. Now that he was back safely, he felt the adrenaline rush fade.

"I'm going to be in the armory since I already have dinner prepared and ready to go into the oven; just let me know when you need my help," Winston told him.

"Will do." Calvin ate the cookies, gulped coffee to wash them down, and took two more with him as he headed to his room.

Once he closed the door behind him, he hung up his suit jacket, removed his tie, loosened his collar, and turned up the sleeves of his shirt. Calvin debated taking a shower and decided to save that in case reading the ruffian's coins left him needing a clean break.

The day was still young. If Owen returned soon, they could go over what they'd each learned and perhaps have time to run down more information before dinner.

Calvin also had to admit that he was curious about how Owen had spent his day and decided that if they were going to be partners then they needed to work together instead of making it a habit to split up.

Even if it gives me blue balls.

He ate the last two cookies, splashed water on his face, and headed to the dining room. On the way, he knocked on the library door to summon Winston, who joined him as he settled at the table with the kerchief-wrapped bundle.

"This might be nothing," Calvin warned. "Money can be hard to read because it gets touched by so many people. But assuming the guy gave me the right coins and that the person who hired him touched them barehanded, I might pick up an insight."

"What should I do?" Winston had brought a coffee pot and more cookies with him.

"Just scrape me off the floor if I fall out of my chair and splash water on my face if I take too long to wake up." Calvin took a deep breath and unwrapped the coins.

Cold calculation, overconfidence, secure in the belief he was protected. Annoyance. And underneath it all, a desire to make the questions go away...

Calvin came back to himself with a startled gasp. Winston watched him, close enough to make a grab if Calvin wavered. He breathed deeply, steadying himself before reaching for the coffee and more sweets.

"Were you able to get anything useful?" Winston looked intrigued.

"I'm not sure. It was more of an emotional read on the person who hired the tough. He didn't like that people have been asking questions, and he felt very sure that he could get away with it. I didn't see or hear him, but my money's on the chief of police or someone who works for him."

"Glad that the reading went well. Is there anything I can do?"

"I'm okay. Thanks. Go on back to the armory," Calvin said. "When Owen comes in, please send him this way."

Calvin walked over to a large painting on the opposite wall and tapped the frame, rotating it to reveal a corkboard. Notes in his writing and Owen's were already pinned from their briefing with Mitch and Jacob. Before he forgot the details, Calvin scribbled down his discussion with the police chief, the most important tidbits from Louisa, and shorthand references to the notes he'd taken at the library.

Before they were finished, there would be additional notes made and red string drawn between the key leads. Calvin knew other agents preferred journals or lists, but he liked being able to see the case laid out like this, where overlooked connections seemed easier to find.

"There you are! Did your day go well?" Owen strode into the dining room, looking windblown and luscious.

How did I think Stephen bore any resemblance? "Pretty well—how about you?"

Owen dropped his lanky frame into the wooden chair across from Calvin. "I got a firsthand look at where the bodies were dumped, talked to one of the men's ghosts, got some inside scoop with some leads we need to run down. And was shot at. Lots to process."

"Shot?"

Owen nodded. "They missed. Don't know which of us they were aiming at, or both."

"Must be the day for it. I got jumped by a guy with a sap." Calvin felt a spark at the concern that flashed in Owen's eyes.

"Are you okay?"

"Yeah. I gave worse than I got." Calvin motioned toward the coffee pot, empty second cup, and the plate of cookies on the table. "Have some. Coffee and sugar are almost as magical as alcohol."

"Hedonist," Owen joked with a snort as he took a cookie and poured a cup.

"Your contact paid off?" Calvin couldn't help his curiosity about who Owen spent the day with.

"Yeah, Ida is a fireball, just like I remembered."

Calvin hadn't expected the way that comment twisted in his stomach. He recognized jealousy when he felt it, even when he had no claim on his partner—and no chance of changing that. "Had yourself a hot time?"

Owen rolled his eyes and gave Calvin a clear look of annoyance. "It's definitely not like that. She's a very dedicated reporter. We're colleagues."

"Sure." Calvin drew out the word just enough to vex his partner. *The only way I'm likely to get a "rise" out of him.*

"Don't be vulgar." Owen drew a notebook out of his jacket pocket. He hadn't paused to leave behind his tie and suit coat before joining Calvin, who appreciated Owen's urgency even if it wasn't personal.

"I spent part of the morning with a showgirl who always hears the best gossip." Calvin felt a petty surge of vindication when Owen's mouth twitched and his lips thinned in disapproval.

"Living down to your dossier?" Owen's tone was teasing, but with a slight edge Calvin wasn't sure how to interpret.

"Just staying in character." Calvin grinned. "Let's get Winston and then go over everything. We might be able to run down a suspect yet tonight if we play our cards right."

Winston joined them, standing ready next to the corkboard to add notes and connections. Calvin listened, impressed, as Owen recapped the ground he and Ida had covered, ending with the bicycle gunman's attack.

"Were you hurt?" Winston gave Owen a head-to-toe glance.

Calvin found that the answer mattered more than it should.

Owen shook his head. "Neither of us got hurt. I'm still not sure whether that was by luck or intent. I have the feeling that if the shooter had wanted to hit us, he could have."

"A warning?" Calvin asked sharply.

"That's what Ida and I made of it," Owen replied. "I think word already hit the streets that we're Davis and Harris's replacements."

Calvin told his story, omitting Louisa's Pinkerton connection and his humiliating lunch at the club. "So what I know for sure is that the chief of police is an asshole, someone who thinks they're untouchable hired a stooge to work me over, and that Ross Swanson is our best bet for the culprit behind the cut up bodies."

"But why would he want to open the gates of hell?"

Calvin and Winston looked at Owen in confusion. "The what?" Calvin echoed.

Owen colored an adorable shade of pink in embarrassment. "Sorry. I must have started that conversation in my head and forgot to say it out loud."

"Gates of *hell?*" Calvin repeated. Winston didn't seem completely surprised.

Owen recounted the legend Ida had shared with him and pinned the note she gave him to the corkboard. Calvin turned to Winston. "Did you know about this?"

"I hear a great many things," Winston replied. "Not all of them are relevant. But now that the topic has arisen, it might do to see if there's truth to the rumor. Although I doubt that we're talking about an actual portal to the afterworld. Perhaps a conduit for dark spirits? I will look into the lore."

Winston's nonchalant reaction made Calvin wonder just how witchy their new assistant really was.

"There's talk that Swanson might not be entirely human," Calvin added. "I spent time reading up on his latest successes in the local paper. He goes about during the day too much to be a vampire—although he could be working with one. He wasn't part of the were-wolf pack you took down, but there's been time for someone new to come to town."

"That still leaves plenty of supernatural creatures who might get a boost from blood and death," Owen mused. "I'd say we should pay him a visit."

Winston cleared his throat. "Before that, I have another item to add to the board. When I went to the farmer's market this morning, there was talk about strange lights in the sky and flying things that couldn't be explained. They didn't happen over St. Louis—it was out in the farmland beyond the city."

"Airships?" Owen wondered aloud. "Meteor showers?

Winston shook his head. "I don't think so. From what the farmers said, there have been strange patterns burned or flattened into their fields, and cattle killed in ways that don't match with the local wild animals. People are scared. The wilder theories claim it might be monsters from another world."

Owen frowned. "Sounds like they've been reading H. G. Wells. He'd come up with something like that."

"I thought the same," Winston replied.

Calvin vaguely remembered reading an excerpt or two from Wells's books that had been published in the paper, and thinking that they were exciting but outlandish. "Monsters from another world? Like we don't have enough trouble with the ones here on Earth?"

Owen shrugged. "No stranger than vampires, werewolves, and vengeful spirits."

Calvin gave him a look. "All which started on this planet. They didn't come from somewhere else to play pranks."

He glanced toward Winston. "Did you get locations for those farms?" At the other man's nod, Calvin continued. "We need to add a map to the board with all the places weird things happen—and overlay the planned path of the railway expansion. I think this ties back to Leland Aiken. The men who were killed and dismembered all had railroad connections. Ross Swanson played a role in some high-profile business deals that eventually rolled up to the new rail lines."

Owen seemed to catch his drift. "Want to bet that the farmers who are being terrorized have land either in the path of the railway or close enough?"

"That sounds like a logical theory," Winston agreed. "I will do some research and add the maps."

Calvin checked his watch. "We have a couple of hours before dinner. Fancy a visit to Mr. Swanson?"

Owen glanced toward Winston, who nodded. "I think that sounds like a perfect way to meet the neighbors," he replied with a grin. "And tomorrow, we can check out the strange flying objects and dead cows."

"I'd like to come with you when you visit the farms," Winston said. "My magic might come in handy."

AFTER CALVIN'S EARLY MISADVENTURE, he and Owen were doubly careful on their way to interview Ross Swanson. They took the trolley, changed direction more than once, and then walked the rest of the way taking a circuitous route.

"Nice place," Owen said as they scouted the Second Empire townhome in a pleasant neighborhood. "Looks like Swanson does well for himself."

"Except that I can't exactly tell what kind of business he's in," Calvin replied. "He doesn't own a store or a factory. He isn't a banker. He seems to be a matchmaker of sorts, introducing investors to people who need business money. I assume he takes a nice cut of the deal.

From what I read, he's from an old-money family, so maybe he's leveraging connections. Although for someone who trades heavily on trust, there have been a number of fairly salacious allegations."

"Let's go see if he wants to work magic for our—ahem—potential business ventures here in St. Louis," Owen said with a gleam in his eye.

The streets they walked were mostly deserted. In the distance, a dog barked. No one was on foot except Owen and Calvin—presumably they were all sitting down to dinner. The scene should have been one of tranquil respectability. Instead, something raised Calvin's hackles. He'd learned a long time ago to trust his gut.

"I don't like it," Owen murmured before Calvin could say anything. "Something's not right."

Apparently, their instincts were in sync.

Calvin went to the left, Owen to the right, meeting in the back. The kitchen door was splintered and hung in ruins from its hinges. Both agents drew their guns, and Calvin took point, with Owen covering his back.

The kitchen showed no sign of struggle other than the broken door. Nothing looked to be disturbed in the dining room, but when Calvin peered around the arched entrance to the parlor, he gestured to Owen that he'd found something.

Ross Swanson lay on the floor in a pool of blood. He wheezed for breath, and Calvin marveled that he was still alive given that half a dozen bullet holes riddled his torso.

Owen stood guard while Calvin warily approached. "Who did this?"

Swanson's head flopped more than turned toward Calvin. "You're too late. My money's gone."

"Were you involved with the men who went missing and got chopped up?" Time wasn't on their side, and Calvin wasn't inclined to be delicate.

Swanson swallowed hard and nodded faintly. "I...didn't pick them. They gave me a list. Had to do it. Blackmail."

"Blackmail about what?"

Blood tinted Swanson's lips. "What I am. That's why they used silver."

Calvin had already figured Swanson couldn't be completely human and still be alive. As his form shimmered and shook, Calvin scrambled back, giving the creature room to transform. But instead of the rough hair, long nails, and sharp teeth of a werewolf, Swanson changed into a different man.

"Shapeshifter, not a were," Owen observed, still keeping his gun raised and ready.

"Explains why he can't heal himself," Calvin said. "Whatever son of a bitch shot him used silver to poison him and make sure it was a slow death."

"Can you tell us anything about who might have set you up?" Calvin figured the desire for vengeance might give the dying shifter enough reason to name his attacker.

"I didn't take the body parts." Swanson's breath rattled as he spoke. "The witch needed them—and the blood. I caught the people on the list and took the bodies. The witch knew about me...I couldn't say no."

"Did that include Davis and Harris?"

Swanson nodded. "I remember those names. They fought back."

"Was Leland Aiken involved?" Calvin figured it was worth a try.

Swanson coughed up blood. His true form looked nothing like the slick businessman he had impersonated. The shifter was stockier, rough-featured, someone who would have fit right in with the gangs of Calvin's youth.

"Maybe. It was all for the railroad."

"Did you kill Swanson and take his place?" Calvin couldn't stifle his curiosity.

"Invented him."

Coughs wracked the shifter's body. Calvin calculated that the shot to the chest had been aimed to graze the heart but not destroy it outright. Swanson's killer wanted him to suffer.

Swanson's body finally failed and he went limp with a deep wheeze.

"Let's get out of here," Owen said. "I'm surprised the cops haven't shown up with all the shots that were fired."

Calvin took one last look around in case they'd missed a clue, but Swanson's parlor, while perfectly decorated, was devoid of personal details.

Then again, he wasn't really Swanson, so his life didn't have real details either.

"What did you make of all that?" Calvin asked as he and Owen walked the last leg of their trip back to the train.

"That should stop the murders—presumably," Owen spoke carefully as if weighing his thoughts with each word. "Good for the city, although I don't imagine people are done dying for the railroad yet. Having a dark witch involved is worrisome, to say the least. But not entirely a surprise."

"And Swanson?"

Owen frowned. "Leland Aiken is my top suspect for blackmailing Swanson, which puts Aiken's witch at the top of the list for who killed him."

Calvin nodded. "I agree. We're thinking alike. That's a good sign." He jokingly bumped shoulders with Owen, enjoying the brief contact.

"What next?"

"I was thinking we should go take a look at the farm where the 'flying objects' were seen. I know it'll be late going after dinner, but if there are lights in the sky and floating orbs, that would be the best time to see them," Calvin replied. "And I have to admit, I'm intrigued at having Winston join us. First outing for the three of us. Should be interesting."

"I can do anything with enough coffee," Owen assured him. "Sounds like a plan."

Winston had dinner ready when they returned, a spicy chicken gumbo with fresh cornbread.

"Spent some time in New Orleans and got the recipe from my landlady," he told them when they praised the flavor. "It's a good meal on a cold night to warm the bones."

By unspoken agreement, Calvin and Owen didn't discuss their trip to visit Swanson until after they finished the meal. Once the plates were cleared and they lingered over a cup of coffee, Winston listened gravely as they recounted what had happened.

"I was also able to learn more about those strange lights," Winston said. "Quite the talk down at the marketplace among the farmers, as you can imagine. Someone went up on a roof to take a better look at the damage and found that the wheat wasn't just flattened randomly—something made very clear marks. Sigils—used in magic."

"To do what?" Calvin asked. "And why?"

"The lights happened when the sigils appeared. Of course, everyone thinks they're 'alien' marks, but I found them in one of the grimoires in the library. They are marks to open or unlock."

"Like opening a gate?" Owen absently let his finger stroke along the rim of his coffee cup.

Calvin looked up sharply. "Your gates of hell theory?"

Winston nodded. "Exactly. And once the lights went away, people on the farms saw 'large black dogs with red eyes' prowling near their barns. Then cattle turned up dead, ripped apart by something bigger than a bear or a bobcat. There's already talk about people moving out."

"Let me guess—the farms aren't far off the new railroad route?" Calvin asked.

"Definitely within the likely right-of-way," Winston confirmed. "But I'm more interested in the black dogs. They sound like hellhounds, or more likely a grim or shuck, neither of which is supernatural nor native to Missouri."

"Just because they started by killing cattle doesn't mean they won't go after people," Owen said. "Sounds like this just became part of our case. But how do we go to a farm at this time of night? The cabbies have gone home, and I'd rather not ride horses in an unfamiliar place in the dark."

"I suspected we'd be making an outing, so I put a bag together with a few things I might need." Winston had a crafty glint in his eye. "And I took the liberty of befriending one of the drivers. He was eager to make some extra money and agreed to lend us the use of his carriage and horse."

"You think of everything, Winston," Owen said. "I take it we can use the carriage tonight?"

"It's on standby for us," Winston replied. "We can go any time."

"Then let's get to it." Calvin stood. "I want to see these 'flying objects' for myself."

***

THE ONE-HORSE CARRIAGE that awaited them was a buggy, not one of the fancier Hansom cabs or the few gasoline-powered runabouts Calvin had seen in town. That suited them just fine since there was nothing special about it to draw attention.

Their lanterns lit the way once they ventured beyond the city's gas lamps. A full moon helped to dispel the darkness, but once the lights of St. Louis were behind them, darkness enveloped the countryside.

After a half hour, Winston pulled the buggy over to the side of the road and looped the horse's reins to a sapling. "We're close now, and we'll do better on foot from here."

Calvin pulled a bag with weapons and other useful items from the buggy, handing off a shotgun to Owen, who also had a long knife sheathed to his belt beneath his coat that matched Calvin's. Owen lit lanterns and passed them out.

Winston lagged behind, walking counterclockwise around the horse and carriage as he murmured under his breath and spread a circle of salt. When he finished, they faded into the shadows, visible only if someone knew where to look and stared intently.

"What did you do?" Calvin blinked with surprise, intrigued and a bit unnerved.

Winston smiled. "Just some minor magic to make the carriage and the horse less noticeable for their protection. If those large dogs with red eyes are here, I don't want to take any unnecessary chances."

Practical witchcraft has its uses, Calvin thought, curious to learn more about Winston's abilities.

They kept their lanterns partially shuttered to avoid drawing notice on the dark stretch of road with large wheat fields and few houses.

"Not a lot of people around to see those strange lights," Owen observed. "Unless it happened closer to dusk when folks might not have gone in yet for the evening or were at the barn doing chores."

Calvin nodded. "If an *entity* wanted to come here without being noticed, why the light show? It's certainly dark enough to come and go without drawing attention."

"This way." Winston guided them toward a corner of the field. In the lanterns' light, they could see where the crops had been flattened.

"Cover me." Winston walked to the edge of the field, careful not to step where the ground had been tilled. He held the lantern with his left hand and stretched out his right arm, palm facing the field, took a deep breath, closed his eyes, and murmured something.

Calvin and Owen positioned themselves so they could watch both directions. Calvin couldn't help stealing a glance toward Winston, fascinated.

Winston's expression tightened in concentration. His jaw clenched, muscles twitching, and his body vibrated with tension. A slight blue glow limned Winston's outstretched hand.

Abruptly, he jerked and stumbled backward. His hand lowered, and the glow faded. In the darkness, Calvin heard rustling amid the wheat and deep growls growing closer.

"Definitely magic—quite certainly dark." Winston panted as if out of breath. "Run!"

They sprinted back toward the buggy as the growling and howls grew louder.

"Watch out!" Owen yelled. His lantern swung crazily as he blasted his shotgun into the darkness, firing toward the red glow of eyes.

Calvin loosed a shot in the other direction as a large shadowy shape bounded toward them, eyes like embers. *A black shuck—what the locals call a "devil dog." Better than a hellhound, but not by much.*

Winston sent a jagged streak of blue fire toward one of the shapes. The creature yelped in pain, and the scent of burnt hair followed.

Calvin spotted at least three devil dogs and wondered if more were coming. He set the lantern to the side and racked another shell, shotgun in one hand and machete in the other. A glance told him that Owen had drawn his knife as well.

"There are four of them," Winston said with uncanny certainty. "Fancy a fight?"

One of the creatures lunged from the shadows toward Winston, teeth bared and eyes blazing. A streak of blue light flared, catching the devil dog in the chest and hurling its large, nearly man-sized body several feet.

Two more advanced on Calvin and Owen, who bided their time for the monsters to get within shotgun range. The two men fell into a back-to-back stance as if they'd been fighting together for years, and despite the newness of their partnership Calvin didn't doubt Owen's protection.

The creature launched at Calvin, covering the gap between them alarmingly fast. He and Owen shot in unison as it lunged. Then Owen swung his blade, landing a deep gash across the monster's right shoulder. Calvin's machete sliced through the shuck's throat, sending dark blood gushing.

Owen wheeled, with one hand reloading and firing in a smooth motion as a second devil dog attacked. His shot caught the shuck in the chest, but it barely slowed. Behind them, Calvin heard Winston chanting and saw another flash of blue lightning.

This time the monster barreled toward Owen, eyes blazing, fanged maw open. His second shell hit left of center, but the creature kept coming. Owen dropped the shotgun and swung the machete with both hands a few seconds too late as the devil dog's massive paw batted him out of the way like a toy, sending the machete from his hand as he tumbled.

Calvin charged, holding the knife like a sword with a two-handed grip. He threw his full weight at the creature, sinking the blessed blade deep between its ribs. Hot black blood fountained from the wound, coating his hands and arms. Calvin dodged to the side as the monster snapped at him, and he spotted Owen's blade on the ground.

The shuck lumbered toward Calvin, who shouted in defiance and swung for the neck this time. The blade bit into the flesh, cutting through matted, coarse hair, severing tendons. With a grunt and a push, Calvin shoved the steel through the spine. The body fell to one side, and the head rolled to the other.

Calvin stood still for a few seconds, heaving for breath, chilled by the rapidly cooling blood that soaked his hair and clothing.

His mind came back on track as he remembered. *Owen.* Calvin stumbled toward where his partner struggled to push up from the ground. "Are you hurt?" Calvin knelt beside Owen, searching for wounds. Owen was dirt-streaked and disheveled, but he shook his head.

"I'm okay," Owen assured him, then took in Calvin's blood-soaked appearance. "My God, Calvin. Is any of that blood yours?"

Calvin stood and gave Owen a hand up, choosing not to examine how hard his heart thudded when Owen had been batted out of the way, or the relief that flooded over him finding that Owen was unhurt.

"Not much, if any," Calvin promised.

Winston jogged over to them, looking unruffled. The bodies of two devil dogs lay in the dirt behind him, and Calvin wondered how he had managed to slay two of the creatures on his own.

"Serious injuries?" Winston gave them both a once-over.

They shook their heads.

"Good. Help me drag the bodies into the wheat, then go back to the buggy. I'll burn the field."

Together they hauled the muscular corpses of the devil dogs to the edge of the field. Calvin noticed that the shucks he and Owen killed had been shot and stabbed, while the creatures Winston killed were charred, matted hair still smoking, looking like they had been struck by lightning.

"Go," Winston said. Calvin and Owen fell back and retrieved the lanterns and their weapons. They remained close enough to intervene if more of the creatures showed up.

Winston fashioned a torch with a sturdy stick and a piece of cloth from his bag, which he lit with a twitch of his fingers. It took only minutes for him to walk along the edge of the field, setting the wheat ablaze before tossing the torch deeper into the field.

"Come on." Winston strode past Calvin and Owen toward where they'd left the carriage. He murmured a word, and the illusion dropped, making the horse and buggy clearly visible. Calvin and Owen crowded into the closed cabin while Winston climbed into the driver's seat.

"You look like you came from a slaughterhouse," Owen observed.

Calvin grimaced. The blood had started to dry, pulling tight in some places and remaining sticky in others. All of it stank. "Not far off the mark. Did it get you with claws?"

Owen shook his head. "No. Thank you for back there—you kept it off me. I thought I'd had it."

"Easier than filing the paperwork if it got you," Calvin joked. He'd examine his feelings later, in private.

Owen seemed to take the joke as it was intended. "My turn to kill the monster next time." He wrinkled his nose. "You reek. And I don't know how we'll get the blood off the seat."

When they got back to the carriage house, Winston stopped by the watering trough. He went into the barn and grabbed a few towels, then tossed one to each of them as he dipped his in the cold water. "See if you can get the worst off." He nodded to Calvin and then turned to Owen. "Give me a hand, please, mopping up the inside."

In minutes they had made the interior presentable, and Calvin no longer looked like he had bathed in blood. Winston told them to wait outside while he returned the horse and carriage to the stable master with a generous tip.

He joined them for the walk back to the Pullman. "Good fighting, lads. You did yourself proud."

Since Calvin was in his early thirties—as was Owen—he bit back a chuckle. He wagered that it had been a while since either of them had been "lads," but somehow, coming from Winston, it seemed right.

"You shot fire at the creatures. Why didn't you light the field that way?" Owen asked.

Calvin wasn't surprised that his bookish partner wanted to know about technicalities.

"I didn't know how it might interact with the sigils and didn't want to risk it," Winston replied matter-of-factly, as if magic were an everyday occurrence.

And for him, I guess it is.

"Did we get them all? The devil dogs?"

"I didn't sense any remaining," Winston replied. "Whoever sent those might magic up more of them, but it will cost time and energy. And they have nothing to do with the devil."

"Were you able to pick up anything about who—or what—made the sigils and called the black shucks?" Calvin asked.

"Yes. It was plain old human magic, hardly aliens from outer space," Winston said. "Probably Aiken's witch. My suspicion is that it's one more step in his 'gates of hell' scheme."

They entered the Pullman through the back, not wanting to make a mess or attract attention. Calvin sent the others on ahead and then stripped down to his underpants, leaving his bloody clothes in the ash bin to be burned.

When he entered the car, Winston was nowhere to be seen, but Owen had lingered, waiting for Calvin.

"I just wanted to make sure you weren't hurt," Owen said, but it was a few heartbeats before he turned away from staring at Calvin's blood-streaked, nearly naked body.

"Uh, no. I'm fine. Thanks." Calvin felt a blush creep to his cheeks, although it was hardly the first time he'd been seen in the altogether. He ducked into his cabin and closed the door, leaning back on it as his heart pounded.

Did Owen just give me a once-over? He definitely got an eyeful. Did he like what he saw? Was it really triage, or was he checking out the goods?

Calvin ducked into the shower, eager to sluice away the blood and dirt. He scrubbed until his skin pinked. As the night's chill and the adrenaline faded, his mind turned back to Owen in the hallway, staring at him.

In the dim light, Calvin couldn't be certain whether the look in

Owen's eyes was arousal or concern. He knew what he wanted to see, and as his hand fell to his cock, slicking it with fast, desperate strokes, his mind filled in the details.

Owen, worried for his safety, taking him into his room and touching him all over, checking for injuries very thoroughly. Pushing him into the shower and stripping down so he could help Calvin wash away the remnants of the fight, hands moving sure but tender. Toweling Calvin down before seeing to himself and then leading Calvin to the bed, inviting him to stay. Taking off the edge, rubbing against each other, or sucking each other off before falling asleep.

Calvin didn't usually stay the night with his lovers, but for Owen he could imagine changing that habit, drifting off tangled up together.

He bit his lip to stifle a groan as he came, riding out the after-shocks and letting the water wash away the evidence. Calvin leaned against the wall and turned off the shower. His daydream left him feeling sad as he dried off, lonely for the touch of someone he was unlikely to ever have.

Chapter 5
Owen

This will help with sore muscles." Winston put a steaming cup of tea that smelled of willow bark in front of Owen the next morning at breakfast. "You took quite a fall yesterday. I can also get ice from one of the brewery cargo cars, if that would help. And if you're still sore this evening, I'll mix up a poultice that will help loosen tight muscles after you take a hot shower."

Owen smiled gratefully. "Thank you. I'll probably take you up on everything. Getting knocked around goes with the job, but it hurts more each year."

Given the danger of his work, Owen knew he was lucky to escape injuries worse than a few broken bones. Even so, he'd been shot, poisoned, stabbed, and hexed, with scars to prove it.

Those scars were another reason Owen avoided liaisons that required him to take off all his clothes or took place outside of dimly lit rooms. The injuries were odd even if he used soldiering as an excuse, and after one casual lover had concluded he must be a criminal on the loose, Owen had made do with quick satisfaction that could be had while mostly dressed.

I wonder what scars Calvin has? What does it say about me that I wanted to jump his bones at the sight of him nearly naked and covered in blood?

Owen had felt rooted in place, mesmerized by the view of Calvin's strong shoulders and flat belly, looking like an avenging warrior out of classical legends. He'd finally gotten his brain to engage, stammered something about checking for injuries, and beat a shameful retreat to his room.

A cold shower hadn't quelled his desire, and Owen had jerked off fast and dirty to thoughts of helping Calvin clean up, and then fucking him hard, proof of life. Owen had silenced his moan with a mouthful of blanket when he came.

Worse, Owen couldn't tell what to make of Calvin's actions. He found himself searching every conversation and gesture for clues to whether Calvin shared his feelings or was simply being friendly. *It's only been a few days. We have time to figure it out. But I might combust in the meantime.*

That morning, Owen heard the shower running in Calvin's stateroom and did his best to pull his thoughts away from the visual that conjured in his mind. He wondered whether Calvin felt the need, like Lady Macbeth, to compulsively scrub away bloodstains long after they were really gone. He thought being soaked head-to-toe in devil dog blood could certainly push a person toward some extra scrubbing.

A few minutes later, Calvin stumbled into the dining room, hair askew, shirt untucked. Owen thought he looked like he'd come off a bender or had managed to sleep through his alarm.

"Morning," Calvin mumbled, accepting the hot cup of coffee Winston pressed into his hands.

Winston spared Calvin a look of amused compassion and returned moments later with a tray of bacon, buttered cinnamon toast, and egg tarts, which he placed in the middle of the table, along with a fresh pot of coffee.

"You had a long day yesterday," Winston said. "Eat up. A solid breakfast sets you right for the whole day."

Owen traded his tea for coffee, trying to chase away the last of his morning fog. After his lusty imaginings, he had fallen into a troubled sleep. In his dreams, the devil dog attacked Calvin, and Owen was too slow to save his new partner. Owen had killed the monster, only to have Calvin bleed out in his arms, the possibilities of what could have been between them forever lost.

He'd woken with wet cheeks and a lump in his throat.

I need to go out tonight, alone, and work off some tension. This is ridiculous. I'm too old to have a crush on my partner.

The clang of a bell pulled Owen from his thoughts.

"That's the telegraph." Winston hurried to the library, with Calvin and Owen close behind, and sat at the desk waiting for the paper tape. Owen translated in his head as the machine clicked. The message repeated then the device went silent.

"It's from Agents Storm and Drangosavich," Winston said. "Watch out for Branson brothers. Ties to Aiken. Follow the money. Good luck."

"Well, that was illuminating," Owen grumbled. "What the hell did it mean?"

Calvin ran a hand through his messy hair, smoothing it mostly into place as they returned to the dining room. "When I was at the library reading back copies of the newspapers, I saw that name. Want to head back there and see what we can dig up?"

"Sure. If Mitch and Jacob thought it was worth a telegram, then there must be a reason for them to suspect it's connected somehow," Owen agreed, actually looking forward to spending time with Calvin when they weren't likely to get eaten by a monster.

Winston walked over to the corkboard and stood with his hands on his hips as if he was searching for something there.

"Follow the money," he repeated, still staring at their pinned notes. "St. Louis is just now getting back on its feet after the war, in many ways. Financially, the city is still fragile. There have been bank panics that shut business down for days at a time," Winston said. "If the Branson brothers are financiers of dubious honor, they might be valuable allies for someone like Aiken."

"I guess we're going as our business investor personas," Owen said.

"You'll find your shirts pressed, fresh collars and cuffs in your drawer, shoes shined, and suits steamed," Winston said without turning.

"I don't know how we would manage without you," Owen replied sincerely, finding himself a little in awe of their very efficient all-purpose assistant.

"All part of a day's work," Winston answered, although he sounded pleased at the praise. "I shall be cleaning the guns, replenishing the shotgun shells, and working up a few new spells."

Calvin turned to Owen. "Ready in fifteen minutes?"

Owen grinned. "Hell, I can be ready in ten."

They went their separate ways and emerged even faster than predicted. A comb and a dollop of Macassar oil tamed Calvin's dark hair. Owen's shorter hair didn't require quite as much effort to stay in place. Owen twisted his head from side to side, trying to loosen up the stiff, starched collar while Calvin fussed with buttoning his cuffs.

"We look remarkably respectable," Owen noted with a chuckle.

"Imagine that," Calvin bantered. "Once we can bamboozle them into thinking we're legitimate businessmen, the sky's the limit."

Owen didn't bother to point out that they were both unusually well-armed for "legitimate businessmen," even for St. Louis, a city that had one foot in the more refined East and one in the Wild West.

He carried his Colt Peacemaker in a holster beneath his jacket and knew Calvin's Smith and Wesson was similarly concealed. Owen had a switchblade in his pocket and a throwing knife in a wrist sheath. He figured Calvin had at least as many knives on him, if not more.

Calvin hadn't put on his jacket, revealing his shoulder rig. Owen shifted slightly as his cock woke up at the way the straps hugged Calvin's body.

"Let's go—and hope we get a nice, quiet day for a change. Tame enough for a stroll in the park and a bowl of ice cream on the way home," Calvin said, sounding a bit wistful.

"And no one shooting at us," Owen added.

"That would be a nice change."

Remaining cautious, they walked beyond the train station before catching a cab, switched to a trolley, and changed directions again.

Both watched for signs of surveillance or anyone tailing them, but relaxed when they reached the library without incident.

"Back so soon, Mr. Springfield?" A pleasant-faced woman with graying hair piled high in a Gibson knot greeted them from behind the reception desk.

"Did you miss me?" Calvin teased with a boyish grin, flirting harmlessly. Even so, Owen felt a flash of irrational jealousy.

"I see you brought a friend," she replied with a laugh, taking his flirting in stride.

"Owen Sharps, ma'am." Owen politely inclined his head.

"We're here to look at the newspapers again," Calvin said. "I promise we'll put everything back as we found it."

"Oh, I know you will. You left everything very neat the last time." With a motherly smile, she waved them on.

Owen waited until they were out of earshot. "She's probably old enough to be your grandmother," he whispered.

"I just have that effect on people," Calvin retorted blithely, unsuccessfully hiding his grin. He seemed to enjoy Owen's exasperation.

The newspaper room was in the basement, a small space with dim electric lighting that flickered whenever a heavy wagon passed by and rattled the window glass. Calvin and Owen pulled the past two months of back issues and made themselves comfortable at the table.

For a while, neither spoke. The scratching of pen on notepaper and the rustling of newspaper pages filled the silence. Owen was surprised to feel the same calm he'd felt on the train, something he'd only sensed with a few close friends after years together.

They had taken seats where they could watch the door, backs to the wall, out of habit. Much as Owen wanted to remove his jacket in the warm room, he didn't want to reveal his holster. He tugged at his collar and dabbed at his forehead with his handkerchief.

"Warm, isn't it?" Calvin said without looking up. "I don't imagine the librarian would appreciate it if we stripped down, but it's tempting."

Tempting didn't begin to cover it. Owen spent the next several minutes trying to force his over-active imagination to let go of the image of a shirtless Calvin and keep his attention on the dusty papers.

"Find anything? The sooner we turn up details, the faster we can go somewhere that has air."

Calvin pushed his chair back so he could stretch. Owen tried not to stare at the way his lean body shifted, something even the suit coat couldn't completely hide. He was glad the library table hid the telltale bulge in his pants.

"The Branson brothers have their fingers in a lot of pies. Land sales and mining rights in particular," Calvin said.

"That matches what I found. They show up in the papers every couple of weeks for some big land deal."

Calvin nodded. "Except that in between the big deals, other things fall apart. There are articles about people being defrauded with bad contracts or mines that run dry in just weeks. The papers don't quite come out and say it, but—"

"There's always a trail of breadcrumbs that connect to the Branson brothers," Owen finished his sentence.

"Which goes back to the police chief being corrupt," Calvin theorized. "It's the only way someone with so many brushes with scandal could beat the odds and emerge unscathed."

"I found articles about the bank panics," Owen cut in. "When people get scared that the bank doesn't have enough money to cover withdrawals, they panic and try to get their deposits out at once. That creates the problem they feared. It's a real mess. When businesses can't trust the banks, everything gets wobbly. And more than once, a bad land deal with ties back to the Branson brothers touched off a run on the banks."

Calvin closed the newspaper he had been reading. "Mitch and Jacob thought they were connected to Aiken. If he's really a smart, immortal vampire, why wouldn't he choose competent allies?"

Owen frowned, thinking. "I don't imagine a guy like Aiken thinks about mortals as 'allies'—more like tools to be used. We could be looking at this all wrong. We're assuming it would be in his interest to work with competent land speculators. But maybe he's gaining something out of the chaos their scandals cause."

"Interesting." Calvin got up and paced. Owen tried and failed to keep his eyes from watching the curve of Calvin's back and the swell of his ass. "I think you're on to something. So what's the advantage? How does Aiken benefit if the local banks break?"

Owen leaned back and crossed his arms. He feared pushing his chair back and revealing the way his pants tented. "In cities with strong banks, bankers rule the roost. Everyone has to bow and scrape to them, and they can impose whatever terms they want. That can go hard on businesses that want to borrow money or people trying to buy land. A strong bank can hold a city hostage to get what its owners want."

"Okay...that makes sense. Aiken is expanding his railroad and wants to buy up land. He's probably also got some secret vampire plan." Calvin picked up on the line of thinking. "If the local banks are always recovering from one panic or another, they can't bully borrowers like Aiken. They'd be more likely to give him good rates and extend his loans. He's more solvent than they are, so he's got the upper hand."

"And to hell with everyone else who gets hurt by the instability." Owen felt his anger spark on behalf of the people who would be harmed by Aiken's scheme. "Some folks lose their life savings when a run on a bank forces it to close. Local businesses can't get loans at good terms."

"Maybe that's part of the plan," Calvin said, still pacing. "Railroads usually bring travelers to a town, and that means new hotels, saloons, restaurants, boarding houses, and other companies that spring up because of the rail hub. If the banks are always on the brink of melting down, other people can't get loans to build things like that. And if Aiken doesn't need the loans, he can build all the businesses that benefit from his railroad—he walks away profiting from everything, and the city gains nothing."

"Unless the Branson brothers are trying to buy up land to do the same thing—which would make them Aiken's rivals," Owen mused. "I can't imagine that will go well for them in the long run."

On their way out they thanked the librarian and walked a couple of blocks to the Land Office. As usual, a line went around the block as eager speculators, would-be miners, and starry-eyed homesteaders waited to buy land or receive permits they believed would make their dreams come true.

"Busy, as usual," Calvin noted. "With that line, none of the clerks are going to have time to answer any questions from us."

Owen took in the area and elbowed Calvin. He tipped his head toward Tomkin's, a saloon that looked like it might cater to the Land Office customers.

"Let's see if the beer is cold and the stories are worth hearing," Calvin said with a grin.

They walked into Tomkin's, and Owen sized up the joint. A sign over the bar promised free pickles, peanuts, and boiled potatoes with every beer. The tables were filled with men in the dungaree overalls of miners and the plain spun clothing of would-be settlers. An upright piano next to a small stage suggested that later in the day those who came for the free-dinner-with-every-beer might get a little entertainment.

Calvin led the way to the bar. Owen and Calvin sat together, taking the only two barstools that weren't already claimed. Their suits made them stand out, and Owen caught more than one critical appraising glance.

The bartender gave them the once-over. "You sure you gents wouldn't rather have lunch over at one of the big hotels in town? I can promise you that the food's better."

"Maybe later," Calvin replied. "I could use a nibble right now—and a beer to go with it."

"Same here," Owen added. The bartender eyed them like he couldn't figure out why they were there, but he shrugged and went to fill their order. When he returned with their beer and bowls of cold, cooked potatoes, dill pickles, and boiled peanuts, Calvin grinned and turned on the charm that seemed to work on men, women, and stray dogs.

"We came to town looking for business opportunities," Calvin said, playing up his role. "Fast-growing place. Looks like everyone has big plans."

No one else clamored for the bartender's attention, so he lingered and wiped down the bar. "People come west to get a new start, a new name, new chance to win big. Sometimes it works. Mostly…not quite like they expected."

From the man's tone, Owen wondered if the bartender was one of those whose experience hadn't matched his expectations.

"To tell you the truth, I'm not sure the people we really wanted to talk to are in the Land Office." Owen raised his glass to his lips but barely sipped. "We were told to connect with the Branson brothers."

Owen could fake a guileless smile and vacuous expression when needed, a necessary subterfuge. The bartender gave him an incredulous look, and conversation at the bar quieted.

"Do yourself a favor," the bartender said with a decidedly less friendly manner than just minutes ago. "Steer clear of them."

Calvin frowned. "We'd been led to understand that they handled a lot of the land transactions in town. Was that not correct?" He managed to look distressed, like the information that sent him west to score a business deal had suddenly unraveled.

"Oh, they'll sell you land," the man to Calvin's right snarled. "They'll fleece you like a sheep and sell your carcass to the butcher."

"They're goddamn speculators," the man beside Owen added. "They scoop up good land, and parcel out smaller pieces. Except they keep the best chunks, and the poor suckers who trust them end up with lousy farmland or tapped out mines."

"They stay in business because there are so many new people coming every week, the stories don't have time to catch up with them," a man farther down the bar put in.

"How do they stay in town without being arrested?" Calvin looked credibly appalled.

The bartender glanced around and lowered his voice. "Because they pay the right people to look the other way."

"Everybody wants a shortcut," the guy next to Calvin said. "There ain't none that don't end in grief. You want decent land, you need to go stand in that godawful line and wait your turn. Trying to cut corners just gets you robbed."

Owen fussed with his collar and tie, hoping he looked flustered. "Well. Glad we asked. We'll come back early tomorrow, I guess."

"Line starts before dawn," the bartender told them. "People used to try to spend the whole night in line, but the police had to break up too many fights."

"Bright and early then," Calvin said. "Thank you for the advice."

The other men went back to their beer, and the bartender moved down to help other customers. Calvin and Owen picked at their food and sipped slowly at their beer, listening to the conversations around them.

Owen heard a lot about the price of corn, how much the town needed rain, and some gossip about a local Vaudeville actor caught in a compromising situation, but nothing connected to their case. After they had lingered long enough for their departure not to look suspicious, they finished up and headed back outside.

"Can't say I care for potatoes done like that, but the pickles were good," Calvin said as they walked back toward the trolley.

"I preferred the peanuts. The beer was terrible," Owen replied. "What now?"

"I thought we'd show up at the Branson brothers' office and see how it goes," Calvin said. "Let's see what kind of a song and dance they put on for the rubes they swindle, and maybe we can figure out whether they're likely to be working *with* Aiken or if he just hasn't gotten around to killing them yet."

"Should be interesting," Owen agreed. "That crowd in the bar sure had them figured. Although I can see how starry-eyed transplants coming in from the countryside could be easy to bilk." He frowned. "That makes it even worse, taking advantage like that."

"Agreed—but it's probably paltry compared to what Aiken's up to," Calvin said. "And that thought scares the crap out of me."

Calvin's admission surprised Owen, although he shared the sentiment. He felt like the vampire was still several steps ahead of them and that they hadn't yet figured out his real game. *Swanson's death might have stopped one set of murders, but I'm betting that if Aiken is involved, there will be more to come.*

As they approached the address for the Branson brothers' office, the street grew more congested. Up ahead, Owen saw a cluster of police officers. The undertaker's black wagon sat conspicuously by the curb.

"Looks like trouble," Calvin said.

Owen glimpsed the man he'd seen pass by when he'd been with Ida and recognized Chief Wyman. After everything they'd heard about the man, Owen had no desire to meet him.

"Why don't you go around and see if you can figure out what's really going on," Calvin said. "I met the chief once before, so I'll go straight to the top with my questions. Try not to get arrested."

"Try not to get shot," Owen replied, only partly in jest. He saw Calvin stride into the tangle of cops, horses, and wagons like he owned the street. He shook his head in appreciation of his new partner's skill.

Owen worked his way around the edges of the chaos. He knew that his suit made him stand out in the crowd, so instead of trying to fit in, he squared his shoulders and raised his head like a city official come to inspect whatever was going on.

The ruse worked. Between the imperious expression Owen affected and the rank implied by his suit, people moved out of his way. He stopped a few feet from the office's door, which was propped open so the black-clad morticians could carry out the bodies on stretchers. Owen sidled close enough to smell the blood and see that the savaged corpses looked more like they had been mauled by a wild beast than shot over a land dispute.

Owen saw Calvin talking with Chief Wyman. He couldn't hear the conversation, but from their stance and gestures, Owen guessed the chief was annoyed at Calvin but straining to keep from antagonizing a potential city investor.

Owen took a notebook and pen from his jacket pocket and pretended to take notes as workers milled around him.

"...could be a bear," one cop said to another as they hung behind the undertakers.

"In the city? How?" his companion challenged.

"Got a better idea?" the first cop retorted.

"It could be like that book where the doctor drinks a potion that turns him into a madman," the other officer said. "He changed into a man-beast and had claws and fangs."

"Penny dreadfuls are going to rot your brain. Can you imagine telling the chief that theory?"

"I didn't say I believed it, the second cop sulked. "Just said it could have happened that way."

"Hey, you!" The first cop finally noticed Owen. "You're not supposed to be here."

Owen lifted his head. "I most certainly am. I'm with the Health Department, and I had an appointment with the gentlemen in this office about precautions to stop the spread of man-eating rats." He dropped his voice. "It's become a big problem."

He didn't know what wild flight of fancy made him say that, but the cop's eyes widened. "Man-eating rats?"

"Have you seen any?" Owen pressed, hoping he didn't look surprised at being taken seriously.

The two officers exchanged a look. "The men inside were murdered. It looked like something gnawed on them. Do you think it could be one of those rats?"

"Hmm." Owen pretended to ponder a moment. "I'm sorry to say it's possible. We think the rats are traveling on the ships coming down the river," he said in a confidential tone.

"How would you know for sure?" the taller of the two cops asked.

"Can you tell me what it was like, inside?" Owen asked. "Don't leave out any details—they might be important."

"A customer came for an appointment and found them," the tall cop said. "Throats ripped out, bodies clawed open, blood everywhere."

"It looked like a bear kill," the other cop confided. "Except we're in the city."

"Is there any chance I might be able to see the room?" Owen pressed his luck. The bodies were gone, but they might concoct a reason to visit the morgue. It looked like Calvin and the police chief were deep in conversation, with Calvin angling for something and the chief unhappy about the request.

The two cops glanced toward their chief. "Could you tell if it's big rats if we let you in? I'm sure the chief would approve if he knew about them."

"They leave traces," Owen said. "I'll only need a few minutes."

The taller cop looked to his companion. "You stay out here." He motioned for Owen to follow him, and they slipped inside.

The office stank of blood. So much pooled on the floor that Owen struggled to step around it. Splatter marked the walls and some even painted the ceiling. *It took strength to make this much mess. And rage. This wasn't an animal that needed to eat. This was assassination by monster.*

"Can you tell? Was it rats?" The cop looked frightened enough to piss his pants.

"Definitely rats," Owen said gravely. "Worst I've ever seen."

"I knew it," the man said. "Damn. How do we get rid of them?"

"Place a line of loose salt all around the doors and windows," Owen told him. "Holy water might also help."

"With rats?" the cop's eyes widened.

"These are demonic rats. It wouldn't hurt to have a priest bless the buildings on this block."

The cop nodded. "Okay. I can arrange that. What about traps? Can we trap them?"

"You should leave that to the professionals," Owen told him, completely serious. "I'll turn in my notes, and experienced hunters will be sent to take care of the problem. It would be very dangerous for anyone else to attempt."

Not a lie...it'll be Calvin and Winston and me. Trained professionals. But first, we have to figure out what the hell killed those men, because it's sure as fuck not big rats.

Owen and Calvin met back up half an hour later at the trolley station. Calvin dropped his charming swagger, looking tired and tense. "What's this I hear about rats?"

Owen started to laugh. "How did you hear that?"

Calvin gave him a look. "Why do I get the feeling that you had something to do with it?"

"Maybe." Owen tried not to laugh even harder.

"The chief was keeping me from getting closer or talking to anyone, and we were almost arguing. I thought I saw you over by the doorway to the office. Next thing I know, some uniform cop is talking about man-eating rats. When he mentioned salt lines, I knew you had to be involved," Calvin replied, and despite his tension he looked like he was biting back a laugh.

Owen gave him a quick recap as they waited for the trolley. By the end, Calvin was laughing so hard that he bent over, one arm across his stomach.

"Oh my God, that's brilliant." Calvin slapped Owen on the shoulder. "You got everything we needed except finding the monster itself."

"Definitely not rats," Owen said.

"Let's go back to the Pullman and fill Winston in, and then I'll go see my contact," Calvin volunteered.

They kept up the subterfuge of changing trolleys and switching directions, reaching the train car without incident. Winston was waiting for them. Owen wondered if the man's uncanny sense of when they would return had anything to do with magic.

"You made good time." Winston set out a pot of fresh coffee and a plate of cookies on the dining room table. "Tell me everything."

Calvin and Owen took turns regaling Winston, who had trouble maintaining his composure when Owen got to the part about the man-eating rats.

"Very quick thinking," Winston said. "But I suspect that devil dogs are more likely. I've spent part of today searching the lore. Legends place the devil dogs and a large cat-monster called a Howler in this area, although they've been scarce since the wilderness has been settled. They have history here, but summoning them requires certain skills that aren't common. And before you ask, being a vampire wouldn't help."

Winston added his notes to the corkboard. "We have new information, but not how it all ties together."

Owen came to stand behind him, hands on hips, studying the information they'd collected. His gaze fell on the note Ida had given him.

"Awakening of the sigil," he mused aloud. "The summoning of the servants. The destruction of the rival…holy shit."

Winston and Calvin both looked at him, surprised at his outburst. "Care to share with the rest of us?" Calvin asked.

"I think the first three gates to hell have been opened." Owen was still a little shocked by his insight. "Awakening of the sigil…the original murder-dismemberments. Maybe Davis and Harris's murders too. Plenty of blood for a ritual to wake something. Then the flying objects and the orbs and the devil dogs—the summoning of the servants, and the Branson brothers' murder—"

Calvin nodded. "The destruction of the rival," he said quietly. "Damn. Three down, four to go."

"Excellent intuition," Winston said. "Your contact who gave you this—she didn't know more about the legend?"

Owen shook his head. "She knew the legend and thought it might be important, but if she'd had something more concrete, she would have told me. I'm supposed to check in with her tonight."

"I'm meeting my contact tonight too. Sounds like we've both got big nights on the town," Calvin said with a grin and a wink.

Owen didn't know how to read Calvin's joking. Sometimes he swore the other man's flirting was sincere, and at other times he figured it was just Calvin's way of communicating—and keeping people at arm's distance in a friendly way.

I don't want to be at arm's distance. I want to be in his arms.

"I've asked around among my friends who are witches," Winston said. "No one wanted to say much, but I got a name—Barclay

Macready. Sells his services to the highest bidder and is willing to use magic to do just about anything if the price is right. He's the top candidate for being Aiken's witch."

"How powerful is he?" Calvin asked.

"Strong enough to make trouble and kill people in creative ways," Winston replied, disdain clear in his voice. "I'd rather not take him on head-to-head until we know more, or have back-up."

Owen moved to the library and sent a telegram to an old friend in New Pittsburgh, a witch who might have insight into the gates of hell theory. Since Mitch and Jacob had sent them in search of the Branson brothers, he cabled a short update—"Bransons dead. Devil dogs? Three gates open. All linked to RR."

He looked up to see Calvin leaning against the doorframe. "News?"

Owen shook his head, trying not to react to how good Calvin looked with his collar unbuttoned and his shirtsleeves rolled up. "Asked a friend for tips, and let Mitch and Jacob know what happened today."

"Did you mention the man-eating rats?" Calvin's grin lit up his eyes.

"I kept it short," Owen bantered. He liked how easy it was to be with Calvin, how well they worked together as if it had been much longer than a few days. He'd never had chemistry like this with prior work partners. He'd gotten along with some better than others. A few he might still count as friends, while others never moved past detached professionalism. One or two he hoped to never see again. No one had affected him like Calvin.

Winston agreed to fix dinner early so they could "go skulking around." The simple meal of roasted chicken, cornbread stuffing, and cooked carrots hit the spot.

Afterward, Owen and Calvin got ready to meet their contacts, and Owen found himself wishing that they didn't have to split up again. *It's efficient. We can cover more territory, and we spent all day working together. Besides, I need a little space. Maybe he does too.* He didn't remember noticing the times he and prior partners had worked together or separately.

"I need to collect some ingredients for a few more spells," Winston said as Calvin and Owen headed out. "If I'm not here when you get back, don't wait up. Some practitioners of the craft keep odd hours."

They stepped onto the Pullman's observation deck, and Owen shivered as a cold breeze howled down the train tracks. "Come back safe," he said to Calvin when they parted ways at the trolley stop.

"I always do," Calvin said with a flash of grin. "You too."

Owen headed for Vincente's Restaurant, where he and Ida had agreed to meet. Vincente was wiping down tables when he arrived and greeted him with a smile and a wave.

"Miss Ida's already here. Go on back. Have you eaten dinner?"

"Just finished," Owen replied, although the aromas were tempting enough to make him consider a second meal.

"I'll bring lemon cookies and coffee," Vincente offered. "Can't work on an empty stomach."

Ida had papers spread out all over one of the long tables. "Thanks for coming," she said without looking up.

"What did you find out?" If he and Calvin had to work separate angles on the case, Owen was grateful to have a sharp contact like Ida to hunt down leads.

"The Branson brothers were murdered earlier today." She repositioned a couple of newspaper clippings amid the layout.

"I know. Calvin and I got to their office not long afterward."

"Stupid cops are looking for man-eating rats," she told him, clearly annoyed. When Owen started to laugh, she looked confused.

"I'm sorry...that's my fault." By the time he explained, she was chuckling as well.

"I regret not being there to see that," she told him. "You're lucky you found two flatfoots who'd actually fall for your story."

Owen shook his head. "It worked and got me inside. I don't think we've seen the last of the devil dogs." He gave her an edited recap of what he and Calvin had run into, and his theory about the gates of hell.

"I wish I could poke holes in your idea about the gates, but I can't," Ida admitted, tapping her pencil against her cheek as she thought. "It makes sense in an odd way."

"It just confirms that Leland Aiken is planning something big, or he wouldn't think he needed demon mojo to make it happen," Owen said.

Ida looked up. "You do know that folks think Aiken is a vampire, right?"

Owen hadn't been planning to let Ida in on that secret, but having her already know made things much easier. "I'd heard that," he replied. "Given some other details, it would make sense."

"A vampire who wants to be a railroad king. I guess immortals need hobbies," Ida said. They fell silent as Vincente brought in the coffee and cookies, and waited until the door clicked after him. Owen poured coffee for both of them bringing their cups and the plate of sweets closer to Ida's workspace, putting them safely on a separate table but within reach.

"I doubt it's a 'hobby,'" Owen mused. "Vampires are good at acquiring power and money to stay safe. So what's his angle?"

Ida handed him a sheaf of papers. "I have a contact in the Registrar of Deed's office. Those are the properties that the Branson brothers registered for themselves, minus the worthless parcels they fobbed off on their marks."

"Have you plotted them to a map, with Aiken's rail line's route?"

"Just got those this morning," Ida said.

"Then let's take a crack at it. We might be able to figure this out by working backward." Owen spread the big map out on another table, and set to penciling in the projected route of Aiken's new railroad. Once that was accomplished, he and Ida marked off the parcels and stood back to review their work.

"They're where it would be natural to put stations," Ida observed. "And at the end of the spurs."

"Perfect places for hotels, restaurants, and businesses for travelers," Owen added.

Ida leaned forward and tapped a place on the map. "There's a bigger piece of land here with a small lake at the end of the spur. Looks like the kind of place railroads like to put an amusement park to get people to ride all the way to the end of the line."

"He might just be a smart businessman looking for ways to make as much money as possible," Owen said, although he doubted it could be that simple.

"Or someone who wanted to lure people out from the city where it might not be noticed if a few go missing." Ida put the same awful thoughts into words that had occurred to Owen.

"It's an expensive way to attract dinner."

"Maybe not," Ida replied. "Railroads take people from places where others know them to places they don't. If some of the passengers never arrive, it could take a while for anyone to realize that—if ever. Not to mention the hobos who ride the rails."

"I wasn't aware that St. Louis had such a large vampire population." Owen wondered why they hadn't been briefed if that was the case.

Ida shook her head. "It doesn't, as far as I can tell—and I've made discreet inquiries on more than one occasion."

She consulted the notes from the Recorder of Deeds and then leaned in to put an "X" within the shaded area. "Here's another mystery. That's a limestone mine that's been abandoned. The Bransons kept it instead of pawning it off to suckers. Why?"

"Damn," Owen said and then glanced up. "Pardon my French."

Ida looked non-plussed. "Language doesn't bother me. What did you think of?"

"You're going to think I'm crazy. Well…even more so after the rat incident," Owen said, feeling heat rise to his cheeks.

"Sometimes 'crazy' sees things everyone else misses," Ida replied. "Spit it out."

"What if Aiken has a special audience in mind for his new railroad and what he's building around it? It wouldn't be difficult to build Pullman cars that didn't have windows. Suppose he's envisioning a vampire migration to the West with plenty of easy pickings for victims?"

"What does that have to do with the mine?" Ida didn't immediately dismiss the central premise which would have sounded insane to just about anyone else, and Owen took that as a win.

"Mines are always dark. Maybe Aiken will build fancy hotels for the mortals, and underground hotels for the vampires. Plenty of escape tunnels—not that anyone sane would try to chase vampires inside a mine. Build the hotel over the mine, for that matter. And if some night shift workers go missing…no one will pay much mind."

Owen spun the theory as he talked, but he felt a chill down his spine as if something in the back of his brain recognized the truth.

Ida gave him a horrified look. "Oh my God. That actually makes sense, in a terrible way."

"He's building an empire," Owen replied. "Big plans. Wanting some demon flunkies or henchmen would fit."

"Insurance," Ida said. "Or enforcers."

"We know he's paying people off, like Chief Wyman," Owen said. "But how many shifters does he have working for him, like Ross Swanson? In Swanson's case, the whole persona was invented. But what's to stop a shifter from killing someone and taking his place? Especially someone who's an important decision maker who wouldn't otherwise go along with the plan?"

Ida put her fingers to her temples and closed her eyes. "My head hurts just thinking about it, but I'm afraid we might be onto something. Not that anyone would believe us, even if the newspaper did print an exposé—which it won't."

Owen felt overwhelmed, bordering on despair. *Did headquarters have any idea of the scope when they sent us? Would they believe us? It's almost too much to fathom.*

Owen finished his now-cold coffee and split the last cookie with Ida. "There's nothing more to do tonight. Let's sleep on it and connect tomorrow. Maybe by then we'll have a plan."

"Sleep on it," Ida echoed with a mirthless laugh. "I'm not sure I'll have sweet dreams after laying out that nightmare scenario."

"If we can't stop Aiken directly, maybe we can find proxies to fight for us," Owen said. "If we could figure out vampire politics, there might be competing families that wouldn't want him getting so much wealth. Or competing railroad barons who might want to stymie a rival. Snarling his plans is almost as good as shutting him down."

Owen mustered a confident smile he didn't completely feel. "I believe that we've only just scratched the surface of devious plans." He gave a playful wink. "And if we pull Calvin in, that goes double."

"I applaud your faith in us." Ida blew out a long breath. "It might take me a bit to catch up."

Owen helped her gather her papers and remove all evidence of their meeting from the room. He waited while she paid Vincente and walked her to the trolley station.

"Are you getting on?" she asked when the car came.

He shook his head. "No. I want to walk a bit, clear my head. I'll be careful," he said, forestalling her warning, and let his elbow bump his suitcoat over his holster, to let her know he had his gun.

"You know who's out there," she said as the crowd began to get on the trolley. "Don't take foolish chances."

Owen tipped his hat in assent and watched to ensure she boarded the car without incident. Then he turned the opposite direction, heading for a bar he remembered from his last visit to St. Louis, and hoped it was still as he remembered it.

Oscar's Bar was tucked into a corner on the east side of St. Louis, nothing special about it to call attention, which was exactly the way its customers preferred. The sign was small and faded, no windows faced the street, and the doorway just around the corner in an alley had no light overhead.

Owen knocked, and a panel at eye level opened. "Green carnation," he said. The panel slid shut, and the door opened.

He was taking a risk, coming to a place like this, a "nancy" bar where men like him could relax and find companionship. Nowhere was truly safe, but places like Oscar's were the best to be had.

Habit made him scan the room just in case he recognized anyone— or anyone who might recognize him. Being found out could be fatal.

Two women were just leaving, arm in arm. Their perfect hair and makeup made Owen guess them to be actresses, and from their manner, they were clearly more than friends. The blonde stared at Owen as she passed, then dropped her gaze and continued flirting with her partner as they headed out into the alley.

A moment's panic flared as Owen feared he had been recognized, but he couldn't remember ever having met either of the women.

Pushing his worry aside, Owen walked into Oscar's main room. It looked like someone had attempted to recreate an aristocratic British drawing room on a budget. Velvet flocked high-backed couches, torchiere lights, and gilt-framed portraits created an atmosphere of comfortable confidentiality.

A large bar and mirrored barback anchored the club at the front. In the rear, a piano player provided lively tunes for those who wanted to dance. The couches were arranged in small groupings for those who wanted privacy or conversation. Owen didn't doubt that there was a back hall offering closet-sized rooms for quick, anonymous fucks.

Oscar's was fairly busy, mostly men but a few pairs of women as well. Safe places were difficult to come by. Now that he was here, Owen felt a mix of relief at being among like-minded men and nervousness at what the evening might hold.

"What can I pour for you?" The bartender was a man Owen guessed to be in his forties with short salt and pepper hair, a well-trimmed beard, and a muscular body. Red sleeve garters held up his shirt, revealing toned forearms.

"Bourbon, neat," Owen replied. The bartender slid his shot to him. Owen downed it. "Another."

"New here?" the bartender asked.

Owen let the first drink burn down his throat and hoped the second would loosen the strain in his shoulders. "Been a while."

"Glad you found your way back. Make yourself at home." The bartender moved off to greet another customer.

"Nice to see a fresh face."

At first glance, out of the corner of his eye, Owen thought it was Calvin—black hair, right height. But the accent was wrong, the body a bit too stocky, and Calvin would never wear suspenders with horses on them.

"Nice to find so many friendly faces." Owen tried to see past the passing resemblance to Calvin. "Looks like everyone's having a good time."

"What are you drinking?"

"Bourbon."

The newcomer flagged the bartender. "Two for me and another round for him." He leaned closer, and his knee gently bumped Owen's leg. "So, where're you from? Folks from everywhere come through St. Louis."

The bourbon sat warm in Owen's stomach, loosening stiff muscles but still leaving him clear-headed. "Baltimore," Owen replied. "You?"

"Memphis, among other places. Rode the rodeo circuit for a while, got tired of the travel." He held out a hand. "I'm Matt."

"Patrick," Owen replied without blinking at the lie. His middle name made an alias that was easy to remember.

They chatted about everything and nothing for a bit. Owen was glad Matt didn't try to rush to the back hallway, giving him time to think about how he wanted the evening to go.

Despite Matt's good looks and his passing resemblance to Calvin, the same spark wasn't present that Owen felt every time his partner brushed by him in the hallway. No one ever said that a quick tug or getting sucked off required anything more than willingness and availability. But Owen had made do on that kind of thing for too long, and although his pairing with Eli had ended tragically, the short time they had together just made Owen that much hungrier for something worthy of being a relationship.

"Still not over him?" Matt broke into Owen's thoughts.

"Huh?"

Matt canted his head with a sympathetic expression. "The breakup blues. You got it in spades. That's okay. You're fun to talk with. We can just play a couple of hands of poker and call it a night if you want."

Owen smiled. "I'd like that." Matt seemed like a decent sort, and Owen felt bad about not being in the mood to do more, especially after he'd been getting his nerve up to visit the bar all day.

They took their drinks and found a game just getting started. Owen pulled a cigar from his pocket, lit it up, and made his wager, glad the bets were low stakes. Matt seemed to know most of the others, and Owen guessed he was a regular.

It had been a while since Owen had visited a bar like this, either because time didn't permit, or because he didn't feel safe looking for connections in strange cities. He had no doubt that his previous work partners would have judged him harshly for his interests had they known, and one or two would probably have done their best to see him arrested.

Which made the situation with Calvin all the more tenuous. Owen felt sure that, on some level, Calvin returned his interest. But he also knew that many men went their whole lives without daring more than anonymous liaisons, for good reason. If Calvin did fancy him, practicality and common sense might still argue for them remaining apart.

Owen figured that meant a lot of very cold showers and frustrated nights.

A ruckus near the door made everyone turn. Owen heard raised voices and the unmistakable sound of punches thrown and bodies falling.

Shit. It's a raid. I'm dead if I'm found here.

Some of the patrons fled so fast they knocked chairs over, scrambling toward the back of the bar where there was presumably an exit. The piano music stopped mid-dance. Owen pulled his handkerchief from his pocket and tied it over his nose and mouth, bank robber style.

I could run—but they've probably got people around back too. I'll lose everything if I'm caught here.

So I'd better not get caught. I'm tired of running and hiding. These are my people. Maybe it's time to fight.

Matt hadn't fled. He also covered his face and gave Owen a look, gauging his decision.

"Let's go," Owen rumbled, as two dozen bar patrons surged back against the attackers.

The men who came to bust up Oscar's weren't in uniform, so it wasn't a police raid, Owen thought. *Just a bunch of assholes.* The attackers didn't bother to cover their faces, clearly feeling no shame and fearing no reprisals over their actions.

They seemed surprised when the patrons fought back.

The attackers were armed with knives, baseball bats, and lead pipes. Owen, Matt, and the others waded in with fists, liquor bottles, and chairs.

The attackers pushed their way in, only to be forced back toward the street. Owen ducked the swing of a bat, downing the man with a kick to the side of his knee and the stomp of his foot on the hand holding the weapon. Matt held his own against two men, clearly an experienced fighter, maybe ex-Army like Owen.

Another attacker got Owen in the face, splitting his lip and bloodying his nose, but Owen's punch sent the man careening into the bar, where he slumped and did not get back up.

The bartender smashed a bottle over a man's head and then menaced the man's friend with the sharp shards. One of the poker players held a man at bay with a chair, poking it at his ribs and belly, forcing him back. Another patron had smashed a chair and held broken pieces in each hand, clobbering the man who rushed him from the left and right until the attacker went down without landing a blow.

A fist caught Owen on the side of the face, sending him back a step. He lashed out, a one-two punch, hitting hard enough that he split the man's eyebrow and felt a snap beneath his fist that made him think he might have broken his cheekbone.

"You bastard!"

Only then did Owen get a good look at his opponent, in the seconds before the man drew his gun.

Chief Wyman. Fuck.

Someone crashed into Wyman, grabbing his arm and shifting his aim. A shot rang out, and the bullet tore through Owen's pant leg, sending searing pain through his calf. Before the chief could fire again, Matt lurched into him, wresting away the gun.

"Go home. Leave us alone," Matt shouted, and the others took up the chant, repeating the phrase as they pushed the attackers from the bar and flowed after them into the street, now on the offensive. The chief and his gang of ruffians left several of their number behind as the chanting patrons took after them with chairs and bottles, chasing them until the mob scattered.

"Get out of here," Owen said, worried about Matt after they had staggered several alleys away from the bar.

"You're hurt."

"I've had worse." Owen gave him a push. "Those guys might come back. Go the long way, and make sure you're not tailed."

"Be careful," Matt replied, and the concern in his eyes was sincere.

Matt wasn't Calvin, but Owen appreciated that his acquaintance was a good guy. *Maybe if I'd met him first, before Calvin, we could have at least had a fling.*

I'm proud of our folks. We stood up, and pushed the mob back. There'll probably be hell to pay for it, but it felt damn good.

He shifted and flinched from the pain. He felt blood running down his calf, and moving his leg sent a hot stab all the way to his hip.

I've got to get back to the Pullman.

Owen stood still and listened. He didn't believe Chief Wyman and his mob would give up so easily. *They're out there, waiting to pick us off one at a time when we aren't together to protect each other.*

He paused where he could see better in the dim light of a gas lamp to check his leg. *Just a graze. Hurts like hell. I can't move fast like this.* He took his handkerchief and wrapped it around the wound to stanch the blood, grateful that the injury wasn't worse.

Follow me, a male voice said.

Owen looked up to see the ghost of a skinny young man beckoning to him from farther down the alley. The boy looked to be in his late teens, gaunt and haggard. *Hurry!*

Owen followed, limping badly. The ghost remained in view, never moving faster than Owen could follow. Several times Owen heard voices and hid in the shadows until the sound faded.

The spirit didn't seem inclined to talk, but Owen could make some educated guesses about his story. Young, alone, and dead, far from family or home, keeping to the side places, helping a guy like Owen. He put a story together in his mind and suspected it might differ from the truth only in minor details.

Hurry. Not safe yet.

Owen wasn't familiar with the part of town the young man's ghost led him through, although a glance to reckon by the stars told Owen they were heading in the right direction. They wound through some of the rougher parts of town, neighborhoods crammed with tenements and flophouses, places where even Wyman and his ruffians might not dare to venture.

His ghost guide moved confidently, and Owen wondered if the spirit had lived here or frequented the area. The boy was ill-dressed for the weather and far too young to be dead.

They won't come here. The ghost led Owen to a train station in a run-down part of town. Owen worried that there might not be another train that night and that he could be stuck spending hours in a precarious haven. But when he checked the printed schedule, he saw that more than one train stopped in the next hour.

"Thank you," Owen said to the ghost.

You fought them—and won. The awe in the boy's voice told Owen that his guesses had, tragically, probably been right.

"I can help you move on," Owen offered. As a medium, he had often helped confused spirits find their way to the Beyond.

The young man shook his head. *Not ready to go yet. Still have things to do.*

"Saving people...like us?"

The ghost nodded. *Maybe keep someone from ending up like me.*

Owen's heart broke for the boy, but he understood, and respected his decision. "Go in peace. And...thank you."

The ghost smiled, and the expression softened his features to show his youth. *Get home safely. We need fighters like you.* He faded to nothing as the train reached the station.

Owen was the only passenger to get on, leaving the lonely platform behind him. His thoughts spun as he watched the stops pass, thinking of the spirit and his one-man rescue mission, he was impressed with the ghost's commitment.

They came for us, and we fought back. Does that mean that they'll think twice before trying again—or come better armed?

Either way, we ran them off. We held our ground, protected what was ours. Stood by one another. I'm proud of that.

As he neared his stop, his thoughts turned to a different question. *What am I going to tell Calvin and Winston? I can't admit to being at Oscar's, and it's sure to come up. I'm going to look a mess, and I've been shot—by the fucking chief of police. How am I going to explain it?*

The lights were on in the Pullman even though by now it was past midnight. Owen hobbled toward the car. Shooting pain ran the length of his leg, his face throbbed where he'd been punched, and his split lip stung.

Owen had hoped to slip in unnoticed, clean up in private, and have the night to come up with a good cover story. The light meant that Calvin—and probably Winston—had waited up for him. Much as it warmed his heart that they were concerned, he felt bad for worrying them, and he tamped down panic at trying to come up with a plausible lie about where he'd been and what happened.

He limped up to the observation deck and let himself in the back, hoping the others had just left a light on for him and gone to bed. He knew he couldn't hide his injuries, but he had hoped for more time to get his story straight with as few lies as possible.

Before Owen had gotten halfway down the hallway, he heard rapid steps and Calvin hurried toward him.

"Owen? Are you all right? My God, what happened to you?"

Chapter 6
Calvin

C alvin stared at Owen, taking in the blood, torn pants, the black eye, and rapidly swelling split lip. He moved toward his partner slowly, like approaching a spooked animal.

"How bad is it? Do you need a hospital?"

Owen shook his head. "No hospital."

"Our cover stories will hold—"

"No hospital," Owen repeated, and Calvin thought he saw a trace of fear in his eyes. *What did you get into?*

"Then come into the lab where the light's better, and I'll patch you up." Calvin opened the door and switched on the light. Owen limped into the room, and Calvin drew out a chair for him to sit.

"You're bleeding." Calvin took in Owen's bloody trousers, bruised knuckles, the damage to his face, and his torn coat. *Fist fight. Did he get mugged?*

"Not much." The split lip slurred his words.

Calvin went to the insulated box where Winston kept a block of ice bought from the beer shippers and split a chunk free. He wrapped it in a clean towel and handed it to Owen, who put it against his face and lip.

"Crack any ribs?"

"Uh-uh."

"Broken bones?"

Owen grunted a negative.

Calvin frowned when he saw the powder burn on Owen's pant leg. "Someone fucking shot you!"

Owen didn't say anything as Calvin knelt and carefully pulled up his pant leg, hiking it above his sock and garter to expose the wound. "You're lucky it's just a graze, but I bet it hurts like a son of a bitch." Calvin talked to keep himself calm. The mix of fear for Owen and anger at his injury had his heart pounding.

He could have been killed.

"Shit, Owen. I need to clean this before it gets infected." Calvin learned basic first aid in the military, and the dangers of being a secret agent had given him far too much practice putting that knowledge to use for himself and others.

He washed his hands in the lab's sink, filled a basin with water, and grabbed a clean towel. First, he washed the wound with soap and water, carefully rinsing it to make sure no fibers from Owen's pants remained. He worked as gently as he could, but it didn't escape his notice that Owen gripped the arms of the chair white-knuckled, breathing quickly from the pain.

Calvin carried the basin and towels back to the sink and went to the well-stocked cabinet, found a bottle of carbolic acid, a pack of clean cotton, linen bandages, and an ointment pot marked "for wounds."

"This is going to sting." He dabbed at the wound with a cotton ball soaked in the antiseptic, wincing as Owen bit back a moan.

"It's not deep—I don't think it needs stitches," Calvin determined. He put a generous smear of ointment over the gash and then wrapped Owen's leg with the bandage. "But don't let it get infected. You need to have Winston or me check it every day until it heals. I've seen men lose a limb over a scratch gone bad."

"No hospital," Owen repeated through gritted teeth.

Calvin sat back on his heels and wondered about the reason behind Owen's insistence. Even if their cover story didn't hold, being caught out as government agents might be inconvenient but wouldn't be disastrous. *What happened, and why does he want to hide it?*

He walked back to the sink, soaked and wrung out a clean towel, and daubed the blood from Owen's face. Calvin moved carefully, trying not to cause pain, surprised Owen permitted his touch.

"Who hurt you?" he asked quietly, his voice a low rumble. Calvin hadn't known Owen long, but he had already admitted to himself that his attraction ran deeper than lust. *I think I could fall in love with you, even though that's a bad idea. Maybe I already have. So you can't get yourself killed.*

"A guy jumped me in an alley." Owen flinched when Calvin touched the wet cloth to his split lip.

"Did you trounce him?" Calvin scooped a dollop from the ointment pot and used his index finger to spread the paste over Owen's swollen cheek and then across his split lip.

Their eyes met, and Calvin didn't know what to make of the emotions he saw swirling there. He looked away, afraid of what Owen might see in his gaze at the intimacy of the gesture.

"I got him in the face twice; think I broke something," Owen mumbled.

Calvin took first one hand and then the other, smoothing the paste over Owen's scraped knuckles. "You've got to stop brawling, or your hands will look like mine." He was surprised at how nervous he felt and realized he had held Owen's hand a tad too long, quickly returning it to his lap.

"That how you did it? Brawling?" Owen's voice sounded lower than usual, raising heat in Calvin's belly.

"Misspent youth," Calvin admitted. "Stay put." He headed for the liquor cabinet in the dining room and came back with a bottle of bourbon and two glasses, sloshing a generous portion into both.

"Medicinal." He gave a sly smile, handing off a glass to Owen before knocking back a gulp himself.

"Thanks for taking care of me." Owen sounded pensive.

"We're partners. That's how it works. I imagine I'll get myself busted up sooner or later, and you can return the favor." Calvin tried to keep his tone light. He didn't want to think of how it affected him to see Owen hurt or examine the feelings that surged through him at the close contact.

"Did he steal your wallet? If you got a look at the bastard, we can make a police report," Calvin added.

Owen's eyes went wide, and Calvin saw naked fear there. "No! I mean, it's not something they'll care about," Owen fumbled to make up for his candid reaction. "I've got my wallet. No sense attracting attention."

There's something about this that doesn't add up. What's he hiding —and why?

"It's late," Calvin said. "Let's get you to your room. A good night's sleep should help. Maybe put a pillow under your leg." He checked the ice in the towel Owen held against his cheek, making sure it hadn't melted.

Owen swallowed down his bourbon and set the glass aside as Calvin finished his own drink. "Come on." Calvin offered a hand to help Owen to his feet.

Owen leaned on Calvin's shoulder as they made their way down the narrow corridor. Calvin put an arm around Owen's waist to steady him, keeping him balanced as the door opened, and helped him hobble to the bed.

"No idea how soundly Winston sleeps. So if you need something, yell for me. I'll hear," Calvin promised. He went to the bathroom and returned with a glass of water and a piece of willow bark to chew for the pain.

"Take it easy tomorrow. I have to run down some leads, but maybe you and Winston can work on research here. Give yourself a chance to heal." Calvin paused in the doorway, unable to look away as Owen leaned back against the pillows, eyes closed. *Still beautiful, despite the injuries. Damn, I'm totally moonstruck.*

"Good night," he murmured and smiled as he heard Owen's soft reply before the door clicked shut.

Calvin poured himself another glass of bourbon and went into the library, too keyed up to try to go to bed. He sat at the table and took a deep breath, trying to regain his composure.

I can deny it all I want, but I think I'm falling in love with Owen. Against my better judgment, against common sense. But it's been so long since someone made me feel. And I don't think anyone's ever gotten to me like Owen.

The longer we're together, the more I think Owen might share my interest. Maybe he just needs to feel safe with me, be sure that we'll be working together long enough for the risk to be worth it. If this is a long assignment, we have time to get to know each other. If they plan on moving us apart after this job, we're probably better off not risking our hearts.

Even though it was late, Calvin went to the telegraph. "How long is the assignment? What plans after St. Louis?" he sent to headquarters. *It's a reasonable question, just for making plans. As agents, our cases come and go, but it's understandable to want to know if I'll be working long-term with the same partner or will be sent on to somewhere new.*

He hoped the answer came back confirming that his partnership with Owen was a long-term assignment. Even if Owen never returned more feelings than friendship, Calvin knew that they still had a special chemistry that would make their work together exceptional.

And maybe, over time, he'll come to feel for me what I do for him.

THE NEXT MORNING, Calvin rose before even Winston was awake, letting Owen sleep as well. He stopped at the train station's small refreshment counter to get a cup of coffee and a pastry then headed for Kearson's Palace, knowing that they would already be open for a bleary-eyed breakfast crowd.

Yesterday his meeting with Louisa was cut short. Kearson's closed early because rumors of a mob fighting at another bar made the owner nervous. Temperance groups had staged protests at saloons, and some of the gatherings had turned violent. Calvin appreciated the bartender's caution, even if he and Louisa hadn't been able to finish the work they planned.

His stomach rumbled when he entered, and he ordered a beer and scotch eggs, then found an open spot to wait for Louisa.

Several of the tables were already taken, men coming off the night shift wanting to eat a cheap breakfast and wash it down with a beer. The rest looked like they had stayed up too late and celebrated too hard, looking to blunt their hangovers with a little hair of the dog. Calvin remembered his wild times when he stayed out all night with the gang, causing trouble and living on the edge.

He suspected that most of his comrades from back then were dead or in jail. *Which would have been me if I hadn't gotten out when I did.*

Gradually, Calvin paid attention to the voices around them.

"…heard it was a nancy bar. No threat to us."

"…one of those molly places. Wish I'd have known—I'd have gone with the mob."

"…big fight, bunch of guys got beat up. Wouldn't be surprised if the cops were behind it."

Calvin's stomach knotted. *They're talking about a bar that caters to men like me. A mob broke in and roughed them up. Just goes to prove nowhere is safe.*

A terrible thought occurred to him. *Owen came home late, looking like he'd been in a fight. He didn't want to go to the hospital, wouldn't report the attack to the cops.*

Oh, God. Was he part of the mob? Have I read him all wrong?

Calvin couldn't breathe. He felt his whole body go cold. *Men like the ones in that mob killed Jeremiah.*

Owen doesn't seem the type, but what do I really know about him? It's only been days working together. People can keep dark secrets. Agents are good at pretending to be what they aren't. Did he fool me? Have I fallen for someone who would hate me, hurt me, if he knew what I really am?

Calvin felt like his heart would break. His hand trembled when he reached for the coffee cup, and he felt numb.

Last night when I sent the telegram, I was hoping they'd say Owen and I would be working together indefinitely. But I can't…not if he'd renounce me or be disgusted if he found me out.

I'll ask for a transfer when we finish this case. It happens, sometimes, that partners don't work out. I can make up a reason. But I can't stay.

"Hey. Are you okay?" Louisa stood next to the table, and from her exasperation, Calvin gathered that she had been trying to get his attention for several minutes.

"What did you hear about the riot last night?" he asked, sounding a little strangled.

She sat across from him and took a gulp of his untouched beer. "A bunch of assholes tried to break up Oscar's. It's a nancy bar several streets over. Nice place. I've gone with Lisbet a few times—one of the places we can be ourselves," she told him. "In fact, I was there last night, but we left a few hours before the excitement—not long before I met you here."

"So it wasn't the Temperance protesters?"

She shook her head. "No. I don't know what set the mob off, but it's been happening here every few weeks. We're sure the police turn a blind eye. I wouldn't be surprised if officers were some of the ruffians."

"Can't believe people don't have better things to do," Calvin muttered, struggling to get his emotions under control, hoping that his feelings didn't show.

"Must have been a full moon because they're not the only ones rioting," Louisa said. "Word got out about the Branson brothers' murder. The people who had deals with them are afraid their deeds won't hold up. They're storming the banks and the Land Office, demanding their money and their deeds."

Louisa took his beer again, and Calvin gave a wave of his hand to let her have it. He refilled his coffee cup from the pitcher on the table he'd paid for to keep from having to return to the bar.

"Are the police doing something to stop the riots? Or are they too busy beating up their constituents?" Calvin couldn't temper the bitterness in his voice.

"Don't know. I'm not working now. Thought maybe we could take a stroll in that direction and have a look for ourselves." Louisa snatched one of the last bits of scotch egg from Calvin's plate.

Calvin finished his coffee and nodded. "Let's go. It'll be interesting to see how this plays out."

Screaming crowds besieged the main branch of the St. Louis Bank and Trust, waving bank books and demanding to be let inside. Calvin and Louisa hung back, watching the angry people push and shove against the locked metal doors, challenging the guards who stood stoically outside.

"The newspaper is on the story." Louisa nodded toward a dark-haired woman with a notepad who was working her way around the people gathered in front of the bank, clearly asking questions and taking notes. "That's Ida Hardin. One of the paper's top reporters. She's got an uncanny sense of when there's something going on."

Ida. Owen's contact. Does he fancy her? If so, his interests are different from what I thought, or he's intent on denying what he can't accept about himself. Just like he'd deny me, if he knew.

Calvin swallowed the lump in his throat and plastered on his cockiest grin. "Want to wade into the fray and take a listen?"

Louisa's eyes lit with the thrill of the chase. "Definitely."

They split up and wove through the crowd, watching and listening. Calvin forced himself to focus on the case, shutting down his feelings and refusing to think about Owen. *There'll be time enough to deal with that later.*

From the comments Calvin picked up as he mingled with the rioters, the rush on the bank sprang from simple panic. People had staked their life savings on the land deals they'd made with the Bransons, and now that the brothers were dead, the rioters feared that their deeds and deals might not be valid.

Given what he'd learned about the brothers, the protesters were probably wise to worry. The police milled about the edges, hanging back but making sure their presence was noted.

Calvin spotted Chief Wyman from the back, and wormed his way through the crowd toward him. "Chief Wyman, if I may have a moment…"

Calvin stifled a gasp when Wyman turned around, revealing a black eye and a badly bruised and swollen face. "Did these rioters do that?" he blurted.

Wyman glowered. "No. Had a run-in last night with some trouble-makers, and one of the sods got in a couple of lucky hits. I got the last laugh because I shot the bastard in the leg."

Calvin's world shifted for the second time in just a few hours.

Owen said he'd punched the man who shot him in the face. Louisa thought the cops were in the mob that stormed the bar. Owen wasn't part of the mob—he was fighting them.

Oh my God. Owen was in the nancy bar. He's like me.

"Hey, did you hear me?" Wyman demanded, pulling Calvin from his spinning thoughts. "I asked why the hell you're here."

Calvin pulled himself back into his persona. "I'm here to look at the climate for making future business investments for our clients. This kind of turbulence does not recommend St. Louis."

Wyman swore under his breath. "Don't judge the whole city by some bad eggs."

Calvin resisted the urge to snort in derision at the hypocrisy. "I will have to make a full report to our investors. They'll be the ones making the decision."

Across the way, Calvin saw Louisa talking with Ida. *Of course they know each other. Two women who don't fit the mold making their way in a frontier city. I wonder what tidbits Louisa will learn?*

Calvin drew back, watching as the cops began to break up the crowd, intimidating the frantic protesters into leaving. The stone-faced guards maintained their posts by the locked doors, and the bankers at the heart of the controversy never deigned to peek out the window.

He drifted down the street and waited for Louisa. As the crowd dispersed, he heard their grumbling and suspected that while the cops ran them off this time, it wouldn't take much of a spark to set the anger ablaze again.

With a few moments to himself, Calvin took the chance to catch his breath. The morning had whipsawed his emotions from betrayal to redemption. Now he berated himself for doubting Owen, although he knew that before he'd gained essential information, the circumstances had been damning.

I'm an investigator. I get to the bottom of things. I wasn't wrong to suspect, given the appearances. But I'm so grateful that I was wrong. Owen was in the group fighting off the cops, and that no good son of a bitch Wyman got what he deserved.

Owen and I might have a future after all.

Louisa caught up with him. "Let's go back to Kearson's and compare notes. This was a very interesting outing."

Calvin felt tense all the way back to the bar, worried that given the outbreaks of violence, something else might flare right in front of them.

"I'm almost positive that Chief Wyman was involved in the raid on that bar," Calvin told Louisa when they were seated at a table. "He as much as told me so."

"Wouldn't be surprised. He's a rotter, and so are a lot of the cops he's hired," Louisa replied, sounding resigned but not surprised. "Sometimes they try to stir up trouble here, but the boss pays them off, and the bartender has a double barrel behind the bar. Keeps things peaceful."

"What did you learn from Ida? She's one of Owen's contacts."

"Interesting," Louisa said, and Calvin wondered if she read more into his comment than he intended. "She's very good at what she does. I told her she'd have made a great spy."

"Does she know about you?"

Louisa shook her head. "She might suspect, but she doesn't know for sure. She gave me a tip about the rail spur that's closest to completion. Says that there've been problems in some of the cemeteries—grave robberies, desecration, vandalism. She mentioned two in particular—one is near the spur, and the other is on the edge of town. Some people say they've seen folks walking around at the construction site who should be dead."

"Worth investigating—if you're free."

"I don't work until tonight, but don't you want to get your partner involved?"

Calvin thought for a moment and shook his head. "He got shot last night—it's a graze, but he should take it easy. Let's run this lead down, and if it's more than we can handle ourselves, we'll get Owen and Winston involved."

Louisa gave him a look that suggested she was trying to parse out the parts of his story he omitted, but let it go—for now. "I'd say we start with the cemetery near the spur, and save the other one for later. The spur is a couple of miles outside of town—best way to get there is to ride. You aren't dressed for it."

Calvin glared. "I have my boots on."

"You're wearing a suit. Not going to blend in with the locals." She held up a finger to forestall Calvin's protest and walked up to a man standing near the stage, talking to the piano player. Louisa returned with a satisfied smile.

"You're about the same size as one of the actors who does a cowboy skit. I asked Ben, our stage manager, if you could borrow dungarees, a shirt, and a jacket. You can change backstage. No one will steal your suit while we're gone." Calvin nodded and went to change.

They headed for the nearby stables where Louisa had a friend willing to rent horses for the rest of the day. They packed water, food, weapons, a map, and compass before leaving the bar. Louisa had rifles for both of them, something the stablemaster did not comment on.

"Nice horse," Calvin said admiringly when the mounts turned out to be better quality than he'd imagined.

"Keeping horses in the city is expensive." She swung up to the saddle, riding astride despite her skirts. "Renting them out cuts costs."

Calvin's borrowed clothing fit reasonably well, with the added advantage of being worn enough to look normal if anyone paid them attention. They rode out of town at a brisk pace, and Calvin felt his worries lighten. He'd always loved riding, and it had been too long since he'd felt the freedom of the open road and a fast horse.

"Whoa there, stud," Louisa teased with a wink. "It's not a race. It would be good if you and the horse can still walk when we get there."

"Very funny," Calvin replied, but he heeded her advice, knowing that it had been a while since he'd been in the saddle.

They stopped first at the railroad cemetery that Ida had mentioned. It was a lonely patch of ground set aside to bury workers killed during construction. Squared-off wooden stakes marked the graves, but Calvin quickly noticed something unusual.

"They're all in Chinese," he said as he and Louisa walked among the markers.

"Makes sense," she replied. "The railroads brought a lot of men over from China for cheap labor. Plenty of folks in this area aren't sure how they feel about that. They don't want to do the work for the low pay, but they aren't happy about anyone else doing it either."

Calvin couldn't imagine what it must be like to come halfway around the world to a place so different from home, only to die.

Louisa bent down to take a better look at the markers. "I've learned enough Chinese to recognize a few names," she told him. "And this is odd—the dates aren't new for most of these graves, but the ground looks like it's been recently disturbed."

"Why would anyone dig up old burials? I doubt the workers or their families could afford to ship the bodies back to China."

"The murders back in the city needed body parts for some sort of ritual, and the witch wanted fresh blood," she mused. "Maybe the grave robber here was after something else."

They rode toward where new rail was being laid, taking a side trail up a rise where they could overlook the construction. They tied their horses in a small copse of trees and moved toward the ridge.

"What makes that track?" Calvin asked, pointing toward a large paw print in the dirt. It looked too large to be a wolf or a cougar and didn't quite match either.

"No idea. Let's hope we don't find out."

Calvin lost the animal tracks where the dirt grew hard, but he wondered about its proximity to the construction work and whether it surveilled the worksite for the chance of an easy meal.

Both Louisa and Calvin had brought binoculars, and they trained them on the workers below.

"Something's very strange," Louisa murmured. "The workmen are moving all wrong."

"Almost like they're bewitched or drugged," Calvin agreed.

"I want to get closer."

Before Calvin could protest, Louisa gathered her skirts and headed down the ridge, keeping low behind the thin stand of trees that stretched along the railroad's right of way.

Calvin followed, cursing under his breath. Despite the muted colors of their clothing, the tree cover was thin, and Calvin felt sure that they'd be spotted if anyone chanced to look in their direction.

I can bluff with something about bringing new business to the area and wanting to see the new tracks, but I have no idea how to explain Louisa.

The closer they got to the construction site, the worse the odor became, the unmistakable stench of decomposition. Calvin thought there might be a dead cow that had wandered from a herd, but the smell intensified until he pulled his handkerchief over his mouth and nose in vain to block the odor.

"I think we've found the bodies." Louisa pointed toward the workers.

Calvin focused the binoculars and caught his breath. With the close-up view from the binoculars, there was no mistaking the hollow eye sockets, mottled skin, and ragged clothing that marked the workers as grave-risen.

"He's using zombies," Louisa said.

"No need to pay or feed them." Calvin was shaken by the realization that Leland Aiken's railroad was being built by reanimated corpses.

"How is he controlling them?" Louisa wondered aloud.

"It has to be a spell of some sort," Calvin replied. "Zombies don't last long as workers. The corpses can't regenerate, so they gradually fall apart. So where are they getting replacements?"

"The railroads have brought in thousands of Chinese workers. They stay in the rail worker shanty villages. Most of them don't go out to regular towns. No one knows them. And no one is looking out for them," Louisa murmured.

"When they die, there's no family. No one to notice." Calvin felt sick to his stomach at the injustice, and the reek of decay.

"So they become the replacements," Louisa finished.

Calvin watched through the binoculars while they talked. The shuffling, jerky movements of the two dozen workers made him wonder how long they lasted before falling apart. *They don't need to sleep. Injuries don't matter, and they won't go on strike.*

Calvin saw a flash of a blue robe and gestured for Louisa to look. A slender, bald man wore what appeared to be scholar's robes. He sat in a chair beneath a parasol, and while Calvin could see him speaking, he was clearly not yelling to direct the workers.

"There's the witch," Louisa said.

"Necromancer?" Calvin wondered aloud and felt a flash of fear. He'd gone up against witches before, but never someone powerful enough to raise the dead. A necromancer also didn't fit with the other magic they'd seen. *Does Aiken have more than one witch?*

"We've got trouble." Louisa scrambled backward.

The man in the robes raised one arm and pointed in their direction. The workers stopped, turned as a unit, and started toward them at a fast stumble.

Calvin already had his rifle out as Louisa reached for hers. "The zombies are a tool. Don't shoot them unless there's no choice. I'll draw them off. Aim for the witch."

He took off running, making himself obvious as he broke from cover. Calvin glanced over his shoulder and saw the zombies change direction. They moved quickly, but he could keep a steady pace to stay ahead of them.

A shot rang out, but either Louisa missed, or the witch evaded the bullet because the zombies never slowed.

They had run far enough that Calvin couldn't see Louisa or the witch—but that meant he couldn't be seen by them either. A desperate plan came to mind, and he abruptly reversed direction, zigging and zagging through the shuffling horde. They grabbed for him with clumsy hands and lurched to tackle him, moving just a bit too slowly.

Calvin dodged through the crowd of pursuers, emerging on the other side, and put on a burst of speed. The zombies milled about as if unable to adjust to the sudden change of plan.

Once he realized the zombies would not be hot on his heels, Calvin slowed, changing his route and circling around. That brought him in on the other side of the tracks, behind where the necromancer sat.

He glanced toward where Louisa had been and saw a flash of color that matched her jacket, but no movement.

Calvin didn't hesitate. He aimed and fired, barely breaking stride.

His shot hit the necromancer in the back of the head, propelling his body forward and out of his chair. Calvin wasn't sure what magic like that might be able to do against a mere bullet, so he fired again at the back of the neck and once more through the heart.

Angry over the misuse of the corpses and frightened for Louisa's safety, Calvin pulled the long knife from his belt and took the witch's head off in one swing.

"I'm betting not even you can come back from that." He gave the severed head a kick for good measure, sending it far from the body.

He ran back far enough to catch sight of the zombies, even though he wanted to ensure Louisa's safety. *It would be bad to get overrun in the middle of a rescue.*

Calvin sighed with relief when he saw the zombies sprawled unmoving on the ground, de-animated with the death of their master.

Louisa.

He ran back, fearing the worst. Louisa lay in a heap in the center of the thicket. "Louisa!" He knelt next to her and felt for a pulse. She looked pale, her heartbeat slow and breathing shallow.

The necromancer didn't kill her outright. Did he siphon off life energy? Can a witch like that damage the soul?

Calvin pulled a flask from his pocket and pressed it to Louisa's lips, managing to get enough into her mouth to make her cough and sputter. Her eyes opened wide, and she struggled as if she didn't recognize Calvin.

"Take it easy. I'm on your side," Calvin assured her, grabbing her wrists to stop her from taking a swing at him, or worse, drawing a knife.

"Calvin? What happened?" Louisa stopped fighting him, and he braced her as she sat.

"I was hoping you knew. I drew the zombies off, but the witch must have realized there were two of us and whammied you."

Louisa muttered a decidedly unladylike curse. "I shot, but I swear something batted the bullet out of the way. And then...I can't recall anything until just now."

Before Calvin could reply, they heard a bone-chilling howl that sounded far too close. "Fuck. Those tracks we saw? I'd rather not meet whatever made them. Can you walk?"

"If the choice is to walk or get eaten, I can walk."

Calvin helped Louisa to her feet, and together they hurried toward where they left the horses. He glanced behind them, wondering if the creature might be drawn to the freshly killed witch. But when they reached the rise, Calvin could see where the zombies had dropped with the necromancer's death, and rooting among the rotted corpses was a monster the likes of which he'd never seen.

"Look," he told Louisa, who turned without slowing her pace.

"What the hell is that?"

"I don't know, but let's get out of here before it notices us."

Louisa insisted on swinging up to her saddle unassisted, although Calvin worried that her color was still off. "I can ride," she assured him.

They kept up a fast trot until they were back to a main road when they slowed their pace for the sake of the horses. Calvin cast surreptitious glances at Louisa to make certain she was okay, but she didn't waver, even if her grip on the pommel was white-knuckled.

The sun was low in the sky by the time they returned the horses to the stable. Calvin offered Louisa his arm for the walk back to Kearson's Palace. When she accepted, he didn't know whether she needed the help or was maintaining the fiction of having gone out for a ride with a beau.

Back inside, Louisa headed straight for the bar. "Give me a whiskey, neat," she told the bartender, who raised an eyebrow but hurried to comply. She knocked it back and let out a long breath. "That helps."

Louisa glanced at the clock behind the bar. "I'm not due backstage yet, and I need to collect my wits. Come sit with me for a few minutes."

They found an out-of-the-way table and sat. Calvin wouldn't have minded either a shot from the bar or a swig from his flask after what they'd seen but decided there would be time enough once he got back to the Pullman.

"I thought the whole way back about what that creature might have been," Louisa said.

"I'll ask Winston, but I wonder if it was an Ozark Howler," Calvin replied, having wracked his mind for possibilities on the ride as well. "If so, they prefer carrion to fresh meat—lucky us."

Louisa nodded, and Calvin didn't mention that her hands shook until she folded them in front of her. "I wonder if the witch had to keep the Howler at bay so it didn't eat the zombies."

"Very likely. It wouldn't be a menace to regular work crews or the witch himself, but I can imagine it might stay close, looking for one of the zombies to wander off," Calvin replied.

"If there's anything to that 'gates of hell' theory, I'd say what we saw should count," Louisa said, managing a wan smile. "Zombies, witches, and monsters. All in a day's work for you, isn't it?"

"Fortunately, not every day is quite this exciting," Calvin answered. "The real question is, did Aiken hire the necromancer and know what he was doing? I can't imagine that someone with that sort of power would be hired by the local manager on a whim."

"With luck we've slowed their plans. It might not be hard to exhume bodies, but skilled necromancers are difficult to find," Louisa mused. "Slowing the rail line's progress buys us more time. I keep feeling like there's something bigger we're not seeing yet."

Calvin laid a hand on her arm, still worried. "That's a puzzle for another day. Are you okay to go on stage tonight?"

Louisa nodded, and a spark came back to her eyes. "Always. Best part of this job is the cover. Much more fun than usual. Can you stay for the show?"

Calvin shook his head. "Another night. I want to have a look at that other cemetery, and then I need to get back and check on Owen."

"There's a bar right outside the cemetery that the gravediggers favor," Louisa told him. "You might want to start there and see if you hear anything. It's late for anyone to still be working in the graveyard —legally, at least. Be careful."

"I'll pick up my suit tomorrow if you don't mind me keeping these clothes overnight. Might help me blend in a bit better at the bar," Calvin said. "I'm sorry I can't see the show, but I have every confidence you'll be St. Louis's Ethel Barrymore."

"Flatterer."

If Louisa was up to verbal sparring, Calvin figured she really did feel better. "I'll check back with you tomorrow. I think we're getting closer—so watch your back."

Calvin found a driver willing to take him to the cemetery and wait for as long as required, no questions asked.

St. Anthony's Bar, named for the patron saint of gravediggers, was an old stone building with a slate roof that ran along the outside of the graveyard wall. Calvin had his gun beneath his jacket, but he still approached the place warily.

He found a place at the bar, ignoring the curious looks he drew, and ordered a shot of whiskey. Calvin didn't look around, but from the mirrored barback, he got a good view of the other patrons. Judging by their clothing, they were workingmen—not just gravediggers, but stevedores, dockworkers, and laborers.

Unlike the clubs and bars Calvin usually frequented, the mood was subdued. No one gathered to play cards or dice. Some sat in groups of twos or threes talking quietly. These men had done hard labor all day, and their exhaustion showed.

Calvin settled in to wait. No one bothered him, remarkable since he was an outsider among people who seemed to know each other. He stayed quiet, drank slowly, and hoped people forgot that he was present.

"...I won't work without a rosary in my pocket," one man said. "And I'm not even Catholic. It's too creepy."

"I've been burying the bodies from the jail and the executions for years, ain't never seen anything like this. Those marks on the hanged men—it's not natural," a second man agreed.

"I've seen those marks," another spoke up. "Thought maybe the police gave them some drug so they didn't fight on the way to the gallows."

"It looks like a bite," the first man said, fingering something in his pocket that Calvin suspected was the rosary. "Two teeth marks, and always on the inside of the elbow."

"From what? It's not from a dog. And why would something bite them if they were already in jail?" the third man countered.

"The marks were deep," the first man said. "And the bodies hadn't bled right. Can't tell anyone else about such things, they'll throw us in the nut house. But I know what I saw."

"We saw it too," the others agreed.

"Whatever did it, let's hope it sticks to criminals," the second gravedigger replied. "At least it happens before they come here."

Calvin stayed where he was, mulling over what he'd heard. He couldn't easily ask questions, but from the description, Calvin wondered if there was something preying on the men who were about to be hanged.

It could be a vampire…but would Aiken risk having any of his people be so obvious? There are other creatures that drink blood. Most of them can put the victim under a spell so they don't fight. Maybe it's not connected to the gates of hell or Leland Aiken or that necromancer.

But if it isn't, that's a hell of a coincidence, and I don't really believe in coincidences.

I'll go back to the Pullman and talk to Owen and Winston. Maybe they'll have ideas about how this fits together. And I can get over my worries about Owen.

If he was at Oscar's, then he's interested in men. Perhaps I haven't imagined that he was flirting with me. He'd be as careful as I am, afraid to give anything away. We've been dancing around each other, worried about what the other might think from the beginning, and it turns out we're heading in the same direction.

At least, I hope so. Now I just have to win his trust.

Calvin paid for his drinks and walked back to where he'd left the cabbie. He stood by the carriage, still thinking about what he had heard and the revelation of Owen's interests.

"Take me back to the train station," he told the driver without looking up.

Someone grabbed Calvin from behind and pressed a sweet-smelling rag over his mouth and nose. "I don't think so," a voice said in his ear. "We have other plans for you."

The world blurred in Calvin's vision. He didn't recognize the man who threw him into the carriage, and he realized the man in the driver's seat was not the cabbie he'd paid to wait for him.

This is very, very bad. Louisa's the only one who knows where I went, and she won't notice I'm missing until tomorrow. Owen and Winston won't know what to make of it, even if they do pick up on something being wrong.

I'm in big trouble. I might not make it out of this.

And if I die, I'll never find out if Owen and I could have been more.

That's a damn good reason to fight like hell.

Chapter 7
Owen

When Owen woke on the day after the fight, it took a moment to remember why everything hurt. He had dropped the wet towel onto the floor when the ice melted, but the ache in his jaw and lip reminded him of why he'd had the pack.

His leg throbbed. With a groan, Owen sat up and checked the bandage, relieved it hadn't shifted during the night.

The memory of Calvin caring for him made Owen's heart pound. His proficiency with a medic kit wasn't surprising in itself, but his gentle touch revealed a side that Owen hadn't seen before.

He knew that the circumstances of his injuries aroused suspicion. Owen felt grateful that Calvin hadn't pressed him last night. But given the nature of their work, trust between them was essential, and Owen would need to come up with an explanation that would preserve his own deniability.

Trying to figure out how to handle the dilemma, Owen sighed. *If it turned out that Calvin liked men too, if he really is interested in me, it would make this whole thing much easier.*

Of course, that leaves the matter of Winston. We'd have to figure out if he could be discreet even if he didn't share our tendencies. Plenty of butlers and valets have witnessed indiscretions—they say men like me are a dime a dozen among the upper crust.

Owen startled at the knock on his door.

"Are you awake?" Winston called. "And can I get you something for discomfort?"

Owen grabbed his robe from a peg and hobbled to the door, knowing his hair was a mess and he needed to shave. *I look like a hobo who lost a fight.*

"How did you—"

"Found a note on the table when I got up saying you'd run into trouble and had been shot." Winston managed to sound concerned and slightly reproving at once. He also avoided the use of their names and their honorifics, which Owen found perversely amusing.

"Wrong place, wrong time," Owen replied, hoping not to lie.

"When you're ready, come out for breakfast. I can give you something for the pain, and I've mixed up a few medicinals from my apothecary to make sure infection doesn't set in. Once you've had something to eat and enough coffee to put yourself right, I'll have a look at that leg."

Winston gave Owen's bruised face an assessing look. "And while you shower, I'll break off a chunk of ice for you. Later, I'll pop down to the brewery cargo car and get another block."

"Thank you." Owen was pleased to read efficiency and concern in Winston's manner and no judgment.

"Need to keep you in fighting shape," Winston said. "There's coffee on the boil and plenty of it."

Owen moved slowly through his morning routine. He chewed a bit of the willow bark Calvin had left for him, hoping it would blunt the soreness. Keeping the dressing on his leg dry was a priority, so Owen did his best to wash the rest of his body while leaving his injury outside of the shower stall.

Shaving posed another challenge since the thought of dragging a straight razor across his bruised and swollen cheek made Owen wince. Although he had never fancied beards, he decided that growing one until his face healed might be a good idea.

Owen looked at himself in the mirror and shook his head. He'd done the best he could and still couldn't hide that he'd been in a brawl. *Maybe I can avoid going out in bright daylight for a few days until the worst fades.*

On the way to the dining room, Owen heard a bell indicating an incoming telegram. Winston was not in sight, possibly gone to get more ice. Owen went into the library as the telegraph started clicking, printing the message on the long paper tape.

Owen recognized the sender as headquarters and figured it was orders for both of them. His breath caught in his throat when he read the message and realized it had been addressed only to Calvin.

"Assignments usually one year, longer if goes well. Why?"

Calvin knows. He figured out I was at Oscar's, and he's so disgusted he's already considering a transfer. I read him all wrong.

Owen leaned against the desk, overcome with a tangle of emotions. Fear that Calvin would expose his secret, losing him his job and possibly his freedom. Anger at being forced to hide. And grief at his fantasy of a relationship evolving with Calvin being dashed.

The best that can come of this is that Calvin asks for a transfer and doesn't expose me. It's the most I can hope for. We'll muddle through this assignment, and he'll leave, and we'll never see each other again. I should have known it was too good to be true.

Owen jumped when Winston came to the library doorway. "I heard the telegraph just as it ended. Is everything okay?" He frowned. "You look pale. Are you in pain?"

"The message was for Calvin. I'll leave it on the desk." Owen was surprised his voice remained steady while he formulated a cover. "I banged my bad leg, and it took my breath away."

"Let's get you to the table." Winston bustled into the room. He took Owen's elbow on the side with his injured leg, helping him hobble to the dining room, where sweet buns, bacon, and egg tarts were set out.

"Where's Calvin?" Owen hoped his voice didn't give away his heartache.

"Off sleuthing," Winston replied as he poured coffee. "The note he left on the table said you'd been hurt and what he'd done for you, asked me to look after you, and said he'd gone to meet with his Pinkerton contact and would probably be out all day."

He didn't even want to face me. How did I get it so wrong?

I could blame myself for risking the trip to Oscar's, but if Calvin feels that strongly against it, we wouldn't have worked no matter what. Better to find out before I lost even more of my heart.

Owen knew his analytical approach was just his way of hiding his pain and disappointment. *Focus on the case. We have a job to do. Be professional. And when it's done, don't look back.*

He forced himself to eat even though his stomach was tight. Coffee turned to acid in his gut, but he knew he needed a boost of energy to compensate for his injuries.

"Now, let's have a look at that leg." Winston helped him to the lab, where Owen couldn't help remembering Calvin triaging his injuries. Despite his pain, Owen had drawn comfort from Calvin's kindness, the touch of his hands and his concern.

Winston moved with the efficiency of a medic in a war zone. He was brusque without being rough, and as he handled Owen's leg and checked the wounds on his face, Winston's touch was gentle but impersonal.

"I hope you got the better of the bastard who shot you." Winston smoothed ointment over Owen's cheek and lip.

"Got in a few good hits," Owen admitted. "Didn't expect the son of a bitch to shoot me."

Winston tugged up Owen's pant leg and gently removed the bandages. Calvin's touch had sent sparks dancing through Owen's body and pooled heat in his belly. Winston was as dispassionate as any Army doctor.

"Lucky it's a graze, but still nothing to ignore." He reapplied the ointment, added a few drops of an elixir from a vial, and a pinch of something dried from a little pouch.

"The paste already does a lot to prevent infection, but what I've just mixed in adds a bit of active magic for more insurance." Winston re-bandaged the wound. "That should help with the pain as well."

"Thank you." Owen tried not to get lost in his thoughts over his disillusionment and broken heart.

"That's my job." Winston gave a hint of a smile. "Got to make myself useful beyond providing breakfast and supper."

"You are very useful, and I'm looking forward to learning more about your magic," Owen said sincerely. *I hope you won't run away too. But then, I guess I'll have to be the one to leave.*

The thought made Owen sad. Romantic fantasies aside, he genuinely liked Calvin. Winston intrigued him, and he enjoyed the witch's droll humor. Not to mention the Pullman, the best lodging Owen ever had on assignment.

I thought I'd finally gotten everything I'd dreamed about, but it didn't take long to turn into a nightmare. Serves me right for thinking that things could work out in this world for a guy like me.

"If you're up for it, I've gotten a tip that someone may have bound the ghost of a Spanish priest to scare away people from the railroad construction sites." Winston mentioned it offhandedly, as if gauging how willing Owen was to venture out with his bum leg.

"What do we need to do?" Owen desperately needed a distraction, and he welcomed Winston's suggestion.

"Thought we'd take a carriage out since riding isn't going to work for you," Winston said. "We could hire a cab for half a day, pay the driver extra not to talk about what he hears or sees. With your abilities, we might be able to get some insights into this errant Spanish priest."

"Do you think someone's threatened the ghost?" Owen felt protective of the spirits who elected to remain behind and hated when anyone tried to take advantage of them.

"Not sure. The tip I got was that the Spanish priest seemed intent on scaring away people from around the construction project," Winston replied. "Maybe the railroad is running through somewhere near where he served a mission. Or maybe someone's forced him into their schemes, which won't do at all."

Owen welcomed a reason to get his mind off Calvin and the

telegram. Winston secured a cab and gave directions to the driver before getting into the carriage with Owen.

"People claim to have seen a man in a Spanish priest's cassock who follows people—making them uncomfortable—until they leave. A couple of accounts say he appeared suddenly in front of them with a menacing expression and waved his arms," Winston said.

"Any idea who the priest might be?" Owen asked.

"Maybe. The rail spur where the ghost has been seen runs through land that used to belong to a Spanish mission from the 1500s. It's been long abandoned and what's left is just a ruin, but the records I could find, mentioned a Padre Garcia."

Winston patted the small bag he'd brought with him. "We have everything we need to handle him if you can't talk sense into him."

"If he's an old ghost, I'm surprised it's a new haunting," Owen mused.

"The mission was located out in the middle of nowhere," Winston admitted. "So perhaps the padre stuck around all these years, and there was no one to see him."

"What happened to the mission?" Owen felt there was a missing piece to the story, something that might explain why the priest's ghost chose now to go on a rampage, or how he was able to be controlled by someone else.

"Spain controlled parts of Missouri until just after the turn of the century," Winston replied. "Their control ended in 1803, and that's close to when the mission was abandoned. I'm betting that without Spain in charge of the land, the priests were recalled to another location, and the building fell into ruin."

"That makes sense," Owen said, still puzzled. "Can we go to the mission ruins before we go ghost hunting? I don't think we have the whole story."

Owen had his gun in a holster beneath his jacket and knew Winston likely had a variety of weapons on him or in his bag in addition to his witchcraft. Confronting a troublesome ghost always made Owen leery.

"Why would Aiken—or his henchmen—want the ghost to scare

people away?" Owen wondered aloud. "I wouldn't think that would be good for keeping workers or, eventually, attracting passengers."

"Maybe the ghost's presence isn't supposed to last forever," Winston replied. "Maybe he's more of a temporary night watchman. After all, people hire security or bring in guard dogs during construction, but they aren't stationed there permanently."

"Good point."

Once they left the city limits, they traveled into the countryside, switching from the main route to smaller and smaller roads until they jostled down a barely visible dirt trail. Finally, the carriage came to a halt. Winston got out to talk to the cabbie and then stuck his head back into the cab.

"He can't go farther without damaging the rig—doesn't want to break an axle," Winston said. "He'll wait here for us. I think we've got another mile to the ruins."

They had dressed for the weather and expected to hike, so they were prepared with equipment and clothing to make the trek. Owen's wounded leg ached, but not so badly that he couldn't walk.

The wind swept over the low rolling prairie, and Owen pulled his collar up to shield his face. He wondered if the land had changed much in the centuries since the mission was built and how the priests adapted to this place so far from their home in Spain.

Were they explorers? Did they come to convert the native people? Maybe they came all this way for contemplation? He wasn't sure he could fathom their motives and wondered if the priests had found what they sought.

"Up there." Winston pointed toward what looked like a heap of rubble. When they got closer, Owen could see blocks of weathered limestone worn by the wind and rain, mostly overgrown by scrub. A few stubborn saplings grew amid the ruins.

Owen hadn't known what to expect from the site. He opened his senses as he got closer, knowing Winston had his back. As Owen walked around the foundation, he felt a mix of emotions wash over him that he felt certain were not his own. Purpose—bordering on obsession. Duty, sharp-edged and implacable, homesickness so raw it took his breath away. And then, rising up like the tide and threatening to overwhelm him, a surge of anger and violence that made him stagger.

"Owen?" Winston kept his distance, but concern laced his tone.

Owen stumbled back a step as the scene unfolded in front of him. He saw the mission as it used to be, a dreary stone-walled outpost adrift on the endless prairie with its relentless wind.

Everything unfolded quickly...frightened faces, men screaming, blood splattering against limestone walls. Corpses sprawled on the mission's floor, and he saw a glint of a silver knife, felt a jolt of pain, and then numbness and a growing chill.

"Owen, what do you see?" Winston stood beside him, jostling Owen's arm to rouse him.

Owen came back to himself with a rush of breath. "Oh, God. They were murdered."

"What?"

Owen's head still swam, and his heart pounded. "I didn't see ghosts, but I had a vision. Sort of like seeing the impression of a place as it was long ago. Strong emotions leave a resonance that can be as powerful as a ghost. A little like what Calvin can do with objects."

"You saw a murder?" Winston prompted, and Owen realized he had been rambling.

"The monks were stabbed. I don't think it was an intruder. I felt such a strong feeling of betrayal—I think one of their group killed them. Maybe...Padre Garcia?"

Winston's eyes widened. "That's a twist to the story I didn't expect. It would explain why the mission was abandoned and left to decay. And it might be what binds the padre's spirit to this area."

"If Garcia went mad, and someone has forced his ghost to manifest, then it's no surprise he's terrorizing people." Owen anchored himself by diving into the particulars of the case. "He was violent before—he's still dangerous, even though all his priests are dead."

"I've heard tell that such things are more common than we'd like to think." Winston looked out over the vast, empty landscape. "People head west wanting to make a new start. Some do. But the hardship and isolation go hard on others, and sometimes they snap." The haunted look in his eyes kept Owen from asking for details.

"That changes how we handle the ghost near the rail line," Owen said. "It's not an innocent spirit who's been forced to do bad things. It's a vengeful ghost who killed before and could certainly kill again. Releasing him isn't mercy—we need to send him on to justice before more people die."

Winston appeared unflustered. "I did my best to anticipate all possibilities. We should have everything that we need."

They hiked back to the carriage and found the driver having a smoke while he let the horses graze. "Did you find what you were looking for?" he asked.

"And then some," Owen assured him. Winston gave the man directions for the rail spur construction site, with instructions to stop out of sight of the workers and to keep hidden. The driver gave him an odd look but accepted the extra bills Winston passed to him and agreeably headed the horses in the right direction.

Owen and Winston walked from where the carriage stopped to the construction site. No one appeared to be working today, although they could see where track had been laid and that the ground was prepared to extend the line.

"I see equipment, a pile of wooden ties, and lengths of rail, but no guards," Winston noted.

"It's a long way to come to steal materials," Owen remarked. "Not exactly where they'd be a temptation."

They walked around the area, guns in hand. Owen also carried an iron knife, while Winston had a bag of salt since iron and salt were known to dispel spirits. The site looked as if the workers had stored their materials intending to be gone for more than a few days.

"What's that?" Winston pointed to a heap of stones that looked out of place. The light limestone didn't match the rest of the land, and the jumble didn't match the neatness of the rest of the site.

Winston moved toward the pile, but Owen grabbed his arm.

"Wait. There's bad energy. Does your magic tell you anything?"

"I'm fidgety, which usually means trouble's brewing." Winston eyed the heap as if it were a snake. "Before we go closer, let me get my things together and work protections."

"I think those are stones from the mission," Owen said as the hunch struck him. "That's how they're binding the priest's ghost. I'll deal with the angry spirit—you do whatever you can to destroy those stones."

Owen stood far enough away to give Winston room to maneuver and then lowered his mental protections, opening himself to his gift. He braced for an assault like at the mission, knowing now that the spirit was the true danger.

"Padre Garcia...I know you killed them. Come out and face me. It's time you moved on."

The temperature dropped suddenly, and the ghost of the old priest stood in front of Owen. It flickered instead of remaining solid. The priest's features were twisted with fury, and he held the ghostly image of a bloody knife raised to strike.

"You don't belong here." Owen slowly backed away from the ghost.

The spirit bared his teeth and came at him again. Owen felt his malice, but the ghost didn't frighten him as it certainly would have someone unprepared for a sighting.

"There were no other ghosts at the mission," Owen told Garcia, gambling that the old priest retained enough sense of who he had been to understand. "They've moved on—and you remain."

Owen gradually edged away from the pile of stones. He didn't know if they affected Garcia's strength as a spirit, but he wanted to keep the ghost distracted so Winston could work.

Garcia's spirit flashed, then re-formed, coming at Owen again. So far, the ghost hadn't tried to grab him, but Owen didn't trust that to last.

Maybe he's sizing me up, trying to figure out how much of an opponent I'd be. Then again, we didn't hear that anyone had been killed here, so maybe Garcia has limits.

"Why are you still here?"

Garcia opened his mouth in a silent scream. Owen couldn't tell whether the man's torment was what had driven him to murder when he was mortal or if the madness had grown worse over the centuries of remorse and isolation.

Owen was focused on Garcia, so he wasn't paying attention to Winston. When the witch began to chant, Garcia's spirit wheeled, riveted on Winston instead of Owen.

Shit. This is bad.

Before he could talk himself out of it, Owen hurled himself through Garcia's ghost. While he had no desire to channel a furious, insane spirit, Owen couldn't let the revenant attack Winston.

Owen felt the ghost's confusion at the involuntary channeling, finding himself suddenly grappling for control of a flesh and blood body for the first time in more than four hundred years.

That confusion gave Owen an advantage because he had experience and training in how to enable a ghost to speak through him without putting himself at risk for harm or possession.

"What are you doing? Where am I?" The voice belonged to Owen, but the panicked entity speaking was Garcia.

You're four hundred years past the time you died, being forced to work for a bad man. I can send you on, Owen told the ghost, a silent argument inside his head.

"I can't move on. Do you know what I've done?" The ghost didn't seem to understand how he was speaking aloud. All the while, Owen wrestled to maintain control of his body, willing to give up his voice if he could keep Garcia from controlling his legs or arms. He had the oddest feeling of brawling with himself as he and Garcia struggled.

I know you killed the other monks. I don't care what else you've done, or where you go from here. I can't let you hurt anyone else.

Fighting a ghost was a battle of wills since he couldn't grab hold of a spirit. Owen seized control, dropping his body to the ground to slow Garcia from trying to reach Winston, who was still chanting.

Owen didn't know how long Winston's incantation lasted or what a banishment spell involved, but he hoped it didn't go on much longer. Struggling with Garcia's ghost drained Owen rapidly, and he wondered if the spirit drew from his life energy to sustain his attempt to break free.

"Let me go!" the ghost shrieked in Owen's voice.

All of Owen's training had been how to keep a ghost from taking control, and how to force out a spirit that overstepped its boundaries. Now, in a desperate bid to protect Winston and end Garcia's campaign of terror, Owen did the opposite, using his ability to temporarily lock the spirit inside his body, trapping him to prevent Garcia from attacking Winston.

The mad ghost shrieked in Owen's mind and screamed so loud it hurt his throat. Once he realized that he could control Owen's body, Garcia started to throw Owen from one side to another, and made him claw at his arms and throat.

You have to move on. You can't stay here, and you can't have my body.

"Make me leave," Garcia challenged. "It's been a long time since I had a form. You look nothing like I did, but this body will do."

Fuck you. Owen surged to the forefront of his consciousness, a surprise attack that left Garcia floundering, out of practice with a body, and inexperienced in sharing awareness. A few seconds of indecision gave Owen the edge he needed to keep control—although he didn't know how long he could maintain it.

"I've got him, Winston. Hurry!" Owen shouted as Garcia's ghost raged inside his mind.

Owen's whole world came down to keeping the spirit contained and not allowing him to gain the upper hand. He felt the struggle sapping his energy, and knew that if he lost consciousness Garcia could escape or try once more to control him.

Winston's voice rose. He chanted in Latin, and while Owen didn't know the translation, he felt power in the words. Even at a distance, Owen sensed the tingle of magic rising like a summer storm. He rolled to look toward the stones and saw a shimmering dome of coruscating energy. A blue glow limned Winston's body, growing brighter as he built toward the climax of the ritual.

Winston gave a triumphant, commanding shout, and the dome over the stones flared so brightly that Owen had to shield his eyes. He heard a crack like thunder, and at the same instant Garcia's spirit was torn free—not escaping under its own power, but jerked away from Owen so abruptly that the pain of separation brought tears to Owen's eyes.

With sight enhanced by his gift, Owen saw Garcia's spirit twisting in the air like a plume of smoke. Garcia screamed and cursed, but his struggles did not slow the pull toward where the stones had been blown to rubble by Winston's magic.

Garcia gave one last piercing shriek as the flames flared toward the sky, burning with an acrid, choking smoke, and then everything went silent.

Owen lay in the dirt, too spent to move. He hoped Garcia was truly gone because he doubted he had it in him to wage another battle. He felt as battered internally as he had been on the outside after his fight at Oscar's. Every muscle and sinew ached, his injured calf throbbed, and he felt scoured on the inside.

"Owen!" Winston's footsteps pounded toward him. Winston knelt next to him, rolling Owen onto his back.

"Did it work?" Owen's voice was raw from screaming.

"Yes. Garcia is gone, and the stones are destroyed. Whoever bound his spirit can't do it again—at least, not in the same way. Are you damaged?"

Owen groaned. "Not permanently. Although I felt like I had a fight inside my body."

"You did. I'm impressed. Very few mediums could do what you managed." Winston had brought his bag with him and unstoppered a vial, which he pressed to Owen's lips.

"Drink this. It will dispel any negative energy the ghost left inside you and replenish your strength. Just don't blame me because it tastes awful."

Owen struggled to swallow a liquid that smelled and tasted like pond scum. But almost as quickly as it left his mouth, he felt it begin to take effect.

Winston helped Owen to his feet, gathered the items from his ritual, and collected their weapons. Owen limped worse than before, and he had gained new bruises from his struggle with Garcia.

To Owen's relief, the carriage and driver were waiting where they'd left them. If the man questioned why Owen was covered with dirt, he didn't ask, and Winston's tip ensured the cabbie's discretion.

"Can't have been good for your leg," Winston said, noting how Owen sat favoring his injured calf.

"It could have been a lot worse," Owen replied. Now that the problem of the padre's ghost was solved, the tangled emotions from earlier rushed back.

Will Calvin have already cleared his things out when we get back? Or will he turn me in?

He hoped that Calvin wouldn't destroy his life by exposing his secret, but Owen had to admit that as quickly as he'd fallen for his new partner, he didn't know him well at all. *I think he's an honorable man, but part of being an agent is becoming whatever someone else needs you to be to get the job done.*

Shit. Was this a setup to confirm someone's suspicions about me? No. That's too complicated, and Winston's not acting strangely toward me at all. I don't need to make this worse than it is—it's already pretty bad.

"You're quiet." Winston shot him a glance as the carriage jostled along the road heading into the city.

"Just tired. It's been a long day, and everything hurts." All of which was true, but Owen omitted the shattered heart.

"I'll have a look at that leg when we get back. I can give you something for the pain, or just hand you the whiskey bottle," Winston said with the hint of a smile. "I'm eager to hear what your partner has uncovered. Hopefully a crucial lead to need such an early start."

"Yeah, I'm sure he's been busy," Owen mumbled, turning away. He knew he would have to find a way to deal with his misery if he was going to complete the assignment with Calvin, but right now with the disappointment so fresh, Owen just tried to go minute-to-minute.

If Winston picked up on his mood, he didn't comment. Owen hoped his silence would be interpreted as pain. He definitely didn't want to explain.

THE PULLMAN WAS STILL DARK when they arrived, which gave Owen pause. Winston also noticed with a frown. "I expected him to be back before we returned. I do hope he hasn't run into trouble."

"Probably romancing a showgirl." Owen hobbled after Winston into the train car.

Winston turned on the lights and made a quick check while Owen limped into the lab. When Winston joined him, his expression lit a spark of worry in Owen's gut.

"He's not here. Nothing's been touched. No sign of struggle—but I'm concerned that he's been gone longer than expected." Winston handed Owen a glass with a few fingers of whiskey. "This should help with the soreness."

They didn't speak while Winston checked Owen's leg and added more ointment. "It's healing, and there's no sign of infection," Winston told him as he re-bandaged the wound. "Did you suffer any damage in the fight with Garcia?"

Owen shook his head. "I'll have new bruises, but nothing broke the skin. Although I feel scalded on the inside from the ghost."

"Then the whiskey should help," Winston replied with an encouraging smile. "I'll let you clean up while I check the telegraph and put dinner in the oven."

Owen went to his room and peeled off clothing which was thick with dust. He let a hot shower wash away the grit and sweat, but felt too discouraged to be interested in jerking off.

I've got to lock the feelings away until this all winds down. It probably won't be long. There'll be time enough to wallow when it's over.

Owen dressed and headed for the dining room, where he stood in front of the corkboard, reviewing their leads.

His gaze fell to Ida's list of gates. *Binding a priest's ghost to do their dirty work sure sounds like the fifth gate—corruption of the pious. But what about the fourth one? Is that what Calvin went to look into? That could mean there are only two left. Are we too late to stop the gates from opening?*

A knock drew him to the front of the car. Winston wasn't in sight, and Owen opened the door to a young man he didn't know.

"I have a message delivery for Owen Sharps," the messenger said, chewing his gum open-mouthed with supreme boredom.

"I'm Sharps." Owen took the envelope. He didn't recognize the handwriting. The young man hadn't moved, one hand extended, and Owen dug out a tip from his pocket.

Should I open this now? I'll wait for Winston. He set the envelope on the library desk.

Owen settled into one of the couches in the parlor and found the newspaper and another glass of whiskey set out for him, along with a plate of cheese and crackers. If Winston had a meal already prepared before they left, it would still likely take an hour to heat in the oven. He was grateful for the snack, which tamed his growling stomach.

Owen resolutely pushed his worries about Calvin out of his mind as he read the headlines and paged through the rest of the news. The comics gave him a pang, remembering Calvin's joy over the funny pages on the train when they met.

How can he have gotten under my skin so deep so fast? And why did it have to happen when I can't keep him? The sounds of the telegraph interrupted his thoughts.

Winston came into the parlor, wiping his hands on a towel and wearing an apron around his hips. "It seems we'll have company after dinner. Agent Storm sent a telegram instructing us to expect a colleague of his—a woman named Renate Thalberg, who is a very talented absinthe witch."

"Do you know her?" The idea of absinthe magic intrigued Owen.

"We haven't met, but we've moved in the same witchy circles," Winston replied. "She has a reputation for high integrity—and fearsome magic. I have to wonder if her close ties with ethical vampires may be a factor in her visit, given that at the heart of this case we have a decidedly *unethical* vampire—Leland Aiken."

Owen knew that not everything supernatural was evil. His own abilities and Winston's magic were evidence of that. The government had vampire, witch, and shifter allies who had a vested interest in quelling panic about the paranormal and keeping certain truths quiet.

"The vampires have been curiously absent in everything we've investigated so far," Owen mused, glad for a chance to get his head back into the case. "They might be behind it all, but they've kept their distance."

"There's no doubt that the Branson brothers were linked to Aiken," Winston agreed. "And I suspect that whoever coerced the shifter into collecting the ritual victims was likely a vampire."

Owen nodded. "That would make sense. Shifters aren't afraid of many other creatures. We don't know who was responsible for the crop sigil and devil dogs."

"But the odds are good that the witch is in league with Aiken," Winston added. "If Aiken has claimed the St. Louis territory, other vampires will stay away unless they want a gang war. That holds for other high-powered paranormals. Witches might have an agreement with Aiken, but he's not likely to look kindly on anyone staying in town who is powerful enough to give him trouble."

"Like your friend, Miss Thalberg?" Owen suspected that Winston was more powerful than he let on and that they had only seen a glimpse of his abilities.

"She won't be taking up residence, I'm sure," Winston replied with a cryptic half-smile. "But if Agent Storm asked for her help, then perhaps he's happened onto more information. It won't hurt to have another ally—assuming she can stay for the fight."

An alarm clock sounded in the kitchen, drawing Winston back to check on dinner. Owen looked at his watch and frowned. *Should we be worried that Calvin isn't back yet and hasn't checked in?*

Is he staying out purposely because he wants to avoid me? That doesn't bode well for working the rest of the case together. The possibility made Owen sad. He would have been happy to have Calvin as a friend, even without any romance. *If he's that judgmental, it would never have worked.*

Winston's dinner of baked chicken and root vegetables with cornbread dressing was delicious. Owen forced himself to eat because he knew he needed sustenance and to forestall having to explain his lack of appetite to Winston. They didn't talk much as they ate, but after having spent the day together Owen figured out they were both mulling over what they had seen and how it all went together.

When they finished eating, Winston cleared the table. "Since we don't know when Miss Thalberg will arrive, I'm going to run over to the beer cooler car to get more ice—your bruises will thank me tonight," he added. "I'll be right back. Keep an eye out, please, for our guest."

Chapter 8
Owen

O wen settled back onto the couch in the parlor with the remainder of his whiskey and the newspaper. One article mentioned the incident at the bank but downplayed it as a "disturbance" instead of the panic-driven riot it really was.

For all their prominence in the city's dealings, the only mention of the Branson brothers was their obituary. It lauded their activity as land brokers and barely mentioned the circumstances of their deaths except to note that the police had an "ongoing investigation."

Given what Owen had seen of the police chief, he doubted that the investigation was going anywhere.

It would make sense for Aiken to have the cops in his pocket. Keeps things from getting messy. Good to have someone who can cover tracks if any of Aiken's henchmen make a mess.

Winston entered the back of the car as a knock came at the front door. "Can you please answer the door? I need to put the ice away." He hurried toward the insulated box in the lab, and Owen made his way to the front door.

A slender, slightly built young woman with light brown hair in a Gibson Girl style stood beneath a light that had grown decidedly dimmer. "I'm Renate Thalberg. Andreas sent me—you're in great danger." She swept past him in a swirl of dark skirts.

"You're very welcome to come in, but I worry that some people might talk seeing you enter the Pullman belonging to three gentlemen." Owen tried to be chivalrous.

Renate made a dismissive gesture. "If it bothers people, I can wipe their memories."

Winston bustled from the back corridor and made a slight bow. "Miss Thalberg. We're honored. This is Agent Owen Sharps. His partner, Agent Springfield, is not here right now. Please come in and have a seat. I'll have tea ready shortly."

Owen bit back a chuckle. Winston seemed positively dazzled. Owen had never imagined that witches had their own celebrities.

Renate took a seat in one of the high-backed wing chairs, skirts spread around her, hands on her lap, and spine stiffly proper. "My great-grandfather is Andreas Thalberg, a powerful vampire witch in New Pittsburgh and an Elder among those who walk the night. He has long known of Leland Aiken, which is why I've been sent to give you information about him that may protect you—and help with your case."

Owen frowned. "We've only been here for a few days, and the train from New Pittsburgh takes a long time. How did you—?"

"I had a vision almost two days ago and left at once."

Winston brought in a tray with the tea service and set it on the coffee table. Renate took the tea Winston poured and sipped it. "Andreas is very old, even for his kind. He and others with...abilities... have allied against those who use their special gifts for their own benefit—and to the harm of others. As you can imagine, it has not made him popular among other vampires."

She paused to sip the tea again. "Leland Aiken is an old foe. He has sparred with Andreas and those like him for lifetimes. Most of the time, Andreas and his colleagues have been able to frustrate his schemes. Sometimes not—with disastrous consequences."

Her sharp gaze pinned Owen. "Understand that Aiken poses no threat to Andreas. He can't hurt him. But Andreas has committed centuries to protecting humans against predators like Aiken. Frustrating him is something of a family business," she added with a droll twitch of her lips.

"This railroad is not what it seems. Aiken wants to help predatory vampires migrate to the West where they can feed on victims in areas where there are fewer protections, less ability for the law to notice disappearances and murders," Renate explained.

"He'll have lightless train cars, hotels customized for their needs, and practically deliver the victims into their hands, like a restaurant. It will be a quiet bloodbath."

Owen and Winston nodded. "We had come to something of the same conclusion," Winston replied. "But without the validation of someone who had firsthand knowledge of Aiken. What do you know of the gates of hell?"

Renate startled. "Why do you ask?"

"It would be easier to show you." Owen and Winston led Renate to the dining room and the corkboard. "A contact with knowledge of the supernatural gave me this." Owen pointed to Ida's note about the gates. "I believe there are five gates opened—two left. That's not good."

"No, it's not," Renate agreed. "Tell me, what's happened?"

Owen and Winston took turns filling Renate in on everything that had taken place since they arrived in St. Louis.

"Your conclusions are valid," Renate confirmed when they finished. "And what you've seen upholds the rumors Andreas heard about Aiken's plans for the railroad." She frowned.

"In my vision, you appeared just as I see you here, and I recognized Winston." She glanced around. "Where is the black-haired man?"

Owen's eyes widened. "Calvin is still out working the case and hasn't returned yet."

"You are all in great danger, especially the black-haired man," she said.

"What did you see?" Winston sounded worried. Owen didn't trust himself to speak. While he grieved the relationship he would never have with Calvin, he desperately wanted him to remain safe.

"Absinthe enables me to transcend and have true visions," Renate told them. "It also enhances my magic. I saw him being attacked by vampires. If he's gone missing, then I fear that they already have him."

"He should have been back by now." Owen's heart was in his throat. "Can we save him?"

"Unclear. What I see is true—but I do not see everything."

Owen frowned. "We need to find him. He's out there—he's depending on us." All of Owen's training and experience didn't prepare him for the panic he felt and the need to take action.

"Running headlong into a nest of vampires won't help Calvin, and it'll just get us killed," Renate said. Her tone offered a mild reproof but wasn't unkind, as if she understood his urgency. "We need a plan, and we need to gather materials."

Owen forced himself to sit and clamped his mouth shut against the argument that swelled inside. *She's right. Don't let your emotions get in the way.*

"There's another piece you haven't heard," Winston spoke up, and both Owen and Renate looked at him. "When I went to the brewery car for ice, I heard the cabbies talking. Someone hired a carriage late this afternoon and never brought it back. They said the driver was attacked—found dead. No sign of the carriage—or the man who hired it."

"Calvin. He must have rented it." Owen exchanged a worried glance with Winston, then remembered the messenger with the envelope.

"Oh my God, I forgot. An envelope came when you were out. Maybe it's a good time to have a look at it." Owen retrieved the package from the library and opened it as he sat at the table. "It's from Ida—my reporter contact."

Owen read the letter aloud. In it, Ida laid out the details about hanged men's bodies with fang marks, drained of blood, and disinterred.

"Another piece of the puzzle—another gate of hell," Owen said. "Want to bet this is the 'desecration of the damned' since the drained corpses were all criminals?"

A knock at the door froze them all. "Are you expecting someone?" Winston asked Owen, who shook his head.

Both men pulled their guns. Owen went to answer the door, while Winston went toward the back entrance.

A woman stood on the step. Her blonde hair was piled in a fashionable top knot, and her black wool cloak had a flattering cut.

"Is Calvin here?"

Owen swallowed, figuring this was further proof that his partner didn't share his inclinations. *Must be the showgirl he's been keeping company with.*

"He's out," Owen replied and started to close the door.

"I'm a Pinkerton." The stranger held up her badge. "Let me in. If Calvin's not here, then he's in a lot of trouble—and I think I know how to find him."

Owen stepped back and let the woman enter. She carried herself with confidence, taking the unusual circumstances in stride. He thought she looked vaguely familiar and had the feeling that she also recognized him from somewhere.

"I'm Louisa Sunderson. I've been working undercover with the Pinkertons as a showgirl at Kearson's Palace for the past year. I met Calvin a while ago on a case, and we kept in touch—on and off—so when he got to St. Louis, he stopped by to see if I knew anything that might help with what you've been working on. Turned out that I did."

Winston and Renate came to join them in the parlor. Renate and Louisa gave each other an appraising glance that was cautious but not outright hostile.

"Winston and Miss Thalberg are colleagues," Owen said. "We're worried because Calvin hasn't come back. Make this quick. We need to be out there looking for him."

Louisa's dress beneath her cloak was dark gray with a narrow silhouette, good for blending into the shadows. She settled into one of the wing chairs while Renate took the other. Winston and Owen sat on the couch.

"I had information about some of the people Calvin was interested in, and I told him what I knew. Early this morning, we went to look into reports that there had been grave desecrations and sightings of people who were supposed to be dead," Louisa told them. "We found a necromancer using the zombies of dead railroad workers to build part of the new line. We took care of it."

"And by 'took care of it,' you mean—" Owen prompted.

Louisa met his gaze unflinchingly. "Killed the necromancer, which stopped the zombies."

The fourth gate—commanding the dead. That's six gates opened. Only one more to go.

"We came back to Kearson's and hashed out ideas. I had to get ready for the show—my cover," Louisa went on. "We had a tip about problems at another cemetery, the one near the jail. More missing people. Calvin said he was going to stop by the gravedigger bar to see if he could pick up any information."

"When?" Winston asked.

"Right before dinner. I did my show, and I couldn't shake the feeling something was wrong, so I went to the cemetery myself. The bartender said he saw a man who fit Calvin's description but that he left on his own hours before. I found a place where a carriage had been parked off to the side of the road. The driver was dead—throat slit, but the body had been drained—and it looked like there'd been a struggle. If someone took Calvin, he didn't go easily."

"The driver's body had been drained?" Renate repeated.

Louisa returned her gaze steadily. Owen hoped the two women weren't going to clash.

"Definitely. And if I had any question about what did it, the vampire who followed me made the answer pretty clear," Louisa replied.

"How did you get away?" Owen asked.

"He got too close, didn't think I knew what he was. Staked him through the heart," Louisa said matter-of-factly.

Owen swore he saw a glint of grudging admiration in Renate's eyes.

"Well done," Renate said. "But do we have any idea what Calvin might have found when he went to the bar—or why the vampires took him?"

"With the first cemetery, it was body snatching—the necromancer rounding up undead workers," Louisa replied. "But the second cemetery was where executed prisoners from the jail were buried. I'd heard a rumor that there was something wrong with the bodies. I don't know the details—but I'm betting now that it had something to do with vampires, and Calvin stumbled into more than he could handle."

"He can handle a lot, so my money is on vampires as well," Winston said. "And if the bodies came from the jail, that shifty chief of police is probably involved, somehow."

"They took Calvin." Owen's heart thudded. He forced down his feelings, knowing that he needed to stay detached if they were going to have a chance to save Calvin. *Or bring his body back.*

"It has to mean something that they kidnapped him." Winston looked worried. "If the driver was killed, the attacker had the opportunity to kill Calvin as well—but he didn't. Why not?"

"The sacrifice of the faithful," Owen murmured, feeling his blood run cold.

"What?" Louisa looked between Owen and Winston.

"The seventh gate." Owen felt stunned. "If the gates of hell theory is right, and there's a ritual at the heart of it, then the last piece is what's needed to finish the spell and open the gate. This is dark magic. It would make sense for the final step to be a human sacrifice." He met Winston's gaze.

"They didn't kill Calvin then because they intend to sacrifice him later." Owen felt the truth of his words in his bones. "And if they do, Leland Aiken will have demons at his command. He'll be nearly unstoppable."

Renate's smile was feral. "Then we'll have to make sure that doesn't happen. It's too late to do anymore tonight. I suggest we get a good night's sleep and regroup here first thing in the morning."

Owen hated the delay, even if he knew she was right. He doubted he would sleep well if at all, worrying about Calvin.

WINSTON AND RENATE argued over magical technicalities in the dining room after they'd finished breakfast. Owen's head throbbed, and he had no patience for squabbles. He escaped to the kitchen, hoping that Winston's pot of coffee remained reasonably hot on the stove.

"You were at Oscar's the night of the riot. I saw you."

Owen turned to find Louisa standing in the kitchen doorway. He ignored his panicked heartbeat and faced her with what he hoped was an inscrutable expression.

"I saw you there too," he replied.

She nodded and raised her hands in a gesture of truce. "I mean you no harm. In fact, I've got as much to lose as you do if the truth were known."

"Why bring it up then?"

"Because I'm tired of seeing Calvin moping about like a lovesick schoolboy," Louisa told him with the barest hint of a smile.

Owen startled, caught flatfooted by her comment. "What?"

She tilted her head and gave him a look as if he were hopelessly slow. "He cares about you," Louisa went on. "He's not good at saying it, so you have to look at what he does. He tries to protect you. He told me that he'd met someone who intrigued him, but he wasn't sure the other person shared his 'interests.'"

"He did?' Owen's head spun.

Louisa nodded. "Calvin doesn't wear his heart on his sleeve. But he's gone for you. I don't know how you feel about him, but have a care, or I'll be forced to kick your ass."

Owen managed a sad smile. "Thank you. But first, we have to save his life."

If he's attracted to me, why did he want to know how long we'd be stuck together? I don't understand the telegram if he isn't interested in leaving.

Owen and Louisa returned to the dining room. He forced himself to take a seat instead of pacing. "We've got to come up with a plan, and we've got next to nothing to go on."

"Not completely true," Renate spoke up from where she stood studying their corkboard. "There's an abandoned limestone mine you've circled on the map as a possible future vampire hotel site. It would also be the perfect spot for Aiken's vampire overseers to hide."

"Odds are he doesn't have a large crew of vamps here yet. He'd want a couple of his high-level people to keep an eye on construction and make sure the seven gates project happens, but too many vampires runs a risk of spooking the mortals," Winston noted.

Louisa nodded. "They'd need to feed, and even with the murders and disappearances to open the gates, that wouldn't satisfy a large nest's basic needs. I haven't gotten word of a sudden uptick in people gone missing in surrounding areas either."

"Even a handful of vampires are a challenge in a fight," Owen pointed out. "And we know Aiken had a witch working for him as well. If it wasn't the necromancer, and he had others..."

Renate shared a look with Winston. "Very likely. Leave the witch to us."

Owen looked to Renate. "Do you know who's working for Aiken?'

"I've heard rumors," Renate replied. "Barclay Macready is the name that's linked most often. Not a necromancer, but he is a slimy son of a bitch. Macready is a competent witch, willing to use dark magic to enhance his power. He's a little too willing to rely on relics or stealing spells from other witches instead of doing the hard work to increase his magic the right way."

"It's very possible that Aiken has human enforcers on site, especially if he's working up to the big sacrifice ritual," Winston said. "Easier than vampires to fight, but potentially just as deadly if we're not prepared."

"Is it true you're a medium?" Renate surprised Owen with the abrupt change of subject.

Owen nodded. "I'm not sure how—"

"A friend of mine is a talented inventor," Renate replied. "He lets me borrow some of his experimental technology from time to time. This is one of his pieces—a Maxwell Box. The frequencies it gives off can attract or repel ghosts. In the hands of a trained medium, those ghosts could be enlisted as spies...or allies."

Owen regarded the box with curiosity and some reservations. "Does it harm ghosts?"

Renate shook her head. "No. I have that on authority from other mediums who have made use of it. Spirits are energy, and they have vibrations, so a complimentary vibration brings them closer. An uncomfortable one makes them flee. No permanent alteration."

Owen thought for a moment. Mining was a dangerous business, and miners died in even the best run operations. Some ghosts were sure to have stuck around the old mine, and they might not like having their solitude disturbed. Those with sentience might object to their final resting place being overrun by vampires and people with bad intentions.

"I like anything that improves our odds," he replied. "What about the witchy stuff?"

Renate raised a well-groomed eyebrow but didn't comment on his choice of words. Winston looked amused.

"It's going to depend on what kind of guards we run into and how the mine is protected," Renate replied. "Leland Aiken is no stranger to magic, and from what you've said, we're likely to encounter witches in the mix. There are a variety of possible magics depending on what we find ourselves confronting, both defensive and offensive."

"It also hinges on whether the mine is warded and if the guards have magical protections," Winston said.

Owen looked to Louisa. "How about you? What's your specialty? You're one of the Paranormal Pinkertons."

Louisa shook her head. "Sadly, no. I don't have any special powers other than wicked good aim and I'm fast on my feet. I learned about the supernatural side of things when Calvin's case and mine intersected a few years ago. I didn't realize the guy I was investigating was a wraith. Calvin gave me the talk about things that go bump in the night. After that, I learned on the job." She grinned wolfishly. "But I do have a couple of cards up my sleeve. I've got a bag full of weapons, a badge, and Ida Hardin and I have come up with a way to tangle Leland Aiken's expansion plans and slow him down."

"How?" Owen asked.

"I've been feeding Ida information, and she's been working her contacts," Louisa replied. "She's submitting a news story today to a friend at the big paper in Jefferson City that will link Aiken to corruption at the state and St. Louis level."

Her eyes held a glint of vindictiveness. "We've documented everything—collusion with the governor, payoffs to the police chief, deals with the Irish and Italian crime organizations. The story won't bring down a guy like Aiken, but it will force his allies to pull back and be less open in their support. While it's front-page news, he'll have to mind appearances and step carefully."

Louisa brushed her nails on the collar of her coat in a gesture of triumph. "Not bad for someone with no magic, huh?"

Owen couldn't help feeling a flash of admiration. *She's impressive. I can see how the right man could fall for her. I'm just glad Calvin isn't the "right" man.*

He turned his attention back to Winston and Renate. "Can you locate Calvin? There's no point in making an assault on the mine if Calvin's not there."

"It's a limestone mine. That type of rock allows energy to pass through it easily," Renate mused. "Depending on how warded the mine is, how deep inside they've taken him, and whether they've used magic to dampen and shield scrying, it might be possible to confirm his location if I scry. Unfortunately, any of those variables could give us a false negative."

"It's worth a shot," Owen felt anxiety rise. Calvin had already been gone overnight. The odds of him remaining alive lessened with every hour that passed. Charging in without preparation would get them all killed and fail at saving Calvin, but Owen still chafed at the delay.

"I've been preparing what's needed for offensive and defensive spells, plus some useful cantrips to make things explode and catch fire," Winston offered. "I'm a generalist witch, for the most part. Practical magic. I found a locator spell that I can do with something that belongs to Calvin as a focus. It might serve to confirm his location."

"We should move soon while it's still light," Renate said. "If there are vampires, they'll be sleeping or sluggish. That means we might only confront the human guards. Any ritual will be after dark when they're stronger. Calvin's running out of time."

Renate prepared her scrying bowl. Winston produced an absinthe fountain from a closet in the kitchen and set it up, providing her with a perfect louche. Then he assembled a tripod with a weighted amethyst pendant over a map, along with a hairbrush retrieved from Calvin's room.

Owen stepped out to the observation platform behind the Pullman and stared up at the sky. Winston and Renate weren't the only ones with abilities, although Owen had shied away from the thought of using his gift for this.

I don't find living people. I talk to ghosts. If I call to Calvin and he answers, it's because he's dead. We'll know for certain. And I'll know he's gone.

Owen swallowed a lump in his throat and blinked back tears. *I don't want to find you like this, Calvin. But we have to be sure. You wouldn't want your friends going into danger for a rescue that's too late.*

Breaking my heart for a good cause. I'm really hoping you don't answer when I call.

Owen closed his eyes and tipped his face up to the sky. He concentrated, opening himself, and focused on Calvin. He remembered Calvin's face, his voice, his stance.

Calvin Springfield...if you can hear me, I need you to answer. Please, show yourself. Your friends will put themselves in danger to save you. But we need to know whether you're still here...or gone.

Owen waited, holding his breath. His hands closed around the railing, squeezing the metal hard enough to hurt. Owen tried not to feel, afraid that worry and grief would block out a reply. The wind whipped past him, chilling him to the bone, mussing his hair and stinging his skin.

No answer came. Owen waited, hoping not to hear from Calvin, needing to be certain. Minutes passed, and nothing broke the silence in his mind. Owen slumped in relief, prying his hands from the cold railing, biting back a sob.

Calvin's not dead. As long as he's alive, there's hope.

"We're ready." Winston stood in the doorway.

"Calvin's still alive," Owen told him and saw an echo of relief in Winston's eyes.

"Then let's get to finding him," Winston replied.

They walked back to the dining room. Louisa stood studying the corkboard while Renate sat in front of a silver bowl and a goblet of absinthe. Her eyes were closed, and she appeared to be meditating.

"He's alive," Owen said.

Renate opened her eyes and smiled. "That's all I needed to hear." She took a sip of the absinthe and looked into the bowl, which held the same light-green liquid. Renate murmured an incantation under her breath, and the liquid in the bowl rippled. She sipped again and spoke another line of the spell, bowing her head over the bowl.

A white mist rose above the emerald liquid. Owen and the others weren't close enough to see whatever images appeared, but Renate studied them with focus.

"He's in the mine. And so are vampires and other humans. I can't get a count, but I can sense their essence," Renate replied. "I can confirm that much."

Winston stood behind the tripod pendant. "My turn." He focused on the pendant, putting one hand on the map and holding the other palm down over the apparatus.

His lips moved in a silent spell, and the pendant began to quiver then made slow circles over the map, untouched. The amethyst zig-zagged, then quieted and came to rest with its tether at an unnatural angle, pointing at a spot on the map.

Winston's hand moved to mark the spot, and he released the magic, letting the pendant swing back to its neutral position.

"He's in this area." Winston grabbed a pencil and circled where the amethyst had pointed. "Third level, down from the entrance."

"What is that?" Owen crowded closer for a better look.

"Ida found a map of the limestone mine when she was searching documents at City Hall," Louisa spoke up. "She thought it might be useful since the mine was located near one of the spurs. Fortunately for us, Ida has a talent for removing documents without being caught."

"We might make a secret agent of her yet." Owen appreciated the efforts of everyone in their unlikely team.

"I hope not," Louisa replied. "Ida's perfect doing exactly what she's doing—shining a light on the cockroaches in power."

Chapter 9
Calvin

C alvin woke in darkness. His head throbbed, and from the way his stomach growled, he knew it had been a long time since he'd eaten.

Slowly, memories returned. Calvin recalled going to the gravedigger's bar and what he had overheard. He had headed back to the carriage, only to be attacked and kidnapped.

He groaned and tried to take inventory of his injuries. The back of his head was sore to the touch and bloody. His body ached from spending the night on a stone floor. The inside of his left arm hurt like he'd been stabbed.

Calvin reached his right arm over to check, and his fingers came away sticky with blood.

No wonder I feel lightheaded. I've lost blood on top of everything else.

Calvin fell back on his training. *Think—where, when, how, who? And…what now?*

He forced himself not to consider the consequences and instead tried to answer the other questions and see if there was a way out.

He felt around, finding only rock, stone floor, rough walls. The air smelled musty and damp, chilly but not as cold as outdoors. *A cave?*

His fingers drifted down the rock and felt straight grooves. *Those were made by pickaxes. This is a mine, not a cave.*

Calvin heard the clink of steel against stone when he moved and realized his left leg felt heavy. When he touched his ankle, he found a metal cuff attached to a chain. His psychometric gift kicked in unbidden, and sensations assaulted him. Calvin heard the screams of past prisoners as their terror and pain flooded him. Worst was the unrelenting darkness.

The vision released him and left Calvin shivering and panting. It took several minutes before his breathing slowed and his heart didn't threaten to burst from his chest. He tried to muffle his gasps, worried that his captors could hear his heartbeat. When he could move again, and the shaking stopped, Calvin ripped his shirt and wrapped the length around his right hand to protect himself from more unwanted revelations as he explored his prison.

The floor was mostly empty, except for a tumble of sticks. Calvin's blood chilled as he realized his error. *Not sticks. Bones. Probably human.*

He followed the links to a pin driven solidly into the rock wall. Calvin pushed up to his feet and staggered, pulled off balance by the weight of the fetter. He went as far as his tether allowed, trying to find the limits of his prison. The chain brought him up short before he had made his way around the whole room.

Fuck. This is probably the abandoned mine near the new railroad.

But why?

What's the point?

They've killed plenty of people—why give me special treatment?

An awful possibility occurred to him.

I'm either a human sacrifice or bait.

Calvin tried to argue himself out of the idea and came up empty. *If they just wanted fresh meat, anyone would do. My psychic abilities aren't powerful enough to be that useful. So they either took me for a ritual, or they grabbed me to draw in the others—maybe both.*

The vampires are working for Aiken. He doesn't need to do the dirty work himself. It's cold comfort that sending his goons after us means we pose a threat.

His right hand closed over his left arm. Calvin didn't need light to know that he'd been bitten.

They didn't drain me. Or turn me. More evidence that I'm bait or they'd have killed me right away. But why feed on me?

There's nothing special about my blood. So maybe it's about something else.

The seventh gate of hell, "Sacrifice of the faithful."

What does "faithful" have to do with anything? Do they suspect that I have feelings for Owen? We aren't a couple. What am I missing?

Calvin sat with his back against the wall and drew his feet up so he could hug his knees, gaining some warmth in the chilly room.

Faithful. I'm true to my friends, my oath to the service, what I believe to be right. I do my best to keep my word. I've been told I'm loyal to a fault. Is that what's going to damn me?

Alone in the dark, Calvin leaned his forehead against his knees. *I'm injured, and no one knows where I am. They probably won't even realize I'm missing until I don't come back at night. How long has it been? Is it morning?*

I'm chained up inside an abandoned mine filled with vampires who might want to sacrifice me, kill my friends, and open the door to hell.

Odds are good I'm not going to get out of this. But can I take any of those sons of bitches with me?

Calvin's heart rose in his throat. *Owen.*

They hadn't known each other long, but Calvin already realized that he had fallen in love with his new partner. He'd made up his mind that if headquarters intended that they work together indefinitely, he would bide his time and see if Owen returned his interest. Deep down, Calvin felt certain that Owen shared his feelings.

Maybe it's better that we didn't have a chance to get started if this is how I'm going to die. Owen will avenge me, and perhaps he'll remember me when he moves on, but even if he harbored some feelings, my death won't break his heart.

I've got a duty to escape and warn the others. And if I can't get clear, I need to find a way to stop the ritual. But first, I've got to get out of these chains.

He didn't hear footsteps until he sensed someone standing right in front of him. *Vampires don't make noise. They can see in the dark—and I can't.*

"You're awake. Nice of you to join us."

A cold hand fixed an unbreakable grip on Calvin's left wrist, jerking him to his knees. Fangs pierced his skin, and lips closed over the wound as the vampire's tongue lapped at the blood. The man let go and shoved Calvin backward onto his ass.

"Your blood is delicious."

Calvin made a rude gesture. It was so dark he couldn't see his own hand, but he figured the vampire could.

"No need for temper," the vampire chided. "It's quite an honor to be taken. You're not dinner—you're a sacrifice. Very mythic. Your death will change the world."

"Go fuck yourself."

The vampire's chuckle sounded more like a humorless growl. "You aren't impressed? You should be. Our master will be unstoppable with demons to do his bidding. And you're going to make that possible."

"You came to gloat?" Calvin had nothing but bravado to sustain him, but he would not give his captors the satisfaction of showing fear.

"Hardly. Just making sure you woke up. Can't have a party without the guest of honor."

Calvin refused to acknowledge the comment and hoped that the vampire could see his glare.

"No one knows you're here. You'll be dead before your friends realize you're gone. They've been annoying, poking their noses into our business. Getting rid of them will be a pleasure."

Calvin fumed, but he forced himself to remain still, not wanting to reveal how the vampire's taunts made his heart freeze.

"Make your peace. It won't be long now."

Calvin felt a rush of air and knew he was alone once more. He took a deep breath to quiet his pounding heart. The vampires had made a mistake in leaving him fully dressed. Calvin worked open his belt and unzipped a hidden inner pocket. Inside was a set of steel lock picks and several safety matches.

Calvin worked the picks with practiced ease, careful not to touch the cuff again barehanded. When it dropped free, Calvin rubbed his ankle and replaced the lock picks. Then he ripped another portion of his shirt and wrapped it around the nearest bone to make a torch, lighting it with one of the matches.

The light might attract attention, but if I fall down a shaft, the escape will be over real quick.

Calvin relied on his hearing since the torch's light didn't reach far in the mine's darkness. Parallel tracks for mine cars ran down the center of the path, disappearing into the shadows in both directions. In the distance, Calvin heard the drip and splatter of water. He stayed close to the wall and took the path that sloped upward, hoping that meant it headed toward the outside.

If the vamps are paying attention, they'll hear me moving, smell the smoke or see the fire. I don't have long.

He didn't take time to explore. Side passageways branched off, but Calvin stuck to the main corridor, following the track and hoping his instincts steered him to freedom. Rooms where mining had removed the limestone opened from the passageway. He let his hand trace the wall, and saw faint images of men in work clothes and helmets, faces streaked with dust.

Up ahead he saw lights and slowed, plastering himself against the wall. He edged forward, straining to hear voices or footsteps. There were muted shouts and sounds in the distance but nothing close. Calvin squinted as he came closer, and once his eyes adjusted, he saw that someone had installed electric lights in part of the old mine. The naked bulbs were strung along the ceiling at intervals that lit the way but left dark shadowed pools in corners and at the edges. Calvin's torch had burned down to a smolder, but he held onto it in case he needed to venture beyond the reach of the lights.

Most of the rooms were dark, but two were lit. Calvin warred with himself, whether to risk discovery by looking inside or hurry toward what he hoped was the exit.

I need to make it out, and bring Owen and Winston back to get rid of the vampires. Anything I can learn now will help us rout them later.

The first room was lit by banks of candles, not lightbulbs. Sigils painted in what appeared to be blood marked the stone walls and floor. Ritual paraphernalia covered tables, and the raised slab in the center was clearly an altar sized to hold the body of an adult sacrifice.

Calvin shuddered, seeing what awaited him. The room was empty now, and he had no desire for the witch and devotees return.

He moved as quietly as possible, knowing that no human's stealth could evade a vampire's hearing. But as he continued his escape without interference, Calvin wondered where his captors had gone.

The next room answered his question. Only one bulb burned overhead, revealing half a dozen sleeping vampires. *It must be daytime. Even here in the dark, the urge to sleep is strong unless they're very old. I'll take any lucky break I can get.*

Calvin felt more than heard a presence behind him. He wheeled, shoved the smoldering torch into the man's face, and bolted. He sensed that the vampire was near and ran headlong into the darkness of a side passage, more worried about being caught than falling to his death.

At first, he ran on sheer instinct, certain at every second that he would feel the vampire's hand close on his shoulder. He kept going, turning off into one passage and then another, still working his way uphill but without any sense of direction.

He stumbled over rail tracks and broken cars, nearly tripping over wooden boxes that littered the corridors. Loose gravel made him slip, and the rough rock walls hurt when he fell against them. The turns took him past the central shaft that opened into the other levels, down to where he could still see the light from the ritual room.

Eventually, he no longer sensed his pursuer and slowed his pace. Calvin leaned against the wall, panting for breath. He was thoroughly lost, without any sense of direction. He could hear some type of commotion, but the way sound echoed, he couldn't determine which tunnel it was coming from. *Looks like I'll die here one way or the other.*

A chill passed through him, and he turned nervously. Several more bursts and an ice-cold wind swept through the tunnel. He waited a moment, but there was nothing more. He reached out to steady himself against the wall, and images of long-ago miners appeared in his mind.

They know the way out. If I can see them in my mind, maybe they'll show me the path.

Calvin took a few steps forward and scraped his shin against something solid. He still held the torch, so he used one of the matches hidden in his belt to light it. The large letters read "TNT," and he scrambled back to keep the torch well away from the explosives.

He paused. In the torchlight, he saw several more boxes. Calvin didn't know how long they had been there or if the dynamite inside would still react. When he saw a pile of rope, a spool of fuse and a box of blasting caps, a desperate idea formed.

He propped the torch a safe distance from the boxes and found that one of the rusted mine cars was still on the tracks. Calvin loaded as much of the TNT into the car as it would hold along with bags of an accelerant that would make the explosion burn hotter. He had used the explosive before and knew how to set it off. Calvin prepared the charges, tied the boxes so they would stay in the cart, and leaned into pushing the small rail car back the way he had come.

Contact with the cart gave Calvin the route back to the shaft. He tried not to think too hard about what he was going to do. *I have a chance to stop the vampires without anyone else getting hurt. I can make sure the ritual doesn't happen with me or anyone else. Throw a wrench in Leland Aiken's plans. And if I don't make it out…well, the odds were against me living through this anyway.*

Except that I'll never know how things might have turned out with Owen. Owen.

Calvin never believed much in regrets. In his life he'd made mistakes, been disappointed, and felt betrayed. Even his days in the gangs back in Boston didn't fill him with remorse. But leaving Owen before they even had a chance to discover what they could be to each other left Calvin's heart aching.

At least he won't get hurt trying to rescue me. If he and the others try to find me here, some of them will die. Maybe Owen. I can stop the vampires, and no one else will be harmed.

Calvin shut down his feelings as he rushed the last few yards. He stopped before the turn at the shaft to light the fuse and set the blasting caps. As the cordite burned, Calvin threw his weight against the cart, making it jump from the tracks, sending it falling down the shaft.

Calvin turned and ran. He kept contact with the wall, familiar now with the images its resonance provided. He didn't know how long he had until the fuse lit the dynamite, but he hoped the explosion would trigger a cave-in and a fire that would put an end to the gates of hell threat and destroy the vampires.

Killing them wouldn't stop Leland Aiken. He'd find more henchmen; his kind always did. But he would fail this time, and it would put him on notice that perhaps he didn't own the world just yet.

More importantly, it would save the man Calvin loved and the friends he'd come to value and had known for far too short a time.

Calvin's self-preservation instinct remained strong enough for him to make a last ditch effort to survive what he had just put in motion.

He sprinted back to where he had discovered the TNT. Calvin spotted one of the mine carts that was turned on its side and huddled inside it.

The explosion echoed through the mine. The floor shuddered, and chunks of the ceiling pelted down onto the steel cart, deafeningly loud. The whole mine shook. Calvin curled into a ball, arms wrapped around his head, knees drawn up.

Chapter 10
Owen

Three hours earlier…

Winston arranged for horses—the three he had previously secured as well as a fourth on loan. Renate and Louisa didn't appear to worry about scandalizing anyone who might see them riding astride. Owen and Renate rode first, constantly scanning for threats. Louisa and Winston brought up the rear, watching carefully to ensure they weren't being followed.

They reached the construction site in the early afternoon and fastened the horses in a thicket where they had shade and grass, distant enough from the mine to be safe.

Now that they were near the mine, they shuffled their order. Winston and Renate led the way, using spells to hide their approach and weaving magical protections. Owen and Louisa followed, armed with a rifle, a pistol, and several knives. The bags they carried had more weapons and ammunition as well as the components for additional spells.

They came ready for war.

Hang on, Calvin. We're going to get you out.

The entrance to the mine loomed ahead. Scrub brush had grown up around the equipment abandoned when the mine closed. Rusted mine cars lay tipped over or upended near the end of the rails that led into the darkness. The limestone mining pre-dated Aiken's railway expansion by more than a decade, so nothing remained of the shoddy wooden structures that once housed the miners, who had long ago moved on to the next big opportunity when this one tapped out.

Owen opened his senses, listening for ghosts. He had the Maxwell Box on a strap over one shoulder. Before he trusted the unproven technology, Owen wanted to assure himself of the ghosts' nature so they didn't find themselves with yet another adversary.

Spirits of the mine—we need your help. The creatures who have intruded on your resting place intend great harm. We want to stop them. They've captured one of our friends, and we hope to rescue him. Help us, and you can rest easy once more.

Owen preferred to reach out to the ghosts and have them respond on their own, without coercion. But given the stakes involved in saving Calvin and stopping Aiken, he had no compunctions about using the Maxwell Box and conscripting the spirits if they did not come willingly.

Louisa carried her rifle with the ease of someone with plenty of experience. She watched the landscape around them with the eye of a trained sniper, wary and resolute. Owen understood why she worked so well with Calvin and why he had trusted her to have his back.

Her assurance about Calvin's interest back at the Pullman assuaged his jealousy and lifted his spirits. Owen was glad she'd thrown in her lot with them and found himself hoping that they could work together when future cases brought them back to St. Louis.

One step at a time. We need to rescue Calvin before that can happen.

Don't give up, Calvin. Keep fighting—and believe we'll come for you.

Owen was twitchy anticipating the danger of the rescue, and anxious over everything that could go wrong. Although he had every reason to trust his new allies, they were all wild cards, experienced but unknown. He was grateful for their help, but they lacked the synchronicity that came with working together over time.

Despite their research and the edge that witchcraft gave them, Owen knew they were walking into a dangerous situation.

Rusting machinery and wrecked mine carts littered the ground around the entrance to the limestone mine, useful cover for Owen and the others to move closer without being seen. A large pile of waste rock provided a vantage point. Louisa took her rifle and ammunition and signaled Owen that she was heading for the high ground.

Winston and Renate moved as far forward as they dared without breaking cover. They put down a braided cord in a circle around where they stood for their magic workspace. Owen shivered as he felt the magic rise around him.

Winston murmured, hands moving in patterns Owen didn't recognize, leaving a faint violet after-image in the air.

Renate took a silver chalice and a flask from her bag. She poured the green liquid into the cup and added a pinch of something that sent green sparks flying. When she ran a finger around the rim counterclockwise, Owen heard a soft ringing sound.

Winston and Renate exchanged a look, and then Winston stomped his foot. "So mote it be."

Renate poured out some of the liquid from the chalice and brought her foot down hard. "As I will it, so shall it happen."

For just a second, Owen thought he saw a complex web of silver light race across the distance between their hiding place and the maw of the mine. It flashed and vanished, but Owen felt like a weight had been lifted from the air around them.

"The traps and wardings are gone," Winston said. "Let's see how long it takes them to notice."

In the next breath, Winston and Renate each turned in slow circles, hands moving as if painting invisible symbols in the air. Owen saw a barely-there sparkle in the air around their hiding place, like the glimmer of heatwaves, except on a day far too cold for that.

"That's protection against magic—depending on what gets thrown our way," Renate replied in a satisfied tone.

Owen gathered his nerve and took a deep breath. He opened his gift and concentrated on the dark opening. Owen sensed the restless spirits in the depths of the pit and called to them.

Wake up. Bad people are defiling the mine where you rest. We've come to stop them—and we could use your help.

Owen found that images sometimes communicated better with spirits than words, especially with ghosts that had been dead for a while. He visualized the gruesome alleyway deaths, the mangled bodies of the Branson brothers, and the murdered shifter.

The men want to open the gates of hell. If that happens, many people will die. They've taken our friend hostage to kill him. Will you help us fight so we can save him and stop them from summoning a demon?

Owen sensed the ghosts like a whispered conversation. He fidgeted, awaiting their decision, and hoped he hadn't miscalculated the likelihood of their support.

Two large men armed with pistols barreled from the mine entrance. Before they had gone more than a few yards, the crack of a rifle broke the silence twice in quick succession, and both men dropped to the ground. Louisa flashed him a triumphant grin.

"Shit," Owen muttered as he saw ten more men pour from the mine. The guards quickly took cover in the junkyard of ruined equipment and opened fire on the area where Owen and the others hid.

Bullets pinged and ricocheted from the overgrown wreckage of mine cars, rock haulers, and crushing machines. Owen ducked, figuring he was as likely to be hit by accident as by aim, although he suspected that the warding Winston and Renate raised helped to misdirect the bullets' trajectory.

From the rubble pile, Louisa fired steadily, keeping the guards pinned down.

Anything you can do to help is appreciated. And I can give you an energy boost, Owen told the ghosts.

He flipped the switch, and the Maxwell Box whined as it powered up. Renate had given Owen a quick overview back at the Pullman, and he hoped she had the details right as he turned the knob to half power, waiting to see if the contraption actually worked.

The guards let loose another torrent of shots. With their attention focused on the scrap heap where Owen and the others took shelter, the guards didn't notice the roiling mist that gathered behind them at the mouth of the mine.

Owen glimpsed faces and bodies in the fog, and even at a distance, felt the chill as a cloud of spirits emerged and bore down on the guards.

Men screamed as the revenants swarmed their hiding places, flowing around and sometimes through their bodies. The guards fired into the mist to no avail. In the chaos, some of the men broke from cover, easy for Louisa and Owen to pick off. The ghosts saw to others themselves, descending on them in a dark cloud until the panicked shrieks fell silent.

Two guards managed to evade the ghosts and started working their way closer, using the ruined equipment to shield them from gunfire as the spirits meted out judgment on their unlucky companions. Owen glimpsed the guards as they ran between hiding places but never for long enough to aim.

Winston stared in the general direction the guards had gone. He raised one hand, palm out, and twisted his wrist sharply to the right. One man tumbled out of his hiding place as if he'd been shoved—or dragged by unseen hands. Louisa dropped him with a single shot.

Renate raised her hands and lifted the second man into the air, holding him still for a moment as his arms and legs windmilled, and then tossed him next to the body of his fallen comrade.

"How many more of you?" Owen shouted to the downed guard. The man had lost his gun in the panic of being tossed through the air, and he crouched, awaiting an opportunity to strike.

"Go to hell," the man snarled.

Renate twitched her fingers, and the man lifted a few inches off the ground then dropped back hard.

"Tell us what we want to know, and we'll shoot you. Clean, easy. Refuse, and we throw you to the ghosts," Owen told him.

The man cast a glance behind him toward where the spirits milled like a thundercloud near the mine opening.

"Two more guards inside."

"How many vampires?"

The man paled further, clearly torn between his terror of the ghosts and fear of the vampires. "Maybe half a dozen. They keep to themselves. We don't mess with them."

"Where are they?" Owen called out.

"Deeper down. Maybe level two or three—we don't go down there. I heard they have some kind of weird church set up with candles and an altar."

"What about prisoners?" Owen's heart was in his throat as he awaited the answer.

"I've only seen one lately. Guy they brought in yesterday. Don't know what they wanted with him—maybe dinner."

"Anyone else?" Owen doubted Aiken housed mortal workers in the mine, but he didn't want to be surprised.

"No. That's all. I don't know anything else. Please, don't give me to the ghosts," the man begged.

A shot rang out, and the man fell sideways as Louisa granted his wish.

"Uh-oh," Winston's murmur drew Owen's attention. A man in a long black morning coat and dark trousers emerged from the mine looking like he should be heading for a meeting at the bank.

The stranger brought his hands together, and the ghosts vanished. Owen could still feel their presence, but the man's power had scattered them and sapped their energy. Clearly they posed him no threat.

"I think we've found the witch," Renate remarked with a tight smile that promised bloodshed. "That's Macready."

The witch thrust his right fist in the direction of their hiding place, and bright red light streaked toward them. Owen braced for impact, but before the bolt could strike a sparkling curtain rose to absorb the energy with a flare that made Owen shield his eyes.

Winston pushed both hands forward, palms out, and spoke a word. Owen sensed the shift in power and saw the effects as a wave of magic swept across the space between their position and the mine like a gale-force wind, pushing away everything in its path.

Macready shouted a countermand, and the wind died, leaving a trail of wreckage. A sustained blast of lightning barraged their magical protections. Owen saw Winston and Renate go still and rigid, and he guessed they were channeling their energy to keep the shielding in place.

"To hell with that," Winston heard Louisa curse as she opened fire. He joined her a moment later, firing their rifles toward the witch's position. His image blurred in an attempt to evade their aim, but Owen bet that the man couldn't keep up the lightning bolts and still avoid being shot.

Seconds later, the lightning winked out, and Macready stood behind a transparent barricade that made their bullets freeze and then drop harmlessly to the ground.

"If you've come to stop the ritual, you're too late," he called to them. "Everything is prepared, and the sacrifice has been made ready. You can't change what has been set in motion."

The sacrifice. He means Calvin.

Renate looked to Winston. "With absinthe, I gain a few seconds where I can see what might happen. If we all hit him at once, with that edge, we can end this."

She tipped back the flask and swallowed a few mouthfuls of absinthe. Winston sent a new volley toward the witch, distracting him. Louisa scrambled to a new vantage point on a piece of equipment that was still within their wards. Owen shifted to the edge of the protected area where he could get a better angle.

"Go," Renate whispered.

Winston sent a streak of white fire blazing at Macready. Louisa fired from the right. Owen shot from the left.

Louisa and Owen kept up the cover of rifle fire. Winston sent strike after strike. Owen cranked up the Maxwell Box to its highest setting, and the cloud of spirits returned, nearly solid with the box at full strength.

Renate stared at Macready, waiting. Her eyes narrowed, and then she struck when the simultaneous hits forced him to split his attention. Her magic raised a green fog that rushed toward the witch's wardings, slipping through the holes punched in the protective shield. The mist went over, around, and through, as the onslaught continued.

Macready staggered, and the warding flickered. Renate's green fog swirled around him as disorienting as the drink from which she drew her magic. Strengthened by the Maxwell Box, the ghosts took form, gray shapes of miners from long ago. They swarmed Macready, tearing at his clothing and clawing at his skin.

As the witch faltered, his shielding failed, thinning and then dropping altogether. Owen's shot tore through the shoulder, and Louisa put a bullet in his leg. Winston's magic pinned the witch to the ground, and Renate's absinthe fog made him insensible. They left it to the ghosts to finish him, stripping skin from bone and tearing him to pieces.

The ghosts vanished, one by one, as the Maxwell Box gave a high-pitched whine and went silent.

"Calvin." The relief Owen felt ebbed quickly, replaced by frantic concern. "We've got to rescue him. The ghosts can get us around the vampires. We can handle them. Without the witch, they can't do the ritual—or at least can't do it right—"

An explosion shook the ground under their feet. Owen turned to the mine entrance in time to watch it crumble, dropping boulders into the opening in a cloud of dust.

What happened? Owen sent a frantic call to the ghosts. *Where is Calvin—the prisoner? Is he still alive? How do I find him?*

Silence answered him, and no matter how Owen strained to recall them, the spirits remained beyond his reach.

Calvin.

"We have to get inside." He stared at the entrance and the tumble of rocks that filled it completely.

Winston frowned and closed his eyes, working a spell. "The explosion caused a cave-in. It's not just the entrance—the whole main corridor is gone."

"What about the vampires? Can they still do the ritual without the witch? Can you tell if Calvin's still alive?"

Renate's green fog swirled and slipped around the rocks. She concentrated, moving her fingers in an arcane pattern, sending the fog to do her bidding. After a few minutes, the fog returned, and then dissipated.

"There's a fire deep in the mine. The cave-in and smoke create a lot of interference. I can't sense any energies—living or undead. But I'm certain that the gate hasn't been opened," Renate told them. "The threat is over."

No energies, living or undead. Calvin's gone.

"There has to be another entrance. It's too big of a mine to have only one way in and out," Owen protested, desperate.

"You've seen the map. It didn't show any other openings," Winston said.

"There must be something." Owen felt panic clawing inside him. "It could be an old map. What if a new entrance was built later? And air holes. All mines have air holes. Maybe—"

"It's done." Winston closed the distance between them. "I'm sorry, but it's over."

Owen ran to the entrance. He tore at the rocks with his bare hands, caring nothing about ripped nails and bloody fingertips. Owen marshaled all his ability to scream for the ghosts and for Calvin, but no answer came. Maybe the mine ghosts were too spent to be of further help, or perhaps they figured their reason to intervene was over. And if Calvin was among them, perhaps being newly dead kept him from being able to respond. He felt their silence like a void.

He slumped to his knees, resting his forehead against his clasped hands atop one of the boulders, chest heaving with exertion.

"We need to go." Renate placed her hand on his shoulder. "There's nothing more we can do here."

Owen wanted to rant and sob. Everything in him fought to argue and throw himself into proving them wrong. At the same time, he felt himself starting to shut down and go cold, unable and unwilling to break down—at least, not now.

Renate led him back to the horses. Louisa and Winston kept the rifles ready, but no new threats emerged. Owen wanted a fight, hungry for the chance to work off the anger and grief that ached inside him.

He hadn't braced himself yet to call again for Calvin—and get a reply. Renate's reading confirmed the worst.

They rode back in near silence. *We won the battle—and lost Calvin. I should be relieved that the gates weren't opened. Aiken won't be invincible. We might have saved the world.*

But Calvin won't be in it. I should try to reach out to him…at least say goodbye before he moves on.

They returned the horses and headed for the train station. When they reached the Pullman, Winston ushered them into the parlor. Owen headed for the liquor cabinet, pulling down glasses for everyone and reaching for a bottle of bourbon. Winston stepped into the library to check the telegraph. He emerged a few minutes later trailing a length of tape.

"Ida Hardin's article ran in the St. Louis paper as well as in the capitol. Leland Aiken announced that the railway expansion is delayed indefinitely. An inquiry is being opened by the state attorney general's office into Aiken's business dealings with the governor. And Police Chief Wyman has been removed from his role and replaced by Deputy Rourke," Winston reported.

Under other circumstances, someone might have cheered. Given the cost of victory, Louisa and the others sat silently, not ready to discuss the battle but unwilling to go their separate ways.

"I'll catch up with Ida tomorrow." Louisa pushed a strand of hair out of her eyes. "She can't report the full story—no one would believe the gates of hell threat—but she'll want to know the basics of what happened. We couldn't have done it without her."

"I head back to New Pittsburgh in the morning," Renate added. "I'll pass along the news to Andreas. He'll find ways to keep tabs on Leland Aiken. I'm sure this isn't the last we'll hear of him. We might not have completely destroyed his plans, but we've killed his witches, and we've certainly changed his timeline…plus delaying the end of the world is a good start."

Owen poured himself a few fingers of bourbon and sat in stunned silence. He didn't fight the numbness because he knew the grief to follow would be worse. He knew he should try to contact Calvin's ghost again but couldn't bring himself to do it. That would make it all too real.

Winston poured a drink for the ladies and for himself, and raised his in a toast. "To Calvin Springfield."

Renate and Louisa murmured in response. Owen couldn't find his voice and looked away.

"I'll make the report to headquarters." Winston shot a worried glance in Owen's direction that Owen didn't acknowledge. "I'll be happy to include or redact your participation, as you request. While I firmly believe in giving credit where credit is due, I understand that these things can be…delicate."

Louisa snorted, and Renate's wry smile answered him better than words.

"Now that the shooting's done and Aiken has been boxed in, I imagine we'll await a new assignment," Winston added. Despite their success in stopping the railroad project and keeping the gates of hell closed, Winston didn't sound triumphant.

Owen knew that he, Winston, and Calvin were barely acquaintances in the length of time that had passed, but shared danger had forged a strong connection even in that short period.

They'll assign me a new partner. Maybe I'll get to keep Winston and the Pullman. Everything will be business as usual, and we'll head out to another city, another case.

But Calvin will always be in St. Louis. We couldn't even do right by him with a decent burial.

Winston invited Louisa and Renate to dinner, but they declined and left shortly after the toast, promising to keep in touch for the aftermath of the case. Louisa laid a comforting hand on Owen's shoulder and gave him a heartfelt look of shared grief. He remained expressionless, fearing that if he let himself feel anything right now, he would lose control.

"I will get dinner underway immediately," Winston told him. "I'll fetch you from the parlor when it's ready."

Owen shook his head. "I don't have any appetite, and I'd be poor company. I'm going to go to bed."

Winston looked sad but not surprised. "Very well. I'll fix something so you can make a plate if you change your mind. In the morning, I'll get provisions and see to the horses, so if I'm not here when you wake, breakfast will be in the oven."

"Thank you, Winston. For everything."

"You are most welcome. And I too mourn the loss of Mr. Springfield." Winston looked like he had more to say but remained silent.

Owen gave him a tight-lipped nod, grabbed the nearly-full bottle of bourbon by the neck, and headed for his room.

Tomorrow, I'll be Agent Sharps again. Probably better at my job for having less heart to break. Tonight, I'm going to grieve a love affair that should have been and didn't happen, and hope that Calvin's ghost comes to me in my dreams.

I guess I've put it off long enough...

Owen closed his eyes and concentrated, opening his senses, and focused on Calvin—picturing him in his mind.

Calvin Springfield, if you can hear me, please come to me. I need to know whether you're still here.

Owen held his breath. His hands clenched, waiting. But as before, no answer came. Minutes passed, and Owen felt his tears running down his cheeks. *Does this mean you might still be alive? Can I hope?* Owen took a deep breath. *I feel like I would know if he'd passed on. Am I lying to myself?*

He didn't want to answer that question. Owen opened his eyes and looked at the bottle of bourbon, finishing it off before sleep finally overtook him.

Chapter 11
Calvin

C alvin guessed he might have passed out for a while and roused, feeling groggy and unwell. He was surprised to be alive, astounded that the cart had protected him, and he wondered if he would discover that the mine had caved in over his refuge, trapping him to a slow death by hunger or suffocation.

Maybe the vampires weren't so bad.

He knew that even if the vamps had given him a faster death, the consequence of opening the seventh gate was not worth his personal salvation. Calvin gathered his nerve and used all his strength to crawl out from under the cart.

Rock dust hung heavy in the air. Calvin sneezed and coughed, drawing his torn shirt over his nose and mouth. Some rocks had fallen from overhead, but the full blast of the TNT had been far away, sparing him from being beneath a cave-in.

He re-lit the torch and ventured back toward the main shaft. Fallen stone blocked the way after a couple of turns. Calvin hoped that meant his gambit had succeeded. If the fire hadn't consumed the vampires, maybe he'd buried them under enough rubble to keep them busy digging out.

Hacking and snorting from the dust, Calvin staggered back past the overturned mine car that had been his refuge, and leaned against the stone wall of the passageway.

His head spun, a combination of blood loss, hunger, and dehydration. Calvin had no idea how much time had passed since he was captured, but he had certainly missed several meals, on top of being a snack for at least one of his captors. The cloth over his mouth and nose did a middling job of filtering out the dust in the air.

If I sit down or sleep, I'll die here. No one will find me. Even if Owen figures I'm in the mine—which would be a wild leap—the route from the center is blocked, and the explosion might have brought down the whole main gallery.

I've got no idea whether there's more than one way out, but it seems likely. This is a big mine. They'd need more than one entrance for all the miners and carts.

I can't ask the ghosts the way Owen could. But perhaps the impressions they left behind can lead me out.

Maybe I won't make it. But at least I can die trying. And if I'm lucky, Owen will find my body.

Calvin started walking. He trailed his fingers along the wall, straining to pick up the resonance of the miners who had trod these corridors years ago. His makeshift torch provided comfort more than illumination. Gradually the air cleared, leaving behind the worst of the dust.

He wended his way uphill, following the faded images he read from the mine's walls. His arm throbbed from the bites, and his whole body felt bruised. Grit filled his mouth, nose, and throat, making the thirst worse.

Calvin kept going uphill, figuring that the ramps and tracks had to lead to the surface eventually. He thought about Owen, and whether his partner and their allies had found a way to successfully counter Aiken's ambitions.

In his delirium, he thought he'd heard Owen calling for him, but the voice had faded and did not come again. Calvin chalked it up to a product of his desperate imagination.

Did Owen figure out that the last of the gates was to be opened here? I hope my explosion kept him and the others safe. Fighting their way inside with those vampires active would have been a massacre. Much as I wanted to be rescued, I couldn't live with the cost.

Were the vampires destroyed or just trapped? I smelled smoke, and there was a lot of TNT and accelerant in that cart. It should have made a nice big fire with the explosion. Bonus for making it unlikely Aiken could turn this mine into some high-end, undead luxury hotel if he does continue his expansion plans.

He stopped for a moment now and then to listen for signs of pursuit, or of survivors digging out, but heard nothing. Calvin wondered what happened to the guards and whether any of the vampires' human helpers had been caught in the cave-in. *Maybe Owen and the others can stop anyone who made it out. There's nothing I can do about it for now.*

The ramp widened and switched back, still heading upward. Calvin sniffed. He felt a breeze, and for the first time since his capture, the air smelled fresh.

"There's got to be an exit." He pushed his battered body onward. The faint images he received from the walls showed tired workingmen trudging home at the end of long shifts. That confirmation buoyed his spirits and kept him stumbling along.

The next time the ramp doubled back on itself, Calvin glimpsed daylight. His dusty throat strangled a shout of triumph into a croak. Calvin staggered onward and came to an entrance overgrown with saplings and brambles.

Caution made him check for guards or workers, but this mine entrance didn't appear to have been used for a very long time, and no other people were in sight.

He burst out of the darkness and into the daylight like it was Resurrection Day. Calvin sucked in hungry lungfuls of fresh air and basked in the sunlight despite the chill in the air. He had no idea where he was or how far away he might be from the main mine entrance. Calvin set out at as brisk a pace as he could manage.

I probably look frightful, covered in dust and blood. If I run into someone, they're as likely to shoot me as offer help. I'd hate to die escaping, but it beats being sucked dry by vampires or sacrificed to raise a demon.

I need to get back to the Pullman.

During what Calvin had believed were going to be his final moments, his thoughts were filled with Owen. Sharp regret plagued him over not testing the waters to see if his feelings were returned. Hunkered beneath the overturned mine car, he had promised himself that if he lived through the ordeal, he would have the courage to see where his affection for Owen might lead.

At the time, Calvin had believed his thoughts to be the pleasant fantasies of a dying man. Now, he held onto those hopes with all his might, using them to keep him moving.

Don't give up on me, Owen. I'm coming back to you, and we're going to figure everything out—together.

Calvin finally reached a macadam road and breathed a sigh of relief. After he had gone about a mile, he spotted a stream and sank to his knees on the damp bank, washing away the worst of the grit and blood. He swallowed handfuls of water to slake his thirst and ease his parched throat.

The only way I'll be able to hitch a ride is if I don't look like an escaped axe murderer. He couldn't see his reflection, but once he'd cleaned the worst off his skin and brushed down his clothing Calvin ran a hand through his hair and buttoned his jacket to hide his torn shirt.

Out here people have farms and are used to a little dirt, not like city folks.

Just as Calvin started to think the road was empty, he heard the sound of a horse and wagon coming up behind him. He stepped to the side and flagged the driver down, hoping his smile looked harmless and friendly instead of deranged.

"Where're you headed, son?" The older man drew the wagon to a stop.

"Closer to St. Louis. I need to meet a friend at the train station."

The driver nodded. "All right, then. Climb into the back. I'm going most of the way, and you'll be able to catch another ride into the city pretty easily from where I'll drop you off."

Calvin thanked the man and crawled into the wagon's bed along with bales of hay and crates of eggs. He kept an eye out to make sure he hadn't been followed, but no one was in sight behind them.

It's daylight. Even if any of the vamps survived the explosion, they couldn't be out in the sun. If human guards were after me, they'd have caught up with me before this.

Figuring he was as safe as he could get for the moment, Calvin dozed, comforted by the rocking of the wagon.

He startled awake, momentarily disoriented, fighting his way clear from dreams of blood and dust. The smell of hay and the creak of the wagon brought him back to the present. The sun was high overhead, and Calvin recognized the outskirts of the city.

Soon afterward, the wagon pulled up at a cargo depot, and the driver climbed down from his bench. "End of the line, but you can catch a ride to almost anywhere from here."

Calvin repaid the man by helping to unload. He thanked him profusely and headed toward the mix of drovers and wagons.

He hitched a ride with a miller supplying barrels of flour and crocks of fresh butter to the city's bakers. That got him into downtown St. Louis. A short trolley ride would have delivered him to the train station, but without cash to pay and looking too bedraggled to be overlooked jumping onto the trolley without a ticket, Calvin resigned himself to a long walk back to the Pullman.

Finally at his destination and wholly exhausted, Calvin climbed the steps to the back observation deck. He found the door unlocked, but when he entered the car it was quiet and most of the lights were off. Worried, Calvin moved slowly, unsure what he might find.

He thought about just going into his room to clean up, but he wanted to find out why the car had been left open and apparently unattended. Calvin was just a few steps past Owen's cabin door when he heard the unmistakable sound of a revolver being cocked.

"I'm hungover, and they said you were dead. What the hell is going on? Am I imagining you?"

Owen's voice sounded like gravel. Calvin froze and raised his hands, thinking it would be a pity to make it this far and be gunned down before he could make his brave confession.

"Not your imagination and I'm not dead, just a little worse for the wear."

"Jesus, did they turn you?" Owen rasped.

"Not dead, not undead, not a werewolf. Just me."

Owen came closer, and Calvin felt the barrel of the gun against his back. He felt a splash of what he assumed was holy water, followed by a fistful of salt against bare skin, and then the shallow slice of a silver knife on his neck.

"Satisfied? Or did I come all this way to get plugged in my own railcar?"

"God, Calvin. We thought we lost you." Owen turned him around, gun disappearing into his belt, and pulled Calvin into a suffocating hug.

Calvin's head swam, no doubt from hunger, thirst, and blood loss, but the feel of Owen's firm body pressed against him and the scent of his partner nearly made Calvin swoon.

Owen finally let go and pushed back but didn't release his hold on Calvin's shoulders. "You're alive. I was afraid..."

Owen looked like he had slept in his clothes. His hair was askew, dark circles shadowed his eyes. Calvin felt certain that he looked worse, but his heart soared.

"I care about you, Owen. You were all I could think about when they captured me, that I'd never see you again. I'd been afraid to hope you could possibly feel the same." Calvin's words came in a torrent, and he didn't dare stop for fear he would lose his nerve.

"I'll accept whatever relationship you want to give me. I won't leave unless you send me away," Calvin continued as if his mouth had a mind of its own. "But if you feel the same—I pray that you do—let's see where this goes between us."

"You talk too much." Owen cupped the back of his neck and drew Calvin in for a kiss, chaste at first, then harder. Owen backed Calvin against the wall, claiming his lips. He drew back moments later after thoroughly plundering Calvin's mouth. "Does that answer your question?"

Calvin nodded dumbly, wondering if he really had died or if this was a deathbed delusion.

"This had better be real, and you'd better not be dying on me, or I'll come after you and drag you back," Owen rasped. "Let's get you into the shower. Then we can patch where you're bleeding and get you some food and water."

Calvin raised a hand to touch Owen's cheek. "For real?"

Owen returned a weary smile, but Calvin saw relief and affection in the other man's eyes. "For real. I care about you too. But I'd rather not have you pass out while we're...together. Let me take care of you, and then I promise I'll show you how glad I am to have you back."

Calvin allowed Owen to trundle him into his room and start the shower. Owen helped him peel away the dirty clothes, checking for injuries.

"What happened to your fingers?" Calvin took Owen's hand and turned it over, frowning at the torn skin and broken nails.

"I lost my mind a little when the mine exploded," Owen confessed. "I tried to dig my way in to find you."

Calvin met Owen's gaze and then lifted his hand and pressed his lips to Owen's fingertips. "Thank you."

"I failed." Owen looked away, shame clear in his expression. "I didn't keep looking; I didn't save you."

Calvin reached up to Owen's cheek, gently turning his head until they were face to face. "Yes, you did. You gave me the courage to keep fighting and find my way out. Where I was, you couldn't have found me. I didn't give up because I wanted to come back to you...see what we could make of this."

Owen stripped off what remained of the torn shirt and froze when he saw the bites on the inside of Calvin's elbow. The wounds no longer bled, but his forearm was dark with dried blood.

"Christ," he whispered. "They fed on you."

"They didn't drain me or turn me. They were keeping me alive for the ritual." Calvin winced at the memory.

Owen's eyes grew dark, a mix of worry and anger. "Did you cause the explosion?"

Calvin managed a tired smile. "I saw a way to take them all down and stop them from opening the gate. At the time, I figured I'd die either way, but if I blew up the mine, I could save you from getting killed."

Owen paused like he was trying to think of the right response then leaned in and kissed Calvin again. "You're an idiot. A brave...hand-some...idiot."

Owen helped him into the bathroom of his sleeping compartment. Calvin showered, letting the hot water ease his sore muscles and wash away the blood and grime. Owen waited nearby, close enough if Calvin needed help. He left boxers and a robe inside the door, and Calvin felt perverse pride at being able to get dressed by himself.

"You look better when you're not bloody." Owen looked him over from head to toe, and the attention made Calvin shiver despite everything.

"Winston's off tending the horses. He said he left food in the ice box. I...wasn't of a mind to eat last night and food didn't sound good this morning," Owen admitted. "Let me tend your injuries and feed you. And then we'll take things from there." His voice dropped low and sent heat to Calvin's belly.

Calvin started to head for the lab, but Owen steered him to the bed in his own room. "Sit down. I brought supplies. I'll fetch food when we're done. You need to recover."

Owen treated the wound on Calvin's arm and bandaged it carefully. He checked for other scrapes and cuts, and when he was satisfied, he helped Calvin sit up in bed. "I'll be right back."

Calvin had barely gotten settled before Owen returned with a tray. "Hope you don't mind breakfast. Winston left plenty." Juice, sweet rolls, and a bowl of fruit looked to Calvin like the best food he had ever seen.

"You said you didn't eat either. Share with me." Calvin gestured to the food.

When they were finished, Owen set the tray aside and hesitated, looking unsure.

Calvin patted the bed next to him. "Stay, please."

Owen met his gaze. "Winston—"

"Wouldn't be the first butler in history to keep secrets about his bosses." Calvin took Owen's hand and pulled him closer.

"What if he turns us in?"

"We go on the run, change our names, join the Foreign Legion. I hear they're not as strict about some things." Calvin managed a smile. "But I think we can trust Winston. Like Louisa."

"You need to rest," Owen protested.

"I need to know we're both alive," Calvin pleaded. "Please."

Owen climbed into bed beside Calvin and drew him into his arms. "What do you want?"

"You. Anything. Just…you." Calvin reached for Owen, pulling him close and initiating the kiss this time. He let his hands glide down Owen's neck, then over his shoulders, down his arms, marveling that his fantasies had become reality.

"Touch me," Calvin begged.

Owen's hands were gentle, exploring Calvin's upper body with careful, reverent touches. If Calvin had wondered whether Owen shared his feelings, the look in his partner's eyes confirmed the truth.

Calvin pulled Owen down to lie on top of him, kissing as they slotted together. He put his hands on Owen's hips and moved so that their cocks rubbed, and they both moaned with the pleasure of the friction.

"I want—" Calvin breathed.

"Yes." Owen dropped his hands to pull Calvin closer. They rutted against each other, and all of Calvin's senses narrowed to focus on the taste, scent, and feel of the man he'd fallen for, who against all odds, shared his feelings.

Calvin's hips bucked, feeling Owen's erection through his pants.

"So good. Want more," Calvin moaned.

"Let yourself go," Owen urged. "Show me."

Calvin's orgasm boiled from the depths of his groin through his whole body. He writhed and jerked against Owen, who was lost in his own release, grinding their cocks together until both of them cried out as they came.

Owen held him through it all, murmuring against his neck and pressing kisses to his collarbone. He finally rolled to the side but kept his arms around Calvin like he would never let go.

Reality was better than anything Calvin had dreamed.

"We're going to be sticky," Calvin said finally.

"We already are."

"That was—"

"Yeah." Owen was silent for a few minutes. "Are you going away?" His voice sounded so vulnerable that Calvin had to meet his eyes.

"I'm not going anywhere," Calvin assured him.

"But the telegram—"

"I asked headquarters for the duration of the assignment to know if this was going to last a few weeks or indefinitely." Calvin ran his fingers through Owen's hair, marveling that the touch was welcomed. "Because I wanted something special with you, something that would last."

Owen blushed. "That night, when I was shot...I was afraid you might have been on the mob's side and that you couldn't stand the sight of me, wanted to get away."

Calvin brushed a finger across Owen's lips. "I jumped to the wrong conclusion at first, and thought you had been with the cops. I ran into Chief Wyman, and when he said he'd shot the man who punched him, I realized I was wrong. I intended to confess how I felt when I got back that night but..." *I got captured by vampires.*

"I was heartbroken, thinking that you would be disgusted by the truth." Owen's voice was barely above a whisper. "Louisa set me straight. We owe her. We also need to let her know you're alive."

"I'll send her flowers." Calvin traced his fingers down Owen's chest and loved the way it made him tremble. "Or maybe buy her a new gun. I'm glad she spilled my secret."

Owen took Calvin's hand and threaded their fingers together. "No more secrets. You don't have to hide from me."

"I want to do this again, naked. I want to see and taste all of you," Calvin said as his strength faded. "But right now, I need to sleep. Stay."

"I'll be here," Owen assured him as Calvin slid down to lie flat, tugging Owen to slide beneath the covers to hold him. Calvin fell asleep to the sound of Owen's heartbeat and his breath, sated, and for the first time in many years—content.

Chapter 12
Owen

H ours later, Owen eased out of bed, letting Calvin sleep. He listened at the door, sure Winston must be back by now. While the Pullman's close quarters would make it impossible for Winston not to suspect their relationship, Owen respected the need for plausible deniability. Until the world changed, he and Calvin would have to keep what they were to each other a secret, except in the privacy of their rooms.

He slipped out of Calvin's cabin into the corridor—and found Winston heading his way. Owen froze. While he was fully clothed, he was also disheveled, with no explanation.

"May I assume Mr. Calvin returned safely?" Winston asked as if nothing was amiss.

"Yes, he's sleeping. I was just looking in on him." Owen fumbled as his heart sank. He knew he didn't sound or look convincing in the least.

"Good news indeed." A smile lit Winston's face as he looked to the door and then back at Owen before he resumed. "Very well. I'll have dinner at the usual time." Winston turned away toward the galley, but not before Owen overheard his last muttered comment. "Finally!"

Did everyone know we were interested in each other before we did? Ida,

Louisa, and now Winston? For being secret agents, we certainly didn't read the clues.

Owen took a long shower. He hadn't left Calvin's side to clean up after his bender the night of the explosion, and he badly needed to wash away the sweat and dust. Although he knew Calvin wouldn't be at full strength for days, Owen optimistically washed *everywhere*.

Hurried hand jobs and the rushed release of being sucked off in a club's bathroom made up most of Owen's experience with sex. But in his short, doomed relationship with Eli years ago, Owen had risked intercourse. He and Eli had been young and horny, adventurous, and willing to give nearly everything a try. Owen had loved giving and receiving, and Eli had enjoyed both as well. Owen never admitted to anyone how much he treasured the intimacy as well as the intense pleasure.

After Eli died, Owen hadn't trusted anyone enough to risk the vulnerability that came with the act. But since he met Calvin, his private fantasies had expanded to the luxury of having time and privacy to explore so much more than a hurried tumble or a quick tug behind a bar. Last night's frot just whetted Owen's appetite for more.

If it was that good together with him half dead and me hungover, I can't wait to see what we're like when we're both healthy.

Unfortunately, Owen knew they had loose ends to tie up before they left St. Louis, and Calvin needed time to fully recuperate.

Maybe not tonight, but soon.

Owen wandered into the parlor to find the past few day's newspapers, a pot of coffee, and a plate of biscuits with country ham. Winston was nowhere to be seen, but Owen thought he heard him whistling in the front of the car near the galley.

He settled into a chair, poured a cup of coffee, and downed two biscuits before unfolding the paper.

"Railroad Magnate Under Investigation: Spells Trouble for New Spur," the headline read. Owen smiled when he saw Ida's byline and a note that the article first appeared in the Jefferson City paper.

Just as Louisa had said, the article laid out Aiken's history of shady deals and questionable business arrangements, including some compromising details that set the state's governor and other prominent business leaders in a negative light. Investors threatened to withdraw support, the Missouri Attorney General recommended a formal inquiry, and Aiken announced that the project would be sidelined "for the foreseeable future."

We weren't able to stop Aiken completely, but we definitely threw a monkey wrench into his plans. Men like him always find a way to scrape the shit off their shoes and try again, but it'll cost him time, and potential supporters might be wary. It's a win, even if it isn't total victory. He'll have to lie low for a while. And we'll be looking for a way to bring him down for good.

Winston bustled in from the galley, a dusting of flour on his apron. "I thought you might like something with a bit of substance since you haven't eaten much."

Owen gave a crooked smile in response to Winston's tactful description. "The biscuits definitely hit the spot. I'll take the rest in for Calvin. He ate a little, but he was so exhausted he fell asleep."

Okay, there might have been a bit of additional activity between eating and sleep, but we'll keep that our little secret.

"I sent messages to Miss Sunderson and Miss Hardin, letting them know of our good news. We can let Miss Thalberg know once she returns to New Pittsburgh. Perhaps take the time to rest, both of you. I suspect we'll be on our way soon enough," Winston said.

Owen raised an eyebrow. "Have you heard from headquarters?"

"I gave them the abbreviated version of what happened at the mine and afterward, as well as an update that Mr. Calvin returned safely. I've written up the full notes for you and Mr. Calvin to review." Winston apparently had settled on a compromise between casual and full formality. "We can send it special post when you've had time to read it over and make additions."

"I'm sure you were suitably thorough," Owen replied.

"When I sent the telegram, their reply was to get ready for a new case, and lay in supplies to be on the move soon," Winston said.

"I wonder what they'll throw at us next?" Since they had started with vampires, Owen figured they had already jumped into the job feet-first.

"Something suitably challenging, no doubt," Winston answered with a grin as if he relished the adventure. In the kitchen, an alarm clock went off. "Ah—I'd best see to dinner. Let me know if either of you need anything." With that, he headed for the galley.

Owen picked up the tray and carried the papers, biscuits, and coffee to Calvin's room. To his surprise, Calvin was awake and sitting up.

"Winston made a snack to sustain us until dinner." Owen placed the tray on the nightstand. "How are you feeling?"

"Better than last night, not quite back to normal. You?"

"Less hungover, which is a plus," Owen admitted.

Calvin looked down. "I worried when I woke up, and you were gone."

Owen sat on the edge of the bed and smoothed Calvin's dark hair out of his eyes. "I needed a shower, and you were sound asleep. I didn't go far. Figured you'd prefer if I didn't stink."

"I didn't have any problems with your scent." Calvin's heated gaze made Owen's cock wake up and take notice. "I'm just glad you came back."

Owen took his hand. "I told you that I would. And by the way—I think Winston figured us out maybe before we did. I don't think we're going to have a problem there."

"Told you so," Calvin teased gently. Owen filled him in on the highlights from the newspapers while Calvin ate the biscuits and washed them down with coffee.

"It sounds like headquarters considers this case wrapped up," Owen told him. "Aiken is in retreat—for now. Even if they weren't destroyed in the mine cave-in, his vampires have no reason to stick around. And any of his remaining Renfields are likely to scatter since their protector is gone."

"Renfields?"

Owen chuckled. "In *Dracula*, there's a character named Renfield who is a human servant. He knows about vampires and chooses to serve them."

"Why the hell would anyone do that?" Calvin finished off one cup of coffee and poured another.

"Power. Immortality. Wealth. Same reason henchmen help bad people," Owen replied with a shrug. "But the point is, St. Louis is safe for a while, so we're on to the next case."

"Do we know where yet?"

Owen shook his head. "No. But that's okay as long as we're working it together."

Two days later, they had left St. Louis behind en route to Chicago. Their new orders hadn't come in yet, but Owen was happy to be on the move again.

A few days of downtime had done wonders, along with food, rest, and a chance to catch their breath. Mitch and Jacob telegraphed congratulations, as did Renate. Louisa and Ida promised to keep them updated on any future news about Aiken or his helpers. Best of all, Chief Wyman had been permanently fired, which gave Owen a personal sense of vindication.

Winston was busy in the galley, and Owen knew he'd be tied up there for several hours. He slipped inside Calvin's room and stopped in his tracks.

Calvin knelt naked on the bed, his back to the door, legs apart, fucking himself on his fingers.

He gave a coy look over his shoulder. "Want to join me? I thought I'd get ready for you...move things along."

Owen's cock filled rapidly, straining against his pants. He retained the presence of mind to lock the door, although he suspected Winston knew better than to barge in on them. He shed his clothing in the few feet between the door and the bed.

"You've done this before? Fucked a man in the ass?" Calvin's gaze made the heat rise in Owen's belly.

"Yes...not for a long time," Owen admitted.

"Ever been fucked?" Calvin's voice smoldered.

"Not often," Owen stammered and cursed himself for his awkwardness. "But I liked it both ways."

"Good—so do I. Since you hadn't offered, I wasn't sure."

"You were still recovering!" Owen protested.

"Nothing heals a near-death experience like hot sex," Calvin replied in a sultry tone. "Now—are you going to stand there and watch me get myself off, or are you going to join in the fun?"

Owen scrambled up behind him and saw a small jar of petroleum jelly on the bed.

"Slick yourself up. I should be open enough to take you—although you're deliciously bigger than my fingers," Calvin directed.

Owen feared that given his long dry spell, this might be over far too soon. "Don't judge stamina by the first time," he warned. "It's been a while."

"I don't care. There'll be plenty of chances for repeats. Just get in me—I want you."

Owen hurried to comply, biting back a moan when he drew his cock through his slippery fist. He spread Calvin's ass cheeks and lined himself up.

"Come on, Owen. I'm ready."

Owen didn't need to be coaxed. He groaned as his cock sank into Calvin's tight heat, filling him until he was fully seated balls deep.

"So good," he whispered, and leaned forward to kiss Calvin's neck.

"Start moving, or I'll flip us, tie you down, and ride you like a prize bull," Calvin said.

Owen shivered, unsure whether that was a threat or an offer. He tightened his grip and began to thrust, savoring the slow drag out and faster plunge in. Need and hunger took over, and soon he had set up a rhythm.

"Knew you'd feel good," Calvin murmured as Owen snapped his hips, hitting the sweet spot inside.

Owen kept up the pace, guessing it wouldn't take long for either of them. He figured Calvin might have fingerprint-sized bruises on his hip and felt a thrill of possessiveness at marking his lover.

He swiveled his hips, then surprised Calvin by sitting back on his heels and pulling Calvin up with him so that he straddled Owen's knees. Owen reached for Calvin's dripping cock, pre-come mixing with the Vaseline to form a slippery channel in his fist for Calvin to fuck into.

Owen shifted his left hand to slide up Calvin's ribs and found the pebbled nubs that contrasted with his pale skin. Calvin let his head fall back onto Owen's shoulder, eyes closed, mouth open, trembling with the nearness of his release.

"Let me see you come," Owen whispered into Calvin's ear, driving his cock deep into Calvin's ass while his hand skimmed the other man's balls and then took a long pull up his stiff prick.

Calvin bit his lip to muffle his shout as his release fountained over Owen's fist. Owen kept up his thrusts, rhythm faltering as his climax overwhelmed him, and he filled Calvin's ass with his come.

When they stilled, Owen held Calvin against him, back to chest, reveling in the way Calvin's breath came short and sharp, and his heart pounded. A sheen of sweat covered both of them, and the room smelled of sex.

Owen nosed the short hair by Calvin's ear. "I think I'm falling in love with you."

Calvin twisted his head to graze Owen's chin with his lips. "I think I already have," he admitted.

Owen brought them over onto their sides, still tangled up together, and held Calvin close. He thought his partner might wriggle loose or try to distance himself from the emotion of the moment, but Calvin seemed content to lie still with Owen's arm around his belly.

"Looks like we're going to need another shower," Owen observed.

"Guess so." Calvin reached for a handkerchief on the bedside stand, which he used to wipe away the jizz on his belly and Owen's hand. Owen slipped out, immediately missing the contact. He walked to the bathroom to wipe himself off and returned with a warm cloth to clean Calvin, keeping eye contact.

"No one's ever done that," Calvin breathed. His expression was open and vulnerable, and Owen felt his heart swell at the trust that implied.

"Get used to it. I take care of my lover."

"I like the sound of that." Calvin stretched up for a lazy kiss.

"I liked the sounds you made," Owen teased in a husky tone. "Want to hear them again and again."

"I can promise that will happen. But maybe...since there's nowhere to be right now...sooner rather than later?" Calvin's blue eyes were an invitation.

Owen grinned. "Oh, I can definitely promise that. It's a long way to Chicago."

Afterword

Language has changed a lot since the 1890s. Words like "heterosexual" hadn't come into use yet, and "gay" just meant happy. There wasn't a polite term for being gay, and the word "homosexual" had just been coined in 1869 and carried stigma. The least offensive terms were "nancy" or "molly"—Victorian slang for effeminate men or those who liked other men. The sting of those terms has eased over time by falling out of use and becoming archaic. I did my best to choose the least offensive terms that were also period-authentic.

Calvin and Owen recognize the danger that being different poses, but they accept themselves as they are, with fairly little guilt or internalized negative views. As agents, they live outside of societal norms, and both have come to see their orientation as nobody else's business.

Where Calvin or Owen think about their "preference" for men, I do not mean to suggest that being gay is a preference. "Sexual orientation" is a contemporary term that would not have been used in 1897, so Calvin or Owen would think of the kind of person they felt drawn to—"preferred"—as a partner. This is also why they frequently think in terms of "men like me." That phrasing enabled me to make the point without requiring labels.

My goal with the choice of language was to minimize negativity and avoid modern hurtful terms while using words Calvin and Owen might have chosen. Given that being gay was illegal at the time, the repression and need to hide is historically accurate, just as it is also accurate that many people remained true to themselves and found companionship and love despite society's prejudice.

If you like Mitch Storm and Jacob Drangosavich, they have a collection of stories and novellas of their exploits titled Storm & Fury. They and Renate Thalberg are also characters in the Jake Desmet Adventures series I co-write with Larry N. Martin, including *Iron & Blood* and the upcoming *Spark of Destiny*.

You will see more of Calvin, Owen, and Winston, so stay tuned!

Acknowledgments

Thank you so much to my editor, Jean Rabe, to my husband and writing partner, Larry N. Martin for all his behind-the-scenes hard work, to my beta readers, and to my wonderful cover artist Deranged Doctor Design. Thanks also to the Shadow Alliance and the Worlds of Morgan Brice reader street teams for their support and encouragement, plus my promotional crew and the ever-growing legion of ARC readers who help spread the word!

I couldn't do it without you! And of course, thanks and love to my "convention gang" of fellow authors for making road trips and virtual cons fun.

About the Author

Morgan Brice is the romance pen name of bestselling author Gail Z. Martin. Morgan writes urban fantasy male/male paranormal romance, with plenty of action, adventure, and supernatural thrills to go with the happily ever after.

Gail writes epic fantasy and urban fantasy, and together with co-author hubby Larry N. Martin, steampunk and comedic horror, all of which have less romance and more explosions.

On the rare occasions Morgan isn't writing, she's either reading, cooking, or spoiling a very pampered dog.

Watch for additional new series from Morgan Brice and more books in the Witchbane, Badlands, Treasure Trail, Kings of the Mountain, Sharps & Springfield, and Fox Hollow universes coming soon!

Where to find me, and how to stay in touch

Join my Worlds of Morgan Brice Facebook Group and get in on all the behind-the-scenes fun! My free reader group is the first to see cover reveals, learn tidbits about works-in-progress, have fun with exclusive contests and giveaways, find out about in-person get-togethers, and more! It's also where I find my beta readers, ARC readers, and launch team! Come join the party! https://www.Facebook.com/groups/WorldsOfMorganBrice

Find me on the web at https://morganbrice.com. Sign up for my newsletter and never miss a new release! http://eepurl.com/dy_8oL. You can also find me on Twitter: @MorganBriceBook, on Pinterest (for Morgan and Gail): pinterest.com/Gzmartin, on Instagram as Morgan-BriceAuthor, on YouTube at https://www.youtube.com/c/GailZMartin-

Author/ on Bookbub https://www.bookbub.com/authors/morgan-brice and now on TikTok @MorganBriceAuthor

Enjoy a free short story about Mitch and Jacob, *Grave Voices*, here: https://claims.prolificworks.com/free/jaNQX

Check out the ongoing, online convention ConTinual www.facebook.com/groups/ConTinual

Support Indie Authors

When you support independent authors, you help influence what kind of books you'll see and what types of stories will be available because the authors themselves decide what to write, not a big publishing conglomerate. Independent authors are local creators supporting their families with the books they produce. Thank you for supporting independent authors and small press fiction!

Also by Morgan Brice

Badlands Series

Badlands

Restless Nights, a Badlands Short Story

Lucky Town, a Badlands Novella

The Rising

Cover Me, a Badlands Short Story

Loose Ends

Leap of Faith, A Badlands/Witchbane Novella

Night, a Badlands Short Story

No Surrender

Fox Hollow Zodiac Series

Huntsman

Again

Fox Hollow Universe

Romp

Nutty for You

Imaginary Lover

Haven

Gruff

Kings of the Mountain series

Kings of the Mountain

The Christmas Spirit, a Kings of the Mountain Short Story

Sins of the Fathers